# SOUL EQUITY, INC.

# SOUL EQUITY, INC.

## CYD PENNY

authorHOUSE®

*AuthorHouse™*
*1663 Liberty Drive*
*Bloomington, IN 47403*
*www.authorhouse.com*
*Phone: 1-800-839-8640*

*Published by AuthorHouse    01/08/2013*

*ISBN: 978-1-4817-0483-0 (sc)*
*ISBN: 978-1-4817-0482-3 (hc)*
*ISBN: 978-1-4817-0481-6 (e)*

*Library of Congress Control Number: 2013900304*

Thanks to: Kevin Hall, Don Sneed, Wendy Smith and the FIU
School of Journalism.
Dave, I couldn't have done it without you.

# PROLOGUE

## Card Sound Road, the Florida Keys

When the black Mercedes-Benz burst through the barricade on the side of Card Sound Road, it was a dazzling-hot South Florida day. The asphalt link between the mainland and the upper Keys shimmered with heat, as gators tucked themselves into rough cord grass just inches from the edge of the Overseas Highway.

The northbound Benz took the turn way too fast. Waves from the mangrove swamp lapped gently, like nature's clock, as the car went out of control. For one split second, there was no sound, creating a moment that was quick and clean and brilliant, as the Benz left the road, twisting high into the air. Then, with the sun flashing off the front of its new grill, the car pirouetted like a graceful Olympic diver into Crocodile Lake.

Saltwater licked at the polished sides as it bobbed briefly. A solitary heron flew over, alighted, and then left, as the car silently disappeared after one great lopsided dip.

Two men were still inside.

# CHAPTER 1

---

## KEY LARGO, FLORIDA

At Key Largo's police substation on the corner of Gun Club Road, Captain Jack Micelli's cold half-cup of yesterday's coffee sat in the middle of his desk. Next to it, a large Dole pineapple fruit box rested, partly filled with the last contents of his desk: a few alphabetically placed files, a stapler, some odd packs of breath mints, loose paperclips, and several odd-matched pens. Always a meticulous planner, Micelli hadn't spent much time considering retirement, at least not this soon. Not at forty-eight years old. But his doctor had been blunt. Invincibility, and a few other things that Micelli had always taken for granted, weren't guaranteed.

Recently wounded in crossfire during a dockside robbery near Whale Tail Bay, Micelli knew his future as a police officer now included a lame left leg and an ever-present throb of pain.

Tall and athletic, with still-thick black hair, he needed to stay busy. He wasn't a super-jock or even someone who was able to finish everything he started, but slowing down wasn't something he felt ready to do. He couldn't imagine sitting in a chair on a balcony somewhere, watching the world go by or attempting to take up a hobby requiring patience and quiet like golf. He still liked the excitement of crime; he liked the way it tasted in his mouth. Reading didn't interest him, neither did television and he wasn't a late sleeper. *Fundamental* was a good word to describe him; fundamental in the best kind of way. He had a lot of energy and curiosity, and he loved police work. It was who he was; it was what he did best.

But now, as the last in a line of three generations of Micelli police officers, he had to face facts. It looked as if his legacy of service was going to end in a recycled fruit box with a Dole pineapple stenciled on the front.

The shooting happened in September, only four months after he moved south from New Jersey's Transit Police Department on Penn Plaza East, to the palm-tree-lined Key Largo Substation. Not surprisingly, he found the town's law-enforcement needs to be mediocre to the point of comedy. But as justifiable compensation, his days were now filled with sun and the warm, wafting smell of suntan lotion. He had dreamt more than once that he was becoming a sort of exotic version of Sherlock Holmes. Coconut oil, warm breezes, and cold beer were better any day than the frozen streets of Jersey.

Truthfully, Key Largo needed a lifeguard more than it needed an experienced police officer. Three times during his first week at the station, Micelli found himself running through traffic across the Overseas Highway to rescue sea turtles from the road. Later that same week, a tourist flying in a glider kite on the beach was picked up and carried south to Islamorada, where he was deposited atop a giant Rum Runner sign on the roof of Mermaid's Mooring. Suffering electrical burns from the wires in the sign, the errant and now toasted tourist jumped twenty feet to the Tiki roof below and slid down, landing next to a fish locker, where he was squarely impaled on Poseidon's spear.

That was about as serious as the law got in these parts.

And the women were good too.

Then, early one May evening, on a sea-slicked wooden dock running alongside Big Daddy Kane's Bar, a robbery of sorts took place. Micelli's timing was an accident; he stopped by the bar to pick up his winnings from a football pool the day before. He knew the place well, being a regular for its tuna melt at lunch and a stop-by beer around dinnertime. When he drove up, at least five bar patrons and Big Daddy's owner, Joe "Daddy" Kane, were outside the bar, shouting and pointing with excitement at a man in a wheelchair rolling away from the bar, down the wooden boardwalk at incredible speed.

"Jacky!" Kane shouted, red-faced and indignant, waving a baseball bat wildly in the direction of the speeding man. "That bastard just stole my whole freakin' till." Kane's knees were skinned and bleeding, and his Miami Dolphin football shirt was half-untucked; Micelli figured Kane must have fallen on the concrete steps coming out of the bar's front door.

Looking down the long boardwalk, Micelli could see the back of the wheelchair disappearing toward the marina office and the parking lot beyond. He was opening his mouth to say something when gunfire erupted from behind the bar in the opposite direction from where the wheelchair was heading. No one on the dock had a gun, and Micelli thought for just a second that all the people looked like giant bowling pins falling sideways in slow motion in front of him.

Diving behind a fish locker next to the building, Micelli looked again toward the fleeing man and saw him glance back over his shoulder; he slowed the wheelchair near a low hedge.

"Halt!" Micelli shouted on his hands and knees from behind the locker. "Police!"

Pandemonium broke out on the dock behind him, as Kane and his regulars scrambled to get to their feet and began a rush toward the bar.

"Daddy! Oh, Daddy!" Kane's overweight girlfriend, Dee-Dee, began shrieking. Her unnatural, too-bright yellow hair streamed out over the rose tattoo on her shoulder as she lost her high-heeled footing and fell heavily on the boardwalk against a small man known to locals only as Crazy Bobby.

"Shit!" Bobby huffed as Dee-Dee, her too-blond locks, and he went down hard to the ground. His chest ached as she landed on top of him, knocking the wind out of him while they rolled together toward the side of the dock near the bar. Kane, stepping quickly into the doorway, closed the door, locking them out as another hail of bullets started.

Micelli crawled to the side of the fish locker and peered down the dock. He watched the wheelchair zigzag and tip crazily as the man leaned down from the right side of the chair, scooped up a gun from under the hedge, and fired a shot back toward the bar. Micelli said later that with bullets coming at them from both sides, he didn't know which direction to shoot first, but when he saw the flash of the man's gun, his reflexes took control. When it was all over, the wheelchair lay on its side, wheels still spinning, and the man was dead—shot once in the shoulder and once in the chest.

The bullet in the shoulder was Micelli's.

But zealous coverage from the *Miami Herald* marked the beginning of the end of Micelli's career. He didn't feel his own wound and walked around the scene for several minutes before succumbing to blood loss and shock. All he remembered seeing was Dee-Dee sitting on the concrete steps to the bar, crying and shaking as she lit a Marlboro.

"Jacky," she gulped as a long exhale of smoke swirled around her face. "You're freakin' shot, honey. Sit down."

Now, standing in the middle of his half-empty office, he picked up the aspirin bottle he kept in his top drawer, dumped four into his hand, and swallowed them with the rest of his cold coffee. *Waste not,* he thought, although a beer would definitely taste better.

Pushing the speaker button on his phone, he called his assistant, Frances. "When you go out to lunch today, can you pick up a couple more boxes at the store?" he asked. "Hey, don't get any more fruit boxes."

There was silence on the line. "You're gonna be picky about the free boxes?" she answered. "I gotta take what they have there. It's finders-keepers, not a box boutique."

"I just don't think fruit boxes are professional," he answered, closing his eyes and trying not to picture her without her sweater. "Try to get some regular, plain boxes."

"By the way." It was a statement. Frances talked that way. "Mrs. Jackman from St. Therese Church called a few minutes ago and said the kids from the neighborhood have opened up the fire main again. She says the chapel is an inch underwater, and she can't find the cat. She thinks the kids took it."

He clapped his hands together resolutely and took a deep breath. It was going to be a busy day.

# CHAPTER 2

## LITTLE HAITI, MIAMI

Cantaloupe-colored morning sun splashed throughout the small front office of Otero Auto Sales in Miami's Little Haiti. Pulling the wooden blinds closed brought a little relief to his pounding headache, but the papers in Pete Otero's hand still wouldn't stop shaking. *Too much Sangria last night,* he thought. *Again.* Turning away from the sun, Otero looked at a young salesman from local television station WFTV sitting slumped against the arm of a worn, brown leather couch. He didn't like the way the man sat.

"What's with this crap?" Otero said, pointing at the paper. "I'm paying you for good advertising copy, and you bring me *this?*"

The young man tried not to roll his eyes. "It's a play on words," he answered, pursing his lips.

Otero leaned back in his chair and looked at the ceiling for a minute before continuing. "I'm buying three spots here. So let me get this straight. In one of them, I'm a 'caretaker of broken auto bodies'?" He scanned the copy again carefully. "What the hell? What the hell is an 'intellectual giant of crankcase credibility'?"

"It's age-related copy," said the ad man. "Your audience is younger now, and you gotta say something snappy. You can't just stand in front of a car with a dog or a kid and expect sales to increase."

Otero stopped reading and closed his eyes for a moment. Opening them, he looked at the young man and said, "I refuse to be a 'friend to the frequently pedestrian.'" He placed the copy on the desk. "Nope." He was shaking his head. "That ain't going to happen."

"So what do you want to say?"

"Auto Sales. Otero Auto Sales."

"Fine." The young ad man's voice was resigned. "The same in all three spots? Great." He stood to walk toward the outside door. "I'll have to change the invoice. You want me to mail it to you?" He sounded bored.

Otero was squinting at him. "You got family at McNeil, right?"

"The penitentiary?" The man looked down at the floor and then up again with a questioning look. "Yeah." He swallowed hard. "My dad's in for a fifteen to twenty." The following pause would have been awkward any other time, but Otero really wanted to look at this kid. He really wanted to see him. So he stared at him until the young man looked away. "Look," Otero finally said. "I'm paying some old dues forward, okay? Just give me the copy I want. I don't want snappy."

Watching the young man walk out into the parking lot, he felt old.

Otero Auto Sales squatted on the west side of Northeast Second Avenue, not far from Little Haiti's intersection with trendy Biscayne Shores in Old Miami. There, an actual railroad track really did separate the two communities. One sprawled gracefully next to the bay, offering air conditioning, butler's pantries, and ornate, wrought-iron entry gates, while the other, littered in crumbling concrete, boasted graffitied storefronts ringing to the sound of raspy-voiced Botanica witches and dust-filled, candlelit Vodou shops.

Once upon a time, Miami-Dade County Commissioner Arthur Teele ruled here. But that was before he shot himself in the lobby of the *Miami Herald* one day before the newspaper planned to print a story about him that was to be titillating—even to South Florida folks. And they had heard everything.

Otero was a seasoned ex-con, an eight-year veteran of McNeil Island Corrections Center. He was balding, younger than he looked, and almost too short to appear threatening. For a time, he'd been one of the most feared and ruthless drug dealers on the East Coast. During his reign on the streets, New York and Atlanta cops came to know him well. Developing a signature punishment for those whose behavior fell outside his parameters of honor in business, Otero carried a shiv or straight razor, easily concealed in a sock, that he could open with practiced, lightning speed. With one fierce uppercut punch, he could stun a man and bind him wrist-to-ankles, bent forward. Plastic cable ties worked just fine. Cutting right through his victim's clothing, he would use the beloved blade to filet his victim, making several very deep, horizontal cuts, slashing one on top of the other, down into the flesh of the buttocks. Cops gave him the facetious nickname, "Butt-Cutter." In this way, Otero's punishment was a lingering, painful warning to those who didn't pay for the drugs he fronted them. The fleshy, fatty cuts oozed tremendously, took forever to heal, and broke open every time his victim tried to sit down. "Pus Pants" was a nickname he scornfully gave to one former colleague who, almost a year after a run-in with the Butt-Cutter, still stood in his presence. *It was a proven and successful marketing tool, this blade, this enforcer,* he thought, remembering how the shiv felt in the palm of his hand. The wounds hurt over and over again, not just once.

Still, Otero had his standards. He thought of himself as a business professional and maintained studiously that he never hurt a woman. He never hurt a cop. In fact, he never hurt anybody who had not stolen from him or lied to him. He was consistent; these were personal qualities that he was proud of.

Eventually though, as all things do, the drugs changed, the music died, and one day it all caught up with him. Arrested by a team of New Jersey cops, including young Trooper Detective Micelli, prison taught Otero an important thing: it taught him to value himself. When you have nothing left in life, you've got to go back to the basics. After existing for eight years in a place that he tried not to remember, Otero vowed at the same time to never forget. After serving his sentence, odd jobs and old connections led him to a weedy lot on the edge of Miami's Little Haiti, where he managed to buy a struggling auto-sales and repair business and start again. Now, only five years later, he watched helplessly as new developments began to encroach toward the foreclosed properties in the neighborhood. Japanese investors were planning a posh new retail center for the lumber yard down the block, and despite the severe economic downturn, a condo project was still on the books to be built behind oak trees covering an abandoned IGA Superette. The all-glass grocery store, leaving glossy-magazine readers breathless, may still be a few years off, but it would come. One of those college-kid developers with cash crawling out of his pockets made Otero the offer of a lifetime, but that had fallen apart along with everything else in real estate. So taking long naps in the afternoon and fishing in the Keys was still a ways off. Somehow, it didn't seem fair.

He had a dog named Anna. She was small and black—an abandoned handful of tongue, eyes, and tail, surrounded by a great puff of bushy, pitch-colored hair. His shop manager told him that she was a chow chow.

"Yo, *Papi*," the man said with a heavy Cuban accent. "This be a mean dog. She bad. *Loco.* You want a chain? My cousin, he got bit in the face by a chow chow. You want to chain her?"

Intently watching his dog then, Otero liked the way she looked at the shop manager. With a kind of scowl like she knew what the man was saying. She was a tough, scrappy little dog, but she seemed to like Otero, guarding the door when he was in the room and following him with her eyes. Otero did not reciprocate the bonding between them at first. He set her outside his house twice, driving away in his car and thinking that she would find her way to somewhere else—somewhere that needed a dog. He didn't do this in an unfeeling way, just in the way a man looks at what room he has left in his life to share.

Both times she had come back, or rather, refused to leave in the first place, curling up on the step outside his back kitchen door. So, naming her after an ex-wife who wouldn't go away either, Otero allowed her in, buying a small dog bed, a food bowl, and a leash. The more time he spent with her, the more he thought they had a lot in common—character-wise. Not wanting, but somehow needing to love something, he opened a small part of his heart to Anna that had long remained closed.

Late in the morning, delivering sales paperwork to a bank manager, Otero drove north through the city and stopped for an early lunch on Biscayne Boulevard.

When the mall exploded, he was standing across the street at Wild Man's Hamburgers. Holding a french fry in one hand, Otero opened the restaurant door to take his lunch back out to the car, when the air seemed sucked away from him and then pushed back—like an omnipotent hand against his chest. The sound of the explosion was so loud that it changed into no sound at all. As he turned, he saw three polished, white marble columns near the entry door of the mall burst outward, sending glass shards flying up into the air like crystal birds, gleaming with sun and dust and swift shards of steel.

*Jesus!* he thought, squinting up into the dust-colored sun. *Madre de Jesus! God, that push felt so good.* Mesmerized, he stood there for a while as the whole scene contracted from an expanding opaque cloud into a rain of chunks of dirt and falling pieces of pipe and wood. Waiting a minute or two longer, gazing up into the air, he stood transfixed as paper bags fluttered down toward the earth in a slow-motion spiral. It was beautiful. It was *goddamn* beautiful. Then, hearing sirens in the distance, he walked quickly to his car and, stuffing french fries into his mouth, drove out the back side of the parking lot toward home. The street was jammed with cars and people running. It would be better for him not to be found at the scene—just a gut feeling.

*There is a smell to an explosion,* he thought, pulling out of the lot. *A smell you don't forget.* He liked it.

# CHAPTER 3

## KEY LARGO, FLORIDA

The phone rang unanswered on Micelli's desk while he finished doing stomach curls on a workout board in the corner of his wood-paneled office. After a visit to Big Daddy Kane's for his tuna melt, this everyday workout kept him, with a six-pack stomach the envy of men half his age. He let the phone ring until he finished his fourth rep and then answered it quickly.

"Micelli. Key Largo Police." He was holding his stomach in. *Always hold your stomach in,* he told himself. *Then you won't have to think about it. Repetition is the mother of skill.*

It was a Sergeant Pitt from the Miami-Dade Police Department, calling about an explosion at the Biscayne Boulevard mall, just north of Miami Shores. There had been a lot of damage and one fatality, a man named Royston Alexander.

According to Pitt, Alexander was an upstanding citizen, a father of two, and the owner of a jewelry store at the mall. He was also a member of the Church Near the Shore in Bal Harbor, where he lived and had just finished a successful run for a seat on the city council. A concrete wall collapsed on top of him in the explosion. What intrigued police were several deep scars cut cleanly across his buttocks. Long healed, the unusual wound didn't happen in the explosion.

"I pulled up some information off the archives about a similar case in New York," Pitt said. "Your name was in the clip. So what's the deal with this Butt-Cutter guy? He went to jail for a long time, I know. Otero, right? Now this guy who used to work with him gets blown up in South Florida, and Otero's not too far away when it happens. We got him owning a car lot in Little Haiti. You think he's working again?"

Years flashed by in Micelli's mind, taking him back to a courtroom in New Jersey. *That was Otero's MO all right,* he thought; *it was pretty hard to beat.* He didn't want to think about Otero. "I'll have to get back to you," he said, finishing the call as Frances handed him a note. "Call your mother," it read. He sighed; his mother had been calling him, and it was starting to become a daily ritual. She was lonely in New Jersey, didn't understand why he felt the need for a transfer, was thinking about visiting him but was afraid to travel, didn't feel well and her neighborhood bridge club was having a potluck for charity. There was always something.

Dialing his mother's number, he asked Frances to pull his files from storage on the Butt-Cutter. She was giggling as she left the room. "The *what*-cutter?"

"Hi, Ma," he said, leaning back in his chair with his eyes closed. "No, I can't come up right now. I have a lot to finish up before I leave the department. Then I'll be able to visit. Soon. Yes, my leg feels much better. Uh-huh."

He placed the receiver down carefully on top of his desk as his mother continued to talk, and walked over to the small refrigerator against the far wall. Glancing into a small mirror above it, he thought he needed a shave; he looked up his nose, reached down, took a can of Coke out of the fridge, popped the top, and went back to the phone. Picking the receiver up from the desk, he cradled it between his chin and shoulder.

"Of course I'm listening to you," he said. There was a knock on the door, and Frances walked in and placed a stack of several files in front of him. She pointed at her watch and rolled her eyes. Micelli rolled his back.

"I gotta go now, Mom. Yes, Mom, me too. Bye. I'll call you next week. Bye. Bye. Good-bye." Frances smiled at him. *She has pretty blue eyes,* he thought. Before deciding for sure on the police academy, Micelli had thought seriously about becoming an optometrist. His mother had been thrilled, but his father was disappointed. Family tradition won out.

"Florida Highway Patrol is holding on line four," she said, picking at a piece of lint on the front of her sweater.

"Line four?" Micelli never got her sarcasm. "Frances, we only have two lines."

"It's the little blinking one," she said, smiling again. "You got tuna in your teeth."

Micelli kept a hand mirror in his center desk drawer and searched for it as he took the call. Two months ago, the Florida Highway Patrol had recovered the bodies of two men from a submerged Mercedes that had gone off Card Sound Road into Crocodile Lake. They were friars from the Monastery of the Vestibule Divine off West Dixie Highway in Miami. The initial coroner's report concluded it to be a fairly routine car accident; the driver was speeding, and the car missed a turn. In fact, Micelli knew that turn, and it was a tricky one. They were always fishing somebody out of the lake after a miss on the hairpin. To him, it sounded like another notch on nature's belt. So he was only half-listening until FHP mentioned something about the coroner and something about the bodies. One of them had strange horizontal cuts across his buttocks. A Sergeant Pitt had just spoken to them about the mall explosion, and after putting two and two together, Otero's name was coming up more times than law enforcement was comfortable with. Two of his ex-partners from Jersey showing up dead in the same general area of South Florida could hardly be a coincidence.

Something was going on. Micelli suddenly felt happy. There was a chance he could be doing investigative work instead of relocating turtles.

Frances stuck her head around the half-closed office door as he hung up the phone. "Busy you," she said. "While you were talking, the FBI called."

She walked in and dropped a stack of papers on the desk in front of him. Micelli hated it when her shoes slapped against the bottom of her feet—it was probably the only thing about her he didn't like. "They faxed this stuff for you to review. Oh, they want you to come to Miami tomorrow afternoon. I told them you weren't doing anything. You're not doing anything—are you?"

# CHAPTER 4

## MIAMI, FLORIDA

Neda Mason was infuriated. But that was a good thing, because for the first time in a long while, she was actually feeling something.

*It's only been a few months,* she thought, but it seemed like forever since Wilson had been killed. Her whole body ached for him. "My husband," she whispered, tasting the words, remembering him in her arms, remembering the smell of his hair, remembering the sounds he made while sleeping. He'd been shot dead for nothing. Shot that night in his wheelchair at Daddy Kane's Bar in Key Largo. Shot dead for nothing at all.

Troubled, she stood in her small kitchen, staring down into a sink half-full of dirty dishes. The dishwasher broke down weeks ago. But there wasn't much need to wash the dirty dishes. Hell, there wasn't much need to eat, for that matter. *Life just goes on,* she thought dully. *This is all there is to it—you just keep waking up.*

Days turned into nights and then back into days and then back into nights. Her life was like a great big, sad clock, ticking away from death and toward death at the same time. Everything seemed colorless in her life now, even the chipped red polish on the nails of her shaking hands. The doctor had given her some medicine to help her sleep, but the sleep that the pills brought didn't come with rest. It was sleep as empty as the house she lived in. As empty as the too-close-to-the-freeway neighborhood off 163rd Street that Wilson's grandmother had called home, long before the city tore through it with an overpass and an on-ramp.

Since Wilson's funeral, she wandered aimlessly around the house, going from room to room, picking something up and then forgetting why, putting something away and then forgetting where. Worst of all was her constant fear that she would inadvertently turn on the stove and somehow start a fire or not notice that the gas pilot had failed to light or overflow the tub—which she had already done. She tried not to look in the mirror, because she wasn't sure she could face what looked back. And all of this was happening because of that job arranged by her former boss, Royston Alexander. Neda called to her brother Andy.

"Hey, fool," she said, surprised at the strength in her voice. "You listen to me now, you hear?"

Andy was asleep in the big chair in the living room, his thin sides rattling as he worked hard to sleep off a binge of cocaine and Red Bull.

"Snark," he said. Drool ran from the corner of his mouth as he shifted to the side and scratched his crotch. He was a harmlessly pleasant-looking man—almost handsome once—but the drugs were doing their work, and he had a hollow look about him now, in a disheveled sort of bewildered way; the way drug-lost people look right before they're actually lost.

Some people thought it was laugh-out-loud funny that Andy was Neda's brother. *The two of us are like a party trick,* she thought once when they were younger. That was because they couldn't have been more opposite. Neda was African-American, and Andy was Caucasian. Where Andy was tall and thin and goofy, Neda was relaxed and graceful and poised. Where Andy had a tendency to stutter, Neda spoke carefully and clearly. After a while, the laughter got old, but Neda expected and understood it. Although they were foster brother and sister, in Neda's heart and in what remained of Andy's, they couldn't be any closer than blood-related siblings.

Both of them had been taken in by a woman known in Key Largo as Mambo Taffy. She was a big, boisterous, happy woman hailing originally from Ile de la Tortue, or Tortuga Island, off the north coast of Haiti. From there, she moved as a young bride of eighteen to the hard knocks of Alabama in the '60s, spending years involved in civil rights, religious work, and foster parenting. Finally settling in the upper Florida Keys, she finished her doctorate and was hired as a professor of English at the University of Miami. Educated and articulate, she proudly carried the title "Mambo" as a fully fledged Vodou priestess, and, seeing no religious inconsistency, was active in her local Catholic church.

It was Mambo Taffy who fostered Neda after she was discovered at the age of two, abandoned and sitting on the floor of a filthy bathroom at a Chevron gas station in Little Haiti. She had fallen asleep there, all alone overnight, with her little head against a pile of used and damp paper hand towels. The thought of this still caused Mambo Taffy to wake up in a cold sweat. And Mambo took Andy in when he was barely four months old, after he was released from the hospital and diagnosed with severe shaken baby and fetal alcohol syndrome. His single mother, who was addicted to methamphetamine, returned to her parents in Minnesota, later dying of toxic shock. Andy was sweet when he was a little boy—always so sweet.

Neda was shouting at him now as she turned away from the sink and stalked into the living room.

"Andy!" Neda bellowed. "Jesus, God, wake up, you!" She could be a pretty woman, but now her brown face was perspiring, her hair stuck out at odd ends, and her hands shook as she made fists and held them together under her chin.

"Whaaa . . ." Andy said. He didn't do mornings, or really afternoons either. Sometimes, Andy didn't do whole days.

Neda stood over him, staring down into his face. "You. Skinny. Idiot," she said. "Maybe you did one thing right—Alexander is dead. But Andy! You blew out one whole side of the mall. We talked about this! We talked about this!" She was huffing and sweating and walking around the room; the glare of the fluorescent ceiling light shone against the sweat across her brow.

"Andy, baby, please wake up." She knelt down next to his chair, pleading. "It was about Wilson. We agreed on that." She clenched her fists again and pressed one against her heart. "My Wilson." Laying her forehead against the side of Andy's arm, she felt nothing but loneliness. "Alexander didn't care. He knew. He knew those men would be there waiting at Daddy Kane's." She felt the tears welling up in her eyes and swallowed hard, trying to fight them back. "He knew." There was a final sound to her words.

"Shump," Andy said, his hands fluttering around his face like little birds. "Bleew uppl."

Never in her life had Neda felt so helpless and so frustrated at the same time. And *there had been times,* she thought, *yes, there had been times.* The most beautiful relationship she ever had with the most beautiful man she had ever known had all come to an end when that stupid, naïve, sweet-tasting man believed what that liar, Alexander, had promised. Neda told Wilson, *Never trust a fast-talker running for city council who didn't wash his hands after he went to the bathroom, didn't stand up when a lady came into the room, and chewed his gum with his mouth wide open.* Neda, above everything else, was a lady.

They could be in big trouble now; she knew that. First she lost Wilson, and now, slowly, Andy was drifting away. *Which would be more excruciating?* she asked herself. *Two losses were two too many.* It was just supposed to be some sort of small retribution. Retribution for Wilson. A love note from Neda to her man. Andy, of course, cranked-out and open wide, had blown half the block up. Now Neda felt guilty because she had seen that in his face when, in a moment of weakness, she said to him, "Andy, listen, let's get some payback from Alexander. I need this. For Wilson." And Andy had opened his eyes for the first time in several days, and actually focused.

Now, news of the explosion at the mall was being broadcast everywhere, and the cops were issuing press releases and patrolling the streets, stopping every passerby and manning barricades.

Neda's only thoughts were of her nights without Wilson, life without the things they wanted to have together, and that stupid son-of-a-bitch dead-now Alexander. *It was so unfair.*

There was an unexpected knock at the front door. Neda swore under her breath as she crossed the small living room and willed her hand to turn the doorknob. Through the gauzy curtains covering the glass top half of the old, wooden door, she could see an outline of a police officer in full uniform. Blinking lights on the top of his car flashed from the curb, as another officer leaned against the car while talking on the radio.

"Andy," she whispered hoarsely, glancing back over her shoulder toward him, "maybe you better go into the kitchen."

# CHAPTER 5

## LITTLE HAITI, MIAMI

Even in religious practice, animal sacrifice is illegal in Miami. So an enterprising Haitian businessman had purchased the goat heads from a local farmer and frozen them before they were delivered to the open-air market in Little Haiti. Available for an agreeable donation to the Brave Myrto Botanica, the heads were kept on ice in a cooler under a table topped with a purple and silver sequined cloth. Otero thought that a decent amount of money was probably being made that fine sunny day, due to the number of Jesus-faced bags he saw being carried out of the market.

He liked working on the weekends and watching the people come and go from the busy market across the street. Scattered conversations in Creole drifted over to the car lot, along with the sounds of giggling children, singing roosters, and squalling babies. Smoke from corner barbeques wafted around the heads of young women in multihued wraps, as they chatted with the age-weary old charm sellers they would someday become. The market was busy. On Saturday, Little Haiti came alive.

Otero walked back into his cramped office, sat down at his desk, and carefully picked up his razor from inside the desk drawer. He ran his finger lightly along its sharp edge and smiled. He cleaned the razor every day, liking the way it made him feel as he sat there at his desk, holding it.

As a little man, he was undistinguished in a crowd. This was both an observation and an ability that he practiced until he was convinced that he had the skill to become invisible. Once, to test this talent, he walked into a local bank, through the lobby and down a hall, opening a door marked "no entry." It was a telephone closet. He walked inside, closing the door behind him, and stood there for a while. All sorts of possibilities occurred to him, and he made a mental note to return at a later date.

Now he looked down at his blade and then held the cool, bright metal under his nose. He could smell it. They had all paid now. It had been a matter of principle. If you stole money from Otero, you paid the price. It was basically predictable, just like day and night, like black and white, like up and down. *Sort of like gravity,* he thought. It made sense in the bigger picture of things, once you knew how to see the whole picture. He saw that as part of his responsibility—to show some people the whole picture.

Reaching down next to his chair, he gently patted Anna on the head. She licked the back of his hand. *She has such a sweet face,* he thought, looking into her black eyes. A flicker across the television screen caught his eye as the Local-6 News anchor started her midday broadcast with video of the mall explosion. Turning the sound up, he watched footage of the debris and listened as she continued her broadcast by surmising which terrorist group had been responsible.

"Unknown terrorists strike, leaving one dead and at least seven injured today when a bomb explodes at New Marlin Mall in Bal Harbor." The camera panned across the front of the mall, showing several marble columns laying in pieces on the ground as "Breaking News" stretched across news lady's chest in bright-red block letters.

Anna's water bowl was empty, and Otero was filling it, so he only half-heard the dead man's name. News lady was saying something about "jewelry" and "city council," and then the face of a man flashed across the television, and Otero was shocked. He knew that man. Reaching for the remote, he turned up the sound for a second time and rummaged through his center desk drawer, pulling out a manila folder. He checked his watch; 3:00 p.m. It had only been two hours since the explosion, and the news crew had already filmed the dead man's "upstanding" wife—emerging artist BlueJean Alexander, as she cried into her handkerchief. *Nobody uses handkerchiefs anymore,* thought Otero. That was real classy. *She* looked real classy. He made himself a mental note: *buy some handkerchiefs.*

Hastily, and with fixed intent, Otero opened a folder and removed an old clipping from the Metro section of the *Miami Herald.* Two friars from this monastery in Miami were dead after their car went off Card Sound Road in the Keys and ended up in the water. There was a picture of the two men and Otero was positive—100 percent positive—that he knew one of them, and the man wasn't a religious person, that was for sure.

Now, seeing this Alexander guy's name and face on the local news, he was starting to sense a pattern. *Well, well,* he thought. *A scam. And not a small one either.* His instincts told him that if the two men were both in South Florida, something was in the making. *Making and shaking.* He could taste it. Particularly since he knew that the fake friar and the jewelry store wannabe city councilman at the mall had been partners years before.

An old feeling of excitement ran through him as he thought back to Jersey. Both of these dead men had been on his payroll. They had underestimated Otero, and that was something they would be very sorry for. It had been a double-cross, and Otero had dealt with them in his own way. The Butt-Cutter found them, and the Butt-Cutter cut them. One at a time. He found Alexander first, in the back of a pharmacy parking lot late at night. It was winter in Jersey, and as his victim's blood spattered to the ground, he watched it shimmer into ice crystals on the black asphalt lot. As the blood froze, Otero thought the streetlights flashed against it like music. *My own tune,* he remembered thinking.

The other one, the man Otero *knew* wasn't a real friar, had been more difficult; the man's small daughter had been with him the whole week, while Otero followed him. Finally, after work late one night, the man stopped for beer and bread at a Farm Store, and he was alone. Otero, dressed in black, walked quickly up to the passenger side of the man's car and slid inside. He forced the stammering man to drive away and pull into an alley. Forcing the man out of the car and then into the back seat, Otero used the shiv. One of his favorite memories remained the smell and the squeal the man made with his lips pressed tightly together. *Cry like a baby,* thought Ortero. *Go on, cry.*

He took a sip of water and read the article again. *Got to have a look around Miami a little bit,* he thought. *Make some calls. Find out what my old friends are up to.*

# CHAPTER 6

---

## NORTH MIAMI BEACH, FLORIDA

Set well back off Dixie Highway in North Miami Beach, the Monastery of the Vestibule Divine was a popular destination for upscale weddings, banquets, and receptions. Chairs were available for a donation of $50 each, a large round table could be borrowed for $450, and absolutely no rice was allowed on the premises. A donation of $2,500 was required up front for a time not to exceed an hour and a half, and guests were advised that it would not be possible to set up a bar on either side of the chapel doors.

The monastery building itself was born in the province of Angoumois, France, in 1238, and had been purchased by Howard Hughes during his movie-mogul phase, packed into eleven thousand wooden crates, and shipped to South Florida. After some misfortune in the form of sea delays, greedy cargo masters, and lost manifests, the building was eventually re-assembled and placed into the mossy arms of a Florida hummock, complete with its French altar and original prayer well. There, stone by stone, it rose again—Phoenix-like, into a religious retreat and a half-tidy tourist attraction.

*Bought for American history,* thought Micelli. *Almost anything could be had for a buck.*

Micelli walked slowly through the stone arches and into the chapel hall. It was the middle of the afternoon, and it seemed he was alone in the building. It was cool and pleasant inside; shafts of light broke boldly through tall windows and splashed across the dark stone floors. Wafts of dust floated up through the afternoon sun and cascaded back down again like dancing fairies with transparent skirts. In the distance, a bell tinkled. His shoes made absolutely no sound as he crossed the heavy stones. Walking over to a wooden bench, he sat down. His leg was hurting. The seam on his dark-blue uniform pant leg was starting to come apart. *Like my career,* he thought, looking at it.

"Can I help you with something, officer?" said a soft voice behind him.

Startled, Micelli jumped and looked around.

A young man was standing next to the bench, and he held out a smooth hand. He wore faded jeans with a hole in one knee, boat shoes, and a black T-shirt that said "Epiphany" on it in white letters. "I'm Friar Bill."

"Just thought I'd have a look around," Micelli said. He felt tired. "I drive by this place all the time, and I've never stopped."

The friar turned his head to one side. "Your badge says 'Key Largo Police' on it; that's kind of a long drive for you, isn't it?" He smiled. "How long does it take to get to Key Largo from here? About two hours?"

Micelli ignored the question.

"Did you know the men killed in the car accident a few months ago, Friar?" he asked. Micelli liked to ask direct questions. Getting quickly to the point often got a surprised but more revealing answer.

The friar did indeed flinch. "I knew one of them very well," he said after more than a few seconds, during which he was looking down at the floor. "Friar Nathan. We called him Master Nathan—he was a genius of a scholar and teacher. The other one, Friar Allen, was new here." He looked up, suddenly annoyed. "He came to us last year from the Cistercian Abbey of Our Lady up in New Jersey. We have, I believe, already answered these questions."

"Sorry," Micelli said. "I'm really not here in any official way. I know about the case, but I really just wanted to have a look around." He stood up from the bench. "This is a beautiful place."

The friar visibly sagged. "This whole incident has been most trying, Officer . . ."

"Micelli."

"Micelli. Most upsetting. It was a terrible car accident, yes, and we've had several visits from the police and yesterday—just yesterday, we had a visit from the FBI. Can you imagine that? For a car accident? That's kind of overkill, don't you think?" He was wringing his hands. "Overkill. I can't believe I said that."

They walked together toward the hand-carved, ancient wooden doors to the main chapel. Micelli wondered himself what the FBI's involvement was but guessed he would find out soon enough. He had a 3:00 appointment that afternoon with a special agent in charge at the North Miami Beach office on Second Avenue.

"I'll just have a walk 'round, if that's okay," he said to the friar. They shook hands, and Micelli took the next left toward a gift shop he'd seen when he came in. His mother loved postcards, and he had seen some nice ones while passing the little room earlier. Once inside, he picked up a couple of the colorful cards and leaned down to look into a glass case by the cash register. A brooch winked at him from in between some pearl earrings. Asking the clerk to hand them both to him, he thought, *why not?* He paid the price on the little gold corner sticker; his mother's birthday was coming soon and she would be pleased by the small gift. He could picture the way she would open the box, take in her breath, and touch her fingers to her throat.

Outside in the parking lot, Micelli walked toward his car and flipped out the postcards, looking at them again. His mother was pressuring him to move back to Jersey after he retired. Why was he finding it so difficult to make a decision? Pulling the velvet box out of the gift sack, he opened the lid and checked the little earrings and the brooch. He clapped the lid shut and turned the box over.

On the bottom it said, "Alexander's Jewelry. Bal Harbor."

*     *     *

Special Agent in Charge Pascale was on time to the minute for their appointment. He offered Micelli a bottle of water and thanked him for coming. The FBI field office wasn't what Micelli expected. Somehow he envisioned that it would be more official looking, with lots of stainless steel and glass walls or a fountain or two. Instead, it looked just like the old State Farm Insurance office where his uncle used to work in New Jersey. There was a lot of aqua. He was disappointed.

"Follow me," said Pascale, as they walked down the slightly shabby hallway toward the conference room. Somehow, Micelli knew it would have dark wood paneling and smell of mold. There would be a fake potted plant in the corner.

"In here."

Pascale opened the door, and Micelli followed him inside.

There, sitting at the end of a long, empty table, nervously smoking a cigarette, was Neda Mason. She smoothed her hands across her skirt and straightened her back. Micelli could see that she'd been crying.

"Have a seat," said Pascale. He motioned Micelli toward a chair opposite Neda, placed a folder in the middle of the table, and stood across from them with his foot on the rung of a chair.

"Mrs. Mason, this is Captain Micelli. He's assisting us in this case, and I'd like him to be present when you talk with us."

Pascale took his foot off the chair, paused, and looked over the top of his glasses down his nose at Micelli, waiting. Micelli thought maybe he should say something but couldn't think what. He looked over at Neda, but she was staring out the window.

Pascale picked up the folder and looked at it. He cleared his throat and looked again over the top of his glasses. "You know you aren't being charged with anything, right, Mrs. Mason? You understand that we just want some information from you about your husband, Wilson. You can have an attorney present if you want, or you can leave now. You don't have to talk to us at all if you don't want to, okay?"

Pascale stopped and looked at Micelli again. Micelli looked at Neda.

"Can I have a tissue?" she said.

Pascale walked over to a side table, picked up a box, and slid it across the table in front of her.

"You were at the bar the night my husband was killed," Neda said, looking at Micelli. It wasn't a question. "I remember your name from the newspaper."

Micelli was shocked. He looked over at Pascale and then back at Neda. "I—yes," was all he could manage.

"We know about the crack," said Pascale, completely ignoring the exchange between the two of them. "We know about Wilson's involvement with the distribution of it in South Florida." He was standing with his legs apart now, hand on his hips. Micelli thought he looked the part—puffed up somehow.

"Face it, Ms. Mason, this time Wilson got in over his head—way over his head. We want to catch the people responsible for his death, and I'm sure you want them caught too, right?"

"They're all caught," she said flatly. She looked down into her lap and turned her hands over, looking at each finger. "Or they might be sitting in this room."

"What?" said Pascale, still oblivious to their conversation. "Alexander's dead, yes, after an explosion at his store. Oh, and I understand that your brother got himself arrested. He likes to start fires, right? Anyway, the monks, or whoever they were—we'll find out—they're dead thanks to a curve in the road. But there's somebody else, isn't there? Somebody else was working with Alexander." He leaned down close to her.

"I don't know," she said. She brushed a stray hair away from her forehead and ran the back of her right finger under her nose. Micelli handed her another tissue. The room was quiet.

"Mrs. Mason?" Micelli said quietly, trying to make his voice sound reassuring. "What you remembered is correct. I was there on the night Wilson was shot. When I got there, the owner told me Wilson grabbed the till. What I'm wondering is why would a man in a wheelchair try a smash-and-grab for the till of a bar? It's probably not reasonable for him to be able to make a quick getaway, now is it? How do you think your husband expected to take the till at Daddy Kane's Bar and ever make it out of the parking lot?"

Pascale stood up. He and Neda both looked at Micelli.

"What?" Pascale started to say.

Micelli talked over him. "I've been thinking about it, and you know what I think? I think Wilson was afraid when he went into that bar." Micelli scooted his chair sideways, moving closer to Neda. "I don't think he went there to rob the place . . . I think he grabbed that money so he could create a diversion and maybe get away from a bad situation. What exactly was his connection with the men from the monastery? You know, I think . . ."

Pascale sounded irritated. "Micelli," he interrupted, "can I see you in the hall?" He looked at Neda. "We won't be long."

The men got up and walked toward the conference-room door. Micelli's leg hurt.

Out in the hallway, Pascale leaned against the wall, sighed, took his glasses off, and rubbed the top of his nose with his thumb and forefinger. "Where are you going with this, Micelli?"

"You could have talked to me before you started the interview," Micelli said. "If I'm supposed to be assisting you, you might have asked me what I know and how I know it." At this minute, he hated the whole system. "You might have asked me if I was available for this interview. Told me who would be here, stuff like that—working together stuff.

You might have asked how I would feel sitting across the table from the wife of the man who shot me."

"Look, I don't care how you feel. We don't need some headline-seeking hotshot on this case," Pascale said. "We need solid police work. You're only here because someone at division headquarters is trying to fry my butt, get it? The best thing you can do is just sit in the room quietly and let me do my job. Be a good boy. Besides, it's my understanding that you shot him back."

Pascale started to walk past Micelli and back into the conference room.

Micelli shook his head and smiled, took a deep breath, and gave Pascale a quick, hard punch in the stomach.

"You were an asshole in Jersey, and you're still an asshole, Pascale," said Micelli.

The door to the conference room opened, and Neda stuck her head out. Pascale was throwing up in a wastebasket.

"Can I use the ladies' room?" she asked.

# CHAPTER 7

## NORTH MIAMI BEACH, FLORIDA

Pete Otero sat in his car in the parking lot of the monastery. *Damn middle age,* he thought, looking down at his belly as it cascaded over his belt. This was one reason he hated wearing suits—every year, he went up one waist size. Stepping out of the car, he picked up his briefcase from the back seat, straightened his tie, and walked onto the grounds of the monastery.

The gardens were brilliant with orchids, bromeliad, and hanging ferns amid an emerald canopy of lush foliage. Otero could hear the sound of splashing water from a small stone fountain as he walked between the cars along a leafy path. He counted four new Mercedes, one Bentley, one Rolls Royce, and two Range Rovers. A battered Volkswagen sat separate from the rest. A sign in the window said, "Kaufman's Kosher Delivery." *Altogether, a lot of money in nuts and bolts,* he mused. *Not an order proselytizing poverty.*

Inside the main building, the stone floors were cool, and the air seemed light and fresh. When his eyes adjusted to the shady halls, he followed what seemed to be the way to the main office.

Passing a group of people standing in a tall double-door, he heard the sound of arguing. "It's policy, Mrs. Martin. I'm sorry," a man was saying. He sounded bored. "The price for the chapel is $1,400. Or you can stand in front of the banyan tree for $1,200. That's not going to include the music, you know."

"Friar," said the woman, "you let Barbara Ramsey do both for only $900. This is outrageous!" Her voice was shrill and loud, and Otero noticed the size and number of rings on her thick fingers. *Money,* he thought. *She was bathed in it.*

"Calling me every hour and coming over here like this won't change the policy, Mrs. Martin. Regardless of what you think Barbara Ramsey paid."

Otero skirted the arguing group and walked through the arched doorway that said "Administration."

"Yes?" a voice said. "May I help you?"

A young man was standing in front of a filing cabinet. A stack of papers teetered on a chair beside him.

"My name is Russell Moore," said Otero. "I'm from Prudential Insurance. We're investigating a crash involving a Mercedes, about two months ago in the Keys. Killed two men. Our records show they were affiliated with your church—or whatever—here."

"I know the crash you're talking about, Mr. Moore," the young man said, sounding exasperated. "I know the men. What kind of information are you looking for? I mean, we've talked to so many people, I can't possibly see what else there is to tell."

"Prudential is doing an independent audit of the crash. Originally we thought it was driver error, nothing more, and you know, we have to fill out those questionnaires. Unfortunately, Father . . ."

"It's Friar. Friar Bill."

"Well, I'm sorry, Friar, but according to the Miami Coroner's Office, toxicology tests have come back with positive results for cocaine in the blood of the driver."

"*Coroner's Office?* That's *impossible.*" The friar looked like he was going to cry. He was sputtering. "You—can't—*possibly*—tell people that."

"Well, of course, our information will remain confidential, that's why I'm coming to speak directly to you."

"Well it *better* remain confidential." The friar slammed the file drawer shut. His face was flushed. "In fact, if it doesn't, I can assure you that you'll have to look both ways when you cross the street to avoid the lawsuit that's going to hit you. What is it you want to know?"

"Well," Otero said, "to start with, I'd like a copy of the personnel files for both men, and then I'd like to have a look at their personal effects."

"I really should check with the police before I give you any material," said the friar. He looked defiant, but Otero noticed that the top of his lip was perspiring.

"Check with anybody you want," said Otero, "but listen. Between you and me, I'm sure those toxicology tests will turn out to be wrong. Your order here is obviously beyond reproach. These mistakes happen. And I'm sure there will be no publicity. I myself, I almost never speak to the press."

There was a sharp knock at the door.

"Barbara Ramsey is nothing but a jealous bitch," said a shrill voice through the door. "She probably made all that up, you know. She doesn't want to admit she doesn't know the first thing about how to have a proper reception."

The friar's shoulders fell. He closed his eyes.

Otero was quiet for a minute, and both men could hear the woman's shrill voice from the hallway. "And another thing. This is very important. I just have to *have* the Iglesias party seated early, Friar." There was another loud knock. Otero started to move toward the door, but the friar shook his head quickly. They both stared at the doorknob as it turned back and forth and then looked back at each other. "There can be absolutely no press," the voice went on. "*Please,* no press."

Friar Bill was staring at the jiggling knob.

The voice outside continued. "And she speaks French like the Spanish cow she really is."

The friar's voice was a whisper. "Well, I suppose I could give you the same information that I gave to the police," he said quickly. "I mean, they already have it."

He reached into a file cabinet and handed Otero a file; then, taking a deep breath, he walked quickly to the door and opened it.

"Oh!" said the shrill voice. "I didn't know anyone was in here."

Friar Bill's face was very red.

Otero rolled his eyes and stepped in between him and the woman.

"Excuse us one minute, ma'am," Otero said. "Friar Bill, you were going to show me the living quarters?"

"We'll be right back, Mrs. Martin," the friar said warmly. He reached out toward her, taking both her hands into his. "Why don't you come in and have a seat?"

"Well I don't know—" she started. Friar Bill stepped out into the hall, danced her into his office, and shut the door.

"Go," he said to Otero, making a motion down the hallway. "Down that hallway take the first left. Just. Go."

*　　*　　*

Cleaning crews come in during the day at FBI headquarters, and so Micelli had to step over a mop and a bucket to get back into the conference room.

Neda had come back into the room and was standing in front of the window, looking out over the parking lot.

"What did Wilson do for a living, Mrs. Mason?" he asked, sitting down at the table behind her.

"He was a certified inspector of fire extinguishers," she said, without looking at him. There was pride in her voice. "He serviced and repaired them. He had his own business—his own shop, and he worked hard."

"So what was the deal with the drugs?"

She took a deep breath and turned around slowly. She looked tired. Reaching out toward a chair at the end of the table, she pulled it toward her and sat down heavily, putting her elbows on the table.

"We didn't have any medical insurance," she said. "Everything was at stake—not just his health, but the business, our house." Her voice was barely audible, and she seemed to struggle. "He ended up a cripple." Her shoulders seemed to sag and then straighten. "That was a long time ago, and I don't suppose it matters now. He's dead." She was looking down at the backs of her hands, and then she looked up into Micelli's face. "Sometimes good people do bad things." Her lips were trembling. "Sometimes even though you know what's right, you still have no other choice but to do what's wrong."

Micelli paused and let the moment pass. *She's pretty,* he thought, *pretty in a sad sort of way.* "How did Wilson get hooked up with Alexander?" he asked.

Pascale walked back into the conference room, holding one hand over his lower abdomen. He seemed stiff as he sat down slowly near the middle of the table. He didn't say anything.

"I knew Alexander," Neda said. "I worked for him off and on as a housekeeper when I was going to school at night—finishing my degree. Once, I told him about Wilson's business, and he asked if he could meet him. Later, I found out they made a deal to smuggle cocaine in some of the fire extinguishers on cruise ships that came into the Port of Miami." She took another tissue and blew her nose. "It was so easy." Her voice trailed away. "Wilson would collect the extinguishers from the ships when they came back into port for regular service, empty out the drugs, refill them with the real chemicals, put on a new certified sticker, and send the extinguishers back to the ship. Worked like a clock."

"What went wrong?"

"What makes you think something went wrong?"

"Wilson's dead, and I got shot in the process," said Micelli. "Something went very wrong at Big Daddy's Bar, didn't it?"

Neda didn't answer.

"Who was Wilson there to meet?"

"He found something in one of the extinguishers," she said. "Something he wasn't supposed to find." She started to cry. Micelli looked at Pascale, who got up and walked toward them, sitting down again next to Neda and across from Micelli. Neda blew her nose into another tissue and let the tears run down into the corners of her mouth. Her eyes were closed.

"I didn't see what it was. But Wilson told me later that there were some floor plans or a blueprint or something rolled up inside one of the extinguishers," she said. "He said they were serious plans with notes written on each page."

"Blueprints?" said Pascale. This was a new development. "Of what?"

Neda's voice was very quiet. "Turkey Point Nuclear Power Plant," she said.

"Power plant?" said Pascale. *He looks like a Doberman*, Micelli thought. Micelli thought a lot of people looked like dogs. "Do you still have the prints?"

She shifted in her chair. "No," she said. "Wilson gave them to Alexander. It was part of their deal. Do you have any coffee or anything?" She blew her nose again.

"Tea," said Pascale, making notes on a piece of paper.

"The FBI doesn't have any coffee?"

"It's a budget thing," Pascale answered without looking up. "It's the end of the month. Tea is what's left."

"Fine. Well, thanks then," Neda said, standing up. "Since whether or not I talk to you is up to me, you can consider that I'm done with this chat."

Micelli stood up. Neda noticed that. Pascale didn't; he was still writing notes.

"Unless you're going to charge me with something," she said, "I'm done. Out of here."

"What?" Pascale didn't seem to hear.

She walked past them to the door of the conference room. "Taxpayer dollars," she said with a sniff, stepping over the mop and bucket. "You'd think they could cover coffee."

# CHAPTER 8

## BAL HARBOR, MIAMI

The guard gate at Fishtail Estates on Bal Harbor Island was broken on the entry side, so all the cars that were trying to get in had to wait for those that were trying to get out. And vice versa. It was a mini-traffic disaster, and it was irritating Jean Alexander. She had just dropped her boys off at her mother-in-law's place in Miami Beach, where they would stay for the next few days, as she tried to get her life and her mind back together. The mall explosion left her a widow for a second time. Her first husband had gone from lung cancer, and now her second sugar daddy in this unbelievable explosion.

She actually overheard her younger son, who was three, say, "Go to work—boom!" to his brother. At the time, through her shock, she wished it could happen to her. Go to the kitchen—boom! She tried to explain it to the boys so they could understand. Daddy went to work, and there was a big sound, and Daddy was dead now, which meant that he would not be coming home.

The jewelry store would be closed. Certainly, the mall would rebuild the space, but it would be without Alexander's Jewelry. She had no inclination to work.

Then, at a cocktail party she attended two nights after his death, she overheard someone referring to her as an "Emmy Award"—well, she guessed that pretty well summed her up. She could be a bit of an actress. But what was she supposed to do? Stay home and practice grief-induced self-mutilation? She drummed her poppy-red fingernails against the steering wheel as a lawn-maintenance driver stopped to talk at the guard gate in front of her. Just because she wasn't cloistered, draped in black, and swooning to Roy's memory didn't mean she didn't love him. True, perhaps leading a toast at the party that began, "Maybe the third time will be the charm for me," might have been construed by some as slightly out of place. But people who knew Jean recognized that above everything else in her entire life, she had never been—well, *appropriate*. Just because Roy was dead, why did everything have to be about him anyway? He wasn't going to actually know that Herb

Meyerhans stuck his tongue down the throat of the grieving widow, now, was he?

Roy was *dead*, for God's sake. Screw what people thought anyway. She laid her palm hard against the horn.

Life had been fine for her and Roy, and nobody needed to understand that but her. It was just fine. He did his jewelry-store, community-service thing and she did her wife-mother-artist thing. He got what he wanted—a family, a portrait in American respectability, and in turn, she was given the style of life that suited her. Besides being shockingly beautiful, she was analytical. Being married to Roy gave her the time—and the money—to indulge in her one great passion: contemporary art. Her paintings were just beginning to be shown; slowly, a budding career was taking place. Signing her paintings with one name, "BlueJean," she used her body as her paintbrush and painted only in her signature color of blue. A market had not yet fully presented itself—but it would.

She had a talent that was difficult to ignore. And she could also paint.

Finally pulling into her driveway, Jean made a mental note to consider moving to a community that had a separate entrance for service people. She was tired of lawn people and pool people; she was tired of all the people in general that it took to keep life going. She could be happy living somewhere out in the woods, she thought, if it had decent shopping.

Throwing her keys down onto a hall table, she started to pick up a few things around the house. With kids, there was always something lying on top of something that needed to be washed. Finally, cleaning her house for the third time after the housekeeper had already done it, she turned her attention to the office next to the family room. Roy had left his briefcase under the mahogany desk that was angled in the middle of the room. He was obsessive about that briefcase. It was either in his hand, or it was under that desk. The room was out of bounds to the kids, and he didn't appreciate it when she went in there either. The case now sat oddly next to his chair, away from its usual safe cubbyhole. *Funny,* she thought, looking at it, *the fabric of our lives is usually made out of a consistent weave—but not always. He must have had other things on his mind.*

She picked up the case and opened it. When she saw the blueprints for the first time, she half-heartedly tossed them aside. It was only after a second look that her eyes narrowed and she felt that a shot of scotch would be a good idea right about now.

Her heels clicked as she crossed the porcelain tile floor toward the wet bar adjacent to the Florida room. A former model, she was tall and fine-featured with a platinum mane of blonde hair stacked carefully and expensively atop her head. Colored by Bruno at the Capillo Salon on Arthur Godfrey Road, the perfect pale locks were part of what Roy liked about the way she looked. Bruno was paid extra to use the color only on her. A lot extra.

She crossed her long legs and let the scotch run to the back of her throat. What to do next? She folded the blueprints and then rolled them back into a tight roll. *Like a nightstick,* she thought. *Could hurt somebody.* She held them in her right hand and slapped them into her left palm. Actually, that was her second thought. Her first was how much money they might be worth—and to whom.

Placing a thick rubber band around the roll, she walked over to a large gilded mirror in the middle of the entryway and gazed at the woman who looked back at her. *Not bad,* she thought, *for two kids and two husbands.* If she held her stomach in and tilted her head back, she could knock off five or six years. The jewelry store and its inventory would leave her enough to get a good start—a damn good start. After that, the insurance money would see that she was comfortable. But maybe there was more.

She picked up her telephone book from the side table and thumbed through it to the number for her attorney. She waited as it rang, making a note to book a bikini wax. "This is Jean Alexander," she said to the woman who answered. "Is Seymour in? Fine. Have him call me back. Oh! Tell him I want to talk to someone who's under arrest. Andy somebody. The guy they arrested after the mall explosion—you know, the guy who blew Roy up."

Maybe this Andy guy could shed some light on what her husband had been up to. It was a place to start.

# CHAPTER 9

## NORTH MIAMI BEACH, FLORIDA

Deep inside the monastery, Otero stood in the middle of the quiet, cool, dormitory-style room. "Thanks, Friar," he said. "I'll just have a look around."

"That's okay," the friar answered. "I'll wait." He folded his arms over his chest and leaned against the doorframe.

There was little to see. It looked like the room had been cleaned thoroughly. There was no paperwork left anywhere. No art or any decoration at all graced the thick rock walls. The floor was bare, polished stone, and the ceiling was crossed by two heavy wooden beams. Two small beds were placed side by side; each was covered with a white sheet and a folded navy blue blanket. A bucket and a mop stood in one corner. A dresser with a small mirror seemed forlorn against the middle wall of the room. Otero was disappointed. He walked over to the closet, opened the door, and ran his hand through the few pieces of clothing hanging there. A brown paper bag in the corner of the closet held a few envelopes along with a magazine and some crumpled maps. A shaft of light beamed through the dust in the air from the window and splayed over a fire extinguisher standing against the corner of the room. He walked into the austere white bathroom and fingered a magazine left on the corner of the counter. *Gardening Wisdom.*

The shower faucet dripped against the porcelain tub as one single stream of rust ran the length of the tub to the drain. He sighed. *Empty,* he thought. *Shit! Well, it was worth a look.* He took a deep breath. *It smells good in here,* he thought; *sort of minty.* His footsteps echoed as he turned to leave the room.

"Well, this is it," the friar said. "This was Brother Allen's room."

"Not a lot here," Otero answered. They looked at each other. The friar shrugged his shoulders. Otero walked back into the small bedroom. "This Brother Allen," he asked, "had he been with you very long?"

"No, he was fairly new to our order. I didn't know him well."

"Did he come from New Jersey?"

"New Jersey? Well, yes, I think he did. Why?"

A door slammed loudly down at the far end of the hall, and both men jumped.

"Friar Bill?" The man's voice seemed far away, but the tone was urgent. The friar stepped into the hall.

"Yes?" he answered.

A flurry of quick steps came to the door of the room. "Oh dear, you'd better come quickly," the voice said.

"What's the matter?"

"It's Barbara Ramsey; she just pulled into the parking lot and ran her car *straight* into Mrs. Martin's Bentley. I couldn't believe it. The two of them are actually throwing gravel at each other right now. It's terrible."

"God," the friar answered. Otero looked at him. "Just a small prayer," the friar said quickly. "I have to go."

"Don't worry about me. I'm leaving," said Otero, following him out into the hallway. One thing was for sure: Friar Allen wasn't a friar. And he was definitely from New Jersey. Otero could personally vouch for that. *Interesting.*

*   *   *

*Maybe it's time to look up an old friend,* thought Micelli as he walked out of the FBI office building and into the parking lot. Pascale's written report had mentioned the Butt-Cutter along with the men who died on Card Sound Road. What could their connection be to Neda? He ran his hand along the back of his neck and wondered if he should give his mother a call. The sun was pounding against the black tarmac so hard, it made a noise in his temples. *Damn paradise,* he thought. *Damn heat.*

He walked over to his car and got in, started the motor, and turned on the air conditioning. Neda Mason had left the FBI building ahead of him and was now standing on the curb under a large banyan tree across the street near the bus stop. The hot breeze moved her skirt as she brushed her hair away from her face. *Might as well wait,* thought Micelli as he reached into his briefcase and pulled out his cell phone. *See what I can see.*

"Mom?" he said after dialing quickly. "It's me."

Micelli watched as Neda dropped her purse and bent over to pick it up. *She has nice legs*, he thought. Then reflecting further, he noted that she had fairly nice everything.

"Hello?" he said into the phone. "No, I'm listening. Sorry."

Neda sighed and glanced at her watch. She looked impatient.

"Look, Mom, I realize your potato salad recipe is very important to you," Micelli said, "but this whole thing is so ridiculous. Aunt Helen didn't use red potatoes in an attempt to communicate secretly with the neighbors. She probably used red potatoes because that's what she had in the house."

A dark sedan pulled up to the curb near the bus stop. Neda seemed nervous. Leaning back against the big banyan tree, she lit a cigarette and then began to walk up the sidewalk away from the car. It followed her, cruising slowly. Micelli fumbled through the console for a pencil to make a note of the plate number as it passed. Neda walked faster, and the car continued to pace her; then she turned quickly and walked in the other direction. The car stopped and began to turn around in the street to follow her. Micelli thought that maybe he should hang up.

"Mom—" he began.

Neda looked back over her shoulder at the car. Micelli could see her face, and she didn't look frightened—she looked angry. He lay the cell phone gently on the seat, speaker side up, and put the car in gear. He kept his eyes on Neda as she crossed in front of him, the car following slowly behind her. Micelli let the car idle as he tried to decide whether Neda was in trouble or not.

Suddenly the car cut sharply in front of her—*too close*, Micelli thought. It lurched forward as the driver slammed on the brakes with the passenger window directly alongside Neda. She gasped and slammed her open hand down hard on the car's roof. The window was down, and Micelli squinted to see a face through the fronds of a palm intermittently blocking his view.

Neda quickly took one step back from the car, dropped her cigarette on the ground, and reached into her shoulder bag, pulling out a small metal can. She pointed a spray nozzle into the car window with her right hand and flicked the lighter she still held in her left. *Hairspray,* thought Micelli in a moment of surprise. The torch burst through the open window and into the car with an audible rush. Micelli's eyes opened wider as he listened to the screams coming from inside the car.

The sedan's tires squealed as it lurched forward and sped jerkily down the street in a zigzag fashion away from Neda. He looked at her and saw her take one deep breath as she put the can quickly back into her bag. She tucked the back of her blouse into her skirt, took a couple of deep breaths, and walked slowly back toward the bus stop.

Micelli swallowed as he picked the phone up from the front seat.

After listening for a minute, he said, "No, Mom, I don't think the neighbors will suspect anything if you bring Jell-O. I'm sure that will be fine."

# CHAPTER 10

## MIAMI SHORES, FLORIDA

Otero let out his breath as he loosened his tie. He stood with his face near the air conditioner as the small unit sputtered to life. A "window rattler," they called it. He had two in his small, Spanish-style house, one in the bedroom and one in the living room. The one in the living room ran all the time in the summer. *Can't leave a little black dog without cool air,* he thought, filling her bowl with water. She rested her head against his leg before drinking. All she wanted was his touch, and knowing this made him smile slightly. He was tired. It had been a long day.

He picked up the *Miami Herald,* pulled out the news section, and scanned the obituaries. Opening a drawer in his bedside table, he found a pencil and plopped down on the bed. He circled one of the listings.

"Royston Alexander, 57, charitable foundation president and owner of Alexander's Jewelry in Bay Harbor, died Monday. Services Saturday, 9:30 a.m. Little Church Near the Shore, Bal Harbor."

His eyes scanned the copy, noting an arrest for the apparent bombing of the mall. He jotted down the name and then flipped through the phone book, looking for an address. Nothing.

"Connections, Anna," said Otero to the dog. "Remember, life is always about connections. We just need to find them."

Then he had another thought. He could suddenly see the friar's room in the monastery in his mind's eye, and he slapped his hand against his forehead.

"Shit!" he said to the dog. "Why was there a fire extinguisher in the corner of a room in a building made out of stone?"

# CHAPTER 11

## MIAMI, FLORIDA

Micelli slowed the car down, easing it over to the curb across the street from Neda Wilson's house just off 163rd Street and I-95, and looked again at the address on the small piece of paper in his hand. *It's terribly hot already,* he thought dully. It was only 8:30 a.m., and already the heat was making him sick. It made his stomach feel hollow and his head hurt. Sometimes he almost missed New Jersey. Maybe after he retired, he'd move back up there; sometimes he had a longing for hills and real trees, and he didn't want to be able to hear the heat anymore. It made a goddamn sound for chrissakes—he was living in a place where the sunshine liked to scream hot and hard right into your face.

It was a tidy block that was trying hard to look respectable. Palm trees swayed against peeling paint, and a neighborhood park was filled with concrete-chipped sections of old cement picnic tables. A dry fountain, covered in long-faded mosaic pieces, sat empty with several Budweiser cans lying near it in the grass.

He waited a few minutes and then saw her leave the house. She dressed stylishly and simply all in black. He figured she would be going to Alexander's funeral, and he was right. Wearing a round, black pillbox hat with a veil, she carried her bag close to her side. Her face was turned away from him as she walked down the street, away from where Micelli was waiting.

Starting the engine, he moved the car slowly forward and then, remembering the hairspray incident, he stopped the car and got out of the driver's side door, calling to her as she walked.

"Mrs. Mason," he called out.

She stopped walking and turned toward him. She didn't speak.

"I'm sorry I didn't call you first," he said, stumbling over his words. "Can I give you a ride to the funeral?"

She looked at him, over at his car, and back again.

"It's hot," he said, shrugging his shoulders.

She looked at him for a long time and then walked over to the passenger side of the car and waited for him to open the door.

They drove across the causeway in silence with the air conditioning on high. The whole world around them seemed to dazzle in the brilliant morning light. Florida's weather palette could be stunning, and Micelli never failed to appreciate the way the sun sparkled into a million points of liquid light across the bay.

"Look," he began, "we didn't get much of a chance to talk the other day, and I'd like to ask you just a few things, if you don't mind. This isn't official; you already know that you don't have to answer any of my questions. If you don't want to, that's fine. We'll just go to the service. I promise."

She turned to look at him, and he could see again how long-ago pretty she was.

"Wilson is dead. Not much I can do about that," she said. Her voice was flat.

"On the dock that night—at Big Daddy's—the bullets were coming from two directions," he said. "Wilson had a gun, and he pointed it at me, and I fired, but it wasn't my bullet that killed him."

"Like I said before, Wilson went to the bar that afternoon to meet some men." Neda sounded weary. "He didn't want Alexander to know he was going down to the Keys. He said if Alexander called that night, to tell him I didn't know where Wilson was."

"What was the meeting about?"

Neda looked down into her lap for a while and then directly into his eyes. "Officer Micelli," she said with all sincerity, "I've never been so freaking scared in my whole life."

They drove on. Micelli waited for her to continue. Micelli was good at waiting.

"I don't know what the meeting was about. It had something to do with a shipment they brought in." She paused, but Micelli figured she had a lot more to say. "Someone has been following me since Wilson died. Calling the house on the phone and hanging up. A few days ago, when I came home from work, I'm sure somebody had been in the house. Things were moved around—just a little, you know, but I could tell."

"Pascale said something about cocaine yesterday. Talk to me about that."

"That was years ago," Neda began and then stopped. She took a deep breath. "Wilson went to jail for smuggling pellets of cocaine—body-cavity smuggling. He put cocaine in . . . up . . ." She stammered, embarrassed.

Micelli was too. He looked out the window and then continued. "Look, we know Alexander and Wilson were smuggling contraband of sorts into the country in the fire extinguishers. What about the papers you talked about?" he said. "Something about a nuclear plant?"

"Pascale and his FBI friends paid me a visit last night, looking for them."

"That was fast."

She nodded. "I don't have them. I'm pretty sure Wilson gave them to Alexander. When he first told me about them, I said to get rid of them. There weren't any other papers in the extinguisher, just those."

Micelli slowed the car, turning the corner onto the street where the chapel was located, and he heard Neda gasp. The street was festooned with police cars and lights. Two ambulances with the back doors open were facing them. People were running across the parking lot toward them, weeping and holding hands. Neda and Micelli looked at each other.

"Stay in the car," Micelli said as he pulled over and stopped. "Don't get out. I'll be back in a minute."

He walked quickly up to a Miami-Dade police officer, showed his badge, and asked what was going on.

"Somebody in a black Ford F250 drove straight through a crowd of people waiting on the sidewalk," the officer answered. "We've called for an airlift, but it doesn't look good for a couple of folks."

"So this was deliberate?" asked Micelli. "You think somebody drove through these people on purpose?"

"Looks like it. Then they drove down the street and out onto I-95. We've got choppers up. News 7 is up there too. I don't know . . . we don't have anyone in sight yet."

"Jesus," said Micelli. He shook his head and thought that this time he had seen it all. He walked over to some of the people lying in the grass and looked down at one of the men a medic was working on.

It was Pete Otero—it was the Butt-Cutter. Micelli stared hard. There was no mistaking the face. It was him. He knelt down next to the medic.

"What's his condition?" he asked.

The medic looked at Micelli's badge. "He was having trouble breathing and had some chest pains," he answered. The medic removed the oxygen cup from the man's face. Otero opened his eyes and looked at Micelli.

"Old friends," the man said without smiling. His voice trailed off. "Help me sit up."

The medic interrupted. "He needs to go with the ambulance. He needs medical attention."

"Go with them," Micelli said dryly. "We can have lunch some other time."

"Can't do it, man. Besides, I've had broken ribs before." Otero answered. "Got obligations at home." He winced and looked at Micelli. "Anna."

"Anna?"

"If they put me in the hospital, well, she can't stay alone—not all night."

"You got a wife now?"

"No." Otero seemed to falter. "I got a dog, man."

"You got a dog? You?" An emotional connection from Otero surprised him.

Otero pulled himself up, shook off the medic, and started walking toward the parking lot. He seemed woozy. Micelli walked beside him into the lot.

"Why are you here?" Micelli asked.

"Why are *you* here?" Otero answered.

"I'm working a case; give me a break."

"Yeah, well, me too," Otero said. "How's your mother?"

"Don't ask me about my mother." Micelli paused and looked down into the window of his car as they passed it in the lot—it was empty. Neda Mason was gone.

"Shit!" Micelli said. "Holy shit!" His eyes scanned the parking lot. Nothing.

"What?" Otero asked. "Damn, it's hot, and it's almost winter. I don't know why I live here sometimes."

"Well, I had somebody with me, and now she's not in the car anymore." He tried the door handle. Locked. *Shit!*

"Yeah? Maybe she's inside the church."

"Nobody's inside the church. The police closed it off."

The two men stood there for a minute.

"What's she look like?" Otero said.

"Tall. Classy. Dressed in black."

"Oh, I see. Unlike anybody else here at the moment, you mean?"

Micelli was annoyed. "Well, she's got really long legs, and her hair is sort of all up and under this small, round hat with a veil on it." He thought for a moment. "Her name is Neda, and she's really nice looking." There was a pause. "Really nice."

Otero looked at him. "Really nice?"

"Look," said Micelli with some urgency, "please. You go around the building to the left, and I'll go around the building to the right. I'll meet you in the back." They parted and walked in different directions into the crowd of people. Micelli made his way around the side of the building, looking down between the service alleys as he passed. He glanced into knots of people and checked behind shrubs. It wasn't a big building, and it didn't take him much time to get to the back. There he saw Otero standing over someone lying on the ground.

"Micelli!" Otero motioned, waving one arm. "I think I found her. And she don't look so good."

Neda lay on the grass, partly obscured by some bushes on the side of the building. Her hat was off, her collar was ripped, and she had a long, bloody gash on one calf. Both shoes were gone. So was her purse. With all the excitement going on, no one had noticed her yet. Otero and Micelli ran over to her and tried to get her to stand up. She was crying.

"I—got—mugged," she said with a tight voice. Her knees were stained by the grass. Micelli couldn't tell if she was crying because she was hurt or because she was mad. He figured it was a little of both.

"Are you okay?" said Micelli, alarmed. "Can you stand up?"

"Who—who could do something like this, at a funeral?" she said.

"Well, this isn't exactly your garden-party type funeral, now is it?" said Otero, looking around at the chaos.

"Who's he?" Neda said to Micelli, brushing pieces of grass and leaves from her dress.

"Nobody," Micelli said.

Otero looked at Micelli. His eyebrows were up.

"Somebody I used to know," Micelli added.

Neda was still crying. "Look at my dress . . . he took my purse . . . and, and," she was gulping tears now, "he hit me in the face."

Otero felt his own face get red. *Micelli was right,* he thought looking at her. *She* is *really nice.*

"Scum," Otero said. "Here." He reached into his pocket and gestured grandly. "Use my handkerchief."

She took it, smiling thinly, and blew her nose.

"I told you to stay in the car," Micelli said, exasperated. "Neda, you weren't supposed to get out of the car."

"I thought I saw somebody I knew," she said.

They helped her stand. She was roughed up but not injured.

"Where are my shoes?" she said. "I want to go home."

"You got my car keys?" Micelli asked.

"They were in my purse."

"Great," he sighed. He put his hand on the back of his neck and rolled his head around. He could feel a headache starting, and the ache in his leg was back.

"Don't worry, I'll drive," said Otero, waving Micelli off. "I'm okay. My car is over there." They helped Neda across the lawn, found her shoes, and walked out through the parking lot over to a pristine white Saab convertible.

"Nice ride," Micelli whistled.

"I'm in the car business now," said Otero. "There are some perks. You like it? It's custom auto paint. Pearl something. It's got—you know, if you look at it in the sun, you can kind of see down inside. It's called 'depth.' Besides, as you know, I was away for a while. I can have some nice things again now."

Opening the car door for Neda, Micelli could see that the passenger seat was filled with appliances. An iron, a toaster-oven, and a coffeepot lay on the seat. Micelli picked them up as Otero started the engine and opened the convertible top.

"What's all this?" Micelli asked.

"Nothing," Otero answered.

"What, you drive around with appliances in the passenger seat all the time?"

"I forget to unplug things," Otero said.

"You forget to unplug . . ."

"Yeah, and I got Anna to think about. I could burn the house down, you know? So I take them with me. That way I know they're unplugged. Enough. Get in. We gotta stop by my place first—it's right here at the end of the causeway."

He took the iron away from Micelli.

"Just put the rest of it in the back."

Helping Neda into the front seat, Micelli squeezed into the back. As Otero pulled out onto the causeway, Neda handed Micelli the bottom portion of a coffeemaker and started to tell Otero how to get to her house.

Nobody saw the black sedan pull out of the parking lot and begin to follow them.

Halfway across the causeway, Neda turned in the front seat and looked at Micelli. "I didn't tell you everything," she said. "There was some other stuff in the fire extinguisher with the blueprints."

"What'd you say about stuff in a fire extinguisher?" said Otero, thinking again about the extinguisher in the friar's room and his theory about connections.

"Other stuff?" Micelli said. "What kind of other stuff?"

"Some other papers, but—well, they were too weird. My brother, Andy, said we should keep them, but then he got arrested, and I didn't know what to do."

"Who arrested him?" interrupted Otero. "What for?"

"He sort of knows about a mall explosion," she answered.

"I'm putting two and two together," Otero said. "I'm good at that."

"Andy looked at the papers, and he said we should keep them. I told the FBI about the blueprints, but not about the papers. I still have them, but they're scary. I didn't want them in the house."

"What do you mean, scary?" said Micelli. "Where are they now?"

"Hey, guys . . ." said Otero.

"Don't interrupt," said Micelli. He looked at Neda. "Where did you put these papers?"

She was quiet for a moment, wondering how much to say. Then she answered. "There was something creepy about the paper and something about the writing," she said. "Micelli—I think the writing was in blood." She seemed to be spitting the words out now. "I'm not kidding you. It was a list written in blood. I'm serious. So I kept the papers, but I got rid of them, you know what I mean?"

At that moment, Micelli wished he *did* know what she meant. "Just tell me where the papers physically *are*," he said, watching Otero weave between the lanes as the speedometer pushed 80 mph.

"I'm good at hiding things," she said with an earnest look on her face. "If I hide something, you're never going to find it." She pushed her hair away from her face and licked her lips. "I put the papers in a lobster pot in the bay behind Big Daddy's Bar in Key Largo. My mother has a house there. Andy helped me. They're in a Scooby-Doo lunchbox with duct tape around it."

"Guys—" Otero started.

"What on Earth? Neda, is the lobster pot still there now?" said Micelli.

"We're being followed," said Otero.

The black sedan behind them came up quickly along the passenger side of the Saab. The driver swerved the heavy sedan into the side of the convertible, and Neda screamed. The sedan pulled back into the other lane, dropped back for a second, and then hurled forward again. Turning around in her seat, Neda picked up a glass coffeepot from beside Micelli and threw it against the side of the driver's window as the sedan again smashed into Otero's car. Glass flew back into the open back seat.

"Jesus!" said Micelli as he covered his face. "Neda, stop it!"

"Hang on," said Otero. He pushed the gas pedal to the floor, and the car lurched forward.

Neda reached back and pulled the iron away from Micelli.

The sedan pulled in behind the Saab, and with the engine screaming, it gathered speed to hit the rear of the car. Neda was on her knees in the front seat now, aiming the iron at the front windshield of the car behind them. Micelli pulled a small pistol from his inside pocket and aimed carefully, steadying his hand against the trunk of the car.

The iron and two quick bullets hit the corner of the roof above the driver's side of the front window at almost the same time.

The sedan lurched to one side and drove off the causeway onto the swale as the Saab flew across the bay toward the city.

"Wait!" Micelli shouted over the wind. "We can't go back to Neda's place. Don't you get it?"

Neda looked at Otero. Then they both looked at Micelli.

"The mugging wasn't random," Micelli continued. "They're looking for something."

Otero slowed the car down to listen.

"Neda, we thought the fact you found blueprints for the power plant meant that someone was planning to do something there. Sabotage it or something, who knows? But I don't think the power plant is what we should be thinking about. The other papers you found—the ones you put in the lobster pot?"

"Yeah?" Neda said, shouting as the wind blew her hair into her face.

"Tell us what's on the papers, Neda," Micelli said. "Tell us what's written in blood."

Otero slowed the car near the end of the causeway as the sound of sirens approached them from a distance. Both men waited to hear what Neda had to say.

"Some of the writing might have been in Creole. But I think most of it was written in French or something similar." She was no longer on her knees in the seat, so she twisted around to face Micelli in the back. "I was going to take it to Mambo Taffy—my foster mother; she was born in Haiti—and ask her if she would look at it. She's much better at reading that kind of stuff than I am. Plus it stinks. Literally. I'm telling you, the paper smells."

"If it's written in Creole, I might be able help you out," said Otero. "I got a business in Little Haiti. We can probably find someone there who can read it."

"I don't know . . ." Neda hesitated. "Like I said, most of it's French—but there's other stuff there I can't understand. It's like something I've never seen before."

"Well, let's not worry about reading them before we get them back," said Micelli. "I just hope they're still there. I have no idea why you would hide documents like that underwater. No offense, Neda, but that's not very bright."

Neda pushed the hair out of her face and shrugged. "I had to hide them really good," she said. "You can call me superstitious; I don't care. I didn't want those pages crawling out of that box and finding their way back to me in the middle of the night. When I want them, I know where they are."

"I think we ought to head to the Keys now," said Micelli. "At least I can get my spare set of car keys, and we can pick up the box as soon as possible. Can you drive, Cutter?"

Neda interrupted. "Cutter? That's your name?" she said, looking at the driver.

"No, my name's Pete," Otero said. "Cutter is, well—my stage name." He gave Micelli a long look in the rearview mirror.

"Sorry," Micelli said. "My slip. Habit."

"I gotta stop by my place first—it's right here—and look in on Anna," Otero said.

Neda was looking at him sweetly. "Oh, you have a family?" she asked.

"No, I got a dog."

Micelli saw Otero's eyes soften for a moment, and then he saw something else. Fright. As the car turned into the driveway of a small corner house, the front door was wide open.

Otero leapt from the driver's side of the car and hurried through a stucco-covered entryway and into the house. Micelli followed, telling Neda to stay back. He could hear Otero calling frantically inside the house for the dog. Micelli started to get a really bad feeling. Tentatively, he entered the small living room and found it in disarray. Whoever had been there was obviously looking for something and had been resolute on finding it. Everything was "turned," as they say in the business. Pictures were off the wall, the rug was rolled back, drawers dumped; it was a mess. Otero was making small puffing noises as he ran past Micelli, back out the front door and around the side of the house. Micelli picked up two halves of a broken decorative plate from the floor and set them on the coffee table. *Some people don't have very much,* he thought, looking at the little room. A dog bed was snuggled between a recliner and the wall in front of the television set. A squeaky toy lay next to a water bowl, just outside the kitchen door.

"I found her!" Micelli heard Otero say as he came back into the room. He was carrying a small, black dog in his arms, hugging it tightly to his chest with his cheek against the top of the dog's head. "Bastards! Bastards!" His voice was shaking uncontrollably, and he sounded like he might be crying. "She was outside by the big tree in the back yard. Good girl. Good girl. Those bastards hurt her. Look at her paw." Micelli could see a long, red gash seeping through black fur.

Neda was standing in the doorway. "Pete, don't worry, she's going to be fine," she said. "I'll get a cloth, and we'll clean out the cut." She walked over to the sink and started looking in drawers.

"I've got to get her to the vet," said Otero, shaking his head. "It could be worse; she could have internal injuries. You just don't know. She's not that young anymore, and dogs get hurt different than people do. I mean, she'd never tell me she was hurt or anything." His words were coming rapidly. Never in a thousand years would Micelli have ever pictured a man like the Butt-Cutter to have any heart at all, much less one so taken over by a small puff of fur with big, black eyes.

Otero set the dog on the floor, and they watched as she limped over to the dog bed. "Is she *limping?*" Otero's eyes were wide now. "What—what if she gets an infection in there and can't walk right anymore?"

"I don't think you need to worry about that right now," said Neda, peering through the front drapes out toward the street. "We've got company."

# CHAPTER 12

---

## MIAMI, FLORIDA

Jean Alexander sent the bail money through Seymour T. Lerner, PA, and so Andy found himself on the street sooner than he ever expected—but the way Andy's mind worked, it only occupied his thoughts for a moment. When he stepped out of the front door of the Miami-Dade County Courthouse, it was Thumbelina who was waiting to pick him up. Her lime-green Ford Mustang convertible slowed to the curb as the former stripper rolled down the window.

"An-bee," she said in a breathy Marilyn Monroe voice that took a lot of practice to sound consistent. "An-bee, baby, get in the car."

He squinted against the heat as he opened the passenger-side door. "Tina?" He was tired. "I'm waiting for three friggin' hours. Where you been?"

"Grocery store," she said. Her voice was sweet. "Are you hungry?"

He shook his head, yes. Her curly blonde hair was pulled into a ponytail high on the top of her head, and she was wearing a tight, red T-shirt that said "GAMER, ALL BALLS ON," in square black letters. Her shorts were short, she wore stiletto heels, and her gum snapped as they drove down the highway. She was Miami's only dwarf stripper, and in her day, she could sell out the house. There was still occasional talk of a comeback. At four feet two, she carried her double-G breasts around the stage in a wheelbarrow as part of her act.

Thumbelina was the love of Andy's life. Following his short stay in jail for arson, the halfway house arranged a job for him as a janitor at her nightclub. At the time, Andy had just come off a three-day relapse and had been fired for not showing up at the club for work. But he'd forgotten that he was fired and went to clean the next day anyway. Since the owner was out of town, Andy worked the entire week for what turned out to be nothing. But the money wasn't important. Fate ended up bringing him to Thumbelina's aid, late one night when some guys were heckling her as she walked to her car, and the two had become inseparable.

A seemingly odd couple, Andy thought Thumbelina, or "Tina" as he could best pronounce—because too many syllables were difficult—was as near perfect as any woman could be. She was the light in his otherwise dim life. When she laughed—and she laughed often—it seemed to fill him up; it was like gasoline to an engine. And she was pretty and tiny, and he liked the way she was put together. When she walked into a room, she became the room. Once, in an Andy epiphany, he noticed that Tina turned her head, and the sun came in through the window—and he knew that it came through the window then *because* she had turned her head. She was like a circle. Because she was in his life, he had a life. Their partnership was the juxtaposition of one soul with a direction and one soul without, but it fit. Like the best kind of life puzzle. Andy couldn't think about a lot of complicated things, but he understood one thing: he needed Tina.

From Tina's perspective, Andy was a good person to have around because he was fairly tall and could be believably menacing in a kind of thin, shrieking way. He was not all that complicated, and she found that refreshing. And he had not once, not ever, mentioned her size, and that was something that had never happened to her before. "Are you a midget?" someone had said once during a lap dance. "No, asshole," she had answered. "I'm a little person. Little and better." Men were always talking about how short she was or how big her breasts were or a combination of both, but Andy didn't seem to see either. Andy liked to play video games, and Andy liked to get high, and beyond that, little else occurred to him other than a small fixation he had with fire and explosives, but Tina figured that was certainly no reason to stop seeing him.

She had planned a special dinner for him tonight; they would have "Indiana hamburgers," like the ones her daddy used to make. Andy liked them a lot; the burgers were topped with chili and frozen corn, and one time she'd put marshmallows in there too. They had laughed and laughed at how silly that was. But Indiana hamburgers with dessert mixed in tasted good. So earlier today, she'd purchased a bag of little, colored marshmallows and thought that later on she would hide some on herself in bed, and Andy could try to find them.

"You got bail?" she said as the bright lights from causeway poles flashed like a camera against the sides of the car. "Who do you know has that kind of cash?"

"It was in this paper I got," Andy said, feeling his pockets. "I can't find it now. Some lady. Can we pick up some beer?"

"I got some already," she answered, drumming her long French-tipped nails against the steering wheel. Aerosmith blasted out into the night. "Let's stop at the club and pick up some real fun. You want to?"

"Yo, Tina," he said, leaning across the console and licking her ear. "No, I got to think straight tonight. I got a very big plan in here." He was tapping the side of his head.

She felt the scratch of his beard against the side of her face, and his hand was in her lap. She was amazed; this was new behavior for sure.

"I got a plan to make a million dollars in just a few minutes," he said as the car pulled away from the curb. "All I need is a copy machine."

*　　*　　*

Surrounded by sticky marshmallows and pieces of hamburger buns, Andy and Tina lay in bed and shared a beer.

"Well, I think you're stupid," she said as she sat up and reached behind a pillow to retrieve her bra. "You're not going to get away with convincing Big Daddy that you didn't come to work at the bar because you won the lottery. You're going to have to tell him you were in jail."

"I'm not stupid, Tina." Andy could barely speak with her breasts swaying in front of him. He wondered how she could possibly walk around all day alone in a sweater with them, and it started to make him feel lightheaded.

". . . fired again for sure this time." She was talking, but he hadn't heard the first part of her sentence. "Xeroxing a bunch of money and flashing it around ain't going to convince nobody."

"Yes it will." He was almost whispering now as he brushed both sides of his face through the middle of her chest. He closed his eyes and took a deep breath through his nose. She smelled so pretty. He reached out his tongue to retrieve a green marshmallow from behind the sweaty-sweet fold of her breast as he pushed her back down onto the bed. She giggled and poured the last few drops of beer down the front of her neck toward his face.

"An-bee," she was saying softly to the ceiling, "I have a better idea. Let's take all that Xerox money, and let's do something smart with it."

"I like smart things," he said, muffled by flesh.

"Good, honey," Tina said, stroking the top of his head. "Well then, let's trade it for some real money."

# Chapter 13

## Bal Harbor, Florida

The more Jean Alexander considered it, the more she didn't believe the fiasco at Roy's funeral. She had the distinct feeling that there was a sinister side to the "coincidence" that some "drunk" had run over the curb and through a crowd of people on the sidewalk. Thankfully, she'd been with her boys inside the church when it all happened, and thankfully again, although there had been injuries, it could have been much worse. She was still arguing with her insurance company about the loss of her diamond ring following the mayhem that was supposed to pass for "an orderly police presence."

During the days following his death, she discovered a whole new side to her husband. He'd always been a meticulous keeper of information—something she never paid attention to prior to his death, and during the time she spent looking at his compiled life, she swore she had to be the stupidest spouse ever, to miss so many details.

First, there were the blueprints—but it was the writing in the margins that interested her. She didn't care about the fact that the blueprints were of a power plant. Whatever somebody had planned at Turkey Point didn't involve her. She was looking for assets. "Roy's Assets"—that might make a good name for a bar someday, she thought.

She looked at copies of their tax returns and balance sheets from the business; in fact, she'd gone through them three times, each time in a slightly happier frame of mind. Roy was making a lot of money. Not just from the jewelry store—it was making a profit—but he was bringing in other cash too. It was funny, because although they never wanted for anything, they weren't extravagant, over-the-top spenders either. Life as Mrs. Alexander had included the best restaurants, top schools for his sons, the newest neighborhood, the most expensive cars, and the finest wine—by Jean's calculations, and she knew how to calculate. All that was good. But all that didn't equal the amount of money that was coming in, and she wanted to find out where it was. A routine sweep of bank statements and an evening with the bank manager had yielded nothing.

Sitting in Roy's big chair at his desk, she looked again at the writing on the edges of the blueprint. In the margins, numbers were written in blue ball-point pen. They were arranged into columns with dollar signs next to each column heading. There was a column $$, a column $$$, and finally, a column headed SEquity. Next to column SEquity were dates.

Additionally, there was paperwork from a monastery not too far from the Alexander's Jewelry store at the mall. Roy had sold some items to their gift shop, but the dollar amounts on these invoices were significantly higher than anything Roy sold. He didn't sell any $300,000 items. There were invoices for three of them.

Then, before she put the blueprints away for the thousandth time, she noticed something else on the back. Squinting, and finally succumbing to reading glasses, she read the following in a square black stamp: SOUL EQUITY, INC.

# CHAPTER 14

## NORTH MIAMI BEACH, FLORIDA

Friar Bill shut the last drawer of the last cabinet in the last room. No blueprint. He was deeply worried. The work of the order was certainly to serve a higher purpose, but you couldn't go around simply misplacing things. If they couldn't find the paperwork, well, that would be the first occurrence of its kind in decades. He feared a long chain of long chains was about to be broken. The documents in question were not found where they should have been—thankfully—because initially the order believed they were in the car that went off the road and into Crocodile Lake.

The Master had been negotiating for a long time to purchase a rare group of papers, along with some sort of blueprint. As to why a blueprint, of all things, was included with religious documents, well, this was not explained to Friar Bill; and as a matter of fact, he'd found the Master to be unusually tight-lipped about the transaction. So, other than his impression that the collection was somehow different, Friar Bill didn't have any specifics about what the collection itself actually contained.

One thing that had made him nervous all along was the cost. Whatever they were buying, it was extremely expensive. Although the Master had acted for decades as the architect of an extensive collection, Friar Bill had never seen such high sums paid for religious documents. Recently, he'd seen a check for $300,000. Now, the Master was dead, and the friar couldn't find any blueprints in the Master's papers, or any notes as to what the collection was comprised of. That meant a lot of money had been spent on a collection no one knew anything about and now couldn't find. This was not good.

That was until an unspeakably crass-sounding woman named Jean Alexander called him and left a message on his voicemail. He pushed a little button on the front of his telephone and listened as the recording played again.

"Whoever is in charge there needs to talk to me," said a woman's voice, followed by an audible exhale of cigarette smoke. "I've got something that might interest you—it's some kind of a blueprint, I think. My husband was a business acquaintance of yours—Roy Alexander? We need to talk. I've got numbers, I've got dates, and I've got bills to pay."

*Such is the state of the world we live in,* sighed Friar Bill as he picked up the telephone to call her back.

# CHAPTER 15

## NORTH MIAMI BEACH, FLORIDA

True, she was slightly out of practice, and yes, maybe times had changed. But Jean Alexander had to keep reminding herself that men were all made the same way, no matter what your condition or circumstances were; they were basic creatures—so predictable. But then, sometimes that was good.

Friar Bill, however, was turning out to be another story. She had an appointment scheduled with him, and she'd planned it out in her head. He, being a friar and everything that went along with that, would be polite and flustered by her. She would wear something very low-cut and lean forward a lot. She would smile at him. If he was short, she would sit down and smile up at him. He was in the business of helping people, so she would impress upon him how emotionally needy she was, but at the same time, she would show him how emotionally strong she intended to be. She would be virtuous in a trampy kind of way, and she would leave with the information she came for. There was a lot of money somewhere, and she intended to find out where that was.

The tables turned almost as soon as she opened her mouth. She was sitting with her back to the window in his office, leaning forward in the desk chair and scanning the room for an ashtray. The clergy would certainly allow grieving people to smoke cigarettes. This was grief, after all. Her French-tipped fingernails drummed on his desk.

"Being a widow, you know, it's all still a very big shock to me," she started, using her best little-girl voice. "I'm so lonely at night when I try to sleep."

Friar Bill didn't comment. He just sat there with his fingers clasped together on the desk in front of him. *He looks like he has snake eyes,* she thought. They were flat and expressionless.

"Roy only mentioned you once or twice," she continued, trying to make some connection. "But I know you had a great impact on him." She smiled warmly. Flattery might work. Friar Bill had no expression.

"As for your business connection," she said, adding a slightly dramatic pause, "well . . ." She cleared her throat. "My husband was always discreet." She gave him a knowing glance. Nothing. This was not going well.

She took a deep breath. "May I have a glass of water?" she said, considering herself a master manipulator. Not getting a verbal response, she'd learned to make a request that required the non-communicating party to move physically. That was an acknowledgement of some sort. She had her skills. Instead, Friar Bill barely moved a finger and without moving his head, said quietly into his speakerphone, "Water."

The door opened immediately, and a heavy, crystal glass of mineral water was placed on the desk in front of her. Not a second had passed between the request and the delivery.

*Try number two,* she thought, lifting the glass to her lips. She called upon a small spasm of grief to well up into her eyes and then she gulped it back as she appeared to accidentally spill the entire glass down the front of her silk blouse. Her black lace camisole appeared as if by magic through the now-transparent beige silk. She turned a practiced crimson.

At this point, he was supposed to rush to help her. Comfort her. Maybe put his arm around her shoulders. She could lay her cheek against his chest. He would become understanding, and she would be grateful. Instead, Friar Bill moved another finger toward the speakerphone and said in a barely audible, flat voice, "Towel."

Again the door opened and closed behind her. Someone placed a small white towel in her lap.

Friar Bill turned his gaze past her to the window. "Thank you for calling today, Mrs. Alexander," he said to the window.

It was a dismissal. She was outraged.

She could feel water running down the back of her right leg and into her shoe. *Maybe he's partially blind,* she thought. *Sometimes you can't tell when people are handicapped. It's not something you ask someone when you first meet them, is it? Hello, I'm pleased to meet you, and by the way, are you partially blind?* If he *was* partially blind, that would explain a lot.

She stood up and tried to look charitable and honest at the same time, qualities she read that people in the Bible often had. She turned to face him and stood there with both hands on the back of the chair she had been sitting in. She looked at him squarely, infuriated.

"Before you go," he said in an offhanded way, flicking the back of his hand at her and resting his head against the back of his chair, "you said something about some documents . . . I did only a limited amount of business with your husband, but there were some papers that I might . . ."

With a great gasp of exhaled air, she suddenly fell, allegedly fainting, to the ground, collapsing completely behind the guest chair. There was a tremendous thump as she hit the floor and her shoe flew off one foot as the heel snapped and skittered across the room.

Certainly *now* there would be a response. Even a partially blind person would have seen what just happened.

She trembled as she waited for him to jump up from his chair and rush to her aid.

She waited.

As an allegedly fainted person, she remained very still. But the friar didn't move either. He didn't move his finger to the speakerphone to call anyone, and he didn't get up from his chair. It was all very quiet. Things were not going as planned at all. She tried to breathe quietly, and she kept her eyes closed with one of them ever-so-slightly open. Minutes went by. She was trying to figure out how long people faint for when she heard the scrape of his chair across the floor. Through her partially open eye, she saw the heel of his shoe as he walked past her, opened the door, and walked out into the hallway. The heavy door closed behind him.

She was alone.

After a few more minutes, she pulled herself up to a seated position on the floor and looked at the broken heel of her shoe.

They were designer. Manolo Blahnik. *Shit!*

The door opened, and a young man in a blue cardigan entered.

"Oh dear!" he said, scurrying to her side. "Are you all right?" He was almost breathless in his concern. "What on earth are you doing on the floor?" He put his arm out for her to take and helped her up, gently touching her waist as he guided her to the guest chair.

"For heaven's sake, this is very distressing!" he continued. "I'm so sorry I'm late." He helped her sit down. "I was hoping that you weren't waiting too long." He picked up the empty crystal glass, looked down into it, and frowned. He pushed the speakerphone button. "Yes, there's an empty glass in here on my desk. Can you please come and put some water in it for Mrs. Alexander? Thank you."

He pulled his chair to the desk and smiled at her.

"Would you like a tissue? I'm Friar Bill. We talked earlier on the phone."

Jean noticed the chair she was sitting in was wet.

*   *   *

Fifteen minutes south, Pascale was standing on the front porch of Otero's house on the western side of Broad Causeway when Neda opened the front door.

"We received a report from Interpol this morning," he said. "Can I come in?" He stepped over pieces of broken glass on the landing and walked into the house. "Having a reunion for old time's sake?" he said, looking over at Otero and Micelli. They were standing in front of the dog bed.

"Wilson and Alexander were involved in document smuggling at the highest levels," Pascale said.

"What?" said Neda. "No." She was shaking her head. "Not my Wilson. Look, he had a history, I'll give you that. He had some bills to take care of, but past that, no, his business was doing fine. He wasn't smuggling, and he wasn't at any 'highest levels.'"

"I'm sorry Mrs. Mason," he said, "but Wilson's fire extinguishers went out filled with fire retardant for use on cruise ships and—some of them at least—came back into the United States filled with fake passports, pornography on jump disks, foreign currency, stolen items—you name it. In addition to drugs, those fire extinguishers were packed with contraband documents, very lucrative, very illegal documents."

Neda had a wary look on her face. She didn't want to believe him, but she remembered the blueprints Wilson showed her. He never talked too much about what he was doing with Alexander. Grudgingly, she had to admit to herself that it was possible.

"How long do you think this has this been going on?" she asked in a whisper.

"We're getting to the bottom of it now," said Pascale. "I have to ask you—has anybody been bothering you? Following you? That kind of thing?"

"No," Otero said, interrupting sarcastically, "my house looks like this because my cleaning lady isn't feeling well. And I'm betting that if you go over to Neda's house right now, it looks somewhat the same."

Neda gave Pascale an even look as he cleared his throat. "Actually, yes, it does," he said. "Again, I'm sorry. That's one reason I'm here. We've been watching your house, Mrs. Mason, but we missed it when they broke in. I thought you might as well know the facts, in case things start to get rough."

"Start?" said Micelli. He took a step protectively toward Neda. "Does the FBI know who's involved in this and exactly what it is they're looking for?

"Well, it's an industry worth a lot of money," said Pascale. "The kind of things Alexander was bringing in—well, these things needed to be hand-carried. One problem with couriers is they can be stopped and searched. And they need to have paperwork; they have to clear Customs, Immigration—it's complicated. Illegal documents have to find a different path to get into the country. The fire extinguishers were perfect."

"*I* want to know who's behind all this," Otero said, looking around the room and over to where Anna lay curled up in bed. He had an expression on his face that Micelli remembered from long ago. "I, personally, want to know."

"We'll track it back," said Pascale. "Anyway, there's just one more question I need to ask. Anybody here know much about Vodou?"

# CHAPTER 16

---

## KEY LARGO, FLORIDA

There was a copy machine that made double-sided copies in the office at Big Daddy's Bar. Andy had worked at the bar on and off during the time he spent living in the Keys. Neda and Wilson talked about what to do after Andy lost his job at the strip club, and they thought it might be best to get him out of Miami. *Going home is always the best medicine,* thought Neda. So they called Mambo Taffy in Key Largo and told her the truth: her son needed to be out of the city. Daddy's Bar was only a short walk from her house, and anybody who hung out long enough at the bar ended up behind it sooner or later.

Some folks like to repeat the saying that anybody who lives in the Keys is either an alcoholic, a recovering alcoholic, or working on becoming an alcoholic. Whether or not that's true, it certainly looked possible when Tina and Andy walked through the door on Daddy Kane's "Buy a Snort, Get a Slider Free" night. The place was heaving with a great thump, thump, thump from the bass guitar played by Ray-Jay and the Sad Snakes under last year's twinkling Christmas-tree lights still sagging from the raftered ceiling. "Trophy bras" were stapled to the walls beside other pieces of clothing, along with biker colors, license plates, ties, cigar packets, and old socks. There had probably never been any paint on the walls. White wine was served in washed-out mason jars; red wine—one kind, Gallo—was served in glass olive bottles, and there was plenty of beer. *Plenty* of beer.

"An-bee," giggled Tina, "I like this place."

Andy liked it too. He felt fine bringing Tina here. These folks had already seen everything.

Tonight, instead of her usual stiletto heels, Tina was wearing cowboy boots, along with a G-string bikini bottom and a black crop-top tank top that said "AMEN" in pink rhinestones.

"I been missin' you, baby," he said. He kissed the top of her head. "I been workin' hard all day." They steered through the crowd, picked up drinks at the bar, and danced their way into the back office, singing along to "Sucking Sorry," a new track on the band's CD for sale at the bar.

Shutting the door behind them, Andy plunked down next to Tina on a flat, wide, slightly sticky couch. As he put his arm around her, she fumbled in her purse for a joint and looked at him. "Did I ever tell you that in high school, I was class valedictorian?" she asked.

For a moment, he was overcome with emotion. Then, touching her chin with his fingers, he looked into her eyes. "Tina," he said softly, "don't *ever* talk about yourself that way. I think you're perfect."

He kissed the end of her nose as he fished around in his pocket and pulled out a million-dollar bill.

Her eyes narrowed as she took the bill from his hand and turned it over in her palm. "An-bee . . . what the hell?"

"It's a million-dollar bill!" He said in a loud whisper. "I made it!"

"I don't think you can do that," she said with her brow furrowed. "Can I have another drink?"

He slid over to the end of the couch and opened the door of a small under-counter fridge against the wall, pulling out two beers. She lit the joint, and they popped the tops, and he laughed. "Sure, I did too win the lottery! Daddy Kane just laughed and laughed when I showed that bill to him and said that's where I been—winnin' the lottery. I ain't fired. Shit!"

"Tell me how you did this," she said. "Serious."

"I read in a magazine and it worked. I took some dollar bills and put them in the sink over there in the bathroom with bleach and they bleached," he said. "Then I dried them up and ironed them out and I copied a picture of a million dollars from a book about the US Treasury. Mrs. Meeks at the library helped me." He was smiling as he ran his finger in circles around the front of her tank top. "Doing it that way, you get the watermarks and the right threads in the right places on the bills. You got the real paper, you see. Then I put the picture on the machine, and it made bills! I don't know why I didn't think of this a long time ago!"

He had an expression of wonder on his face. Tina thought he looked beautiful.

"They feel real," she whispered. "How many of these bills did you make?"

"About ten or fifteen," he said, taking a long hit off the joint. "I think that actually makes me a billionaire. I'm not sure."

"You really *are* a millionaire!" she squealed, taking another hit off the joint. "This is *so* cool! What about if we make up a bunch of twenties?" Her eyes were wide. "Nobody will look at those twice around here. What do you think—we can use these big bills in Miami, where they seen 'em before. But can we make up some twenties?"

"Sure," he said, reaching around behind her and feeling for the clasp on her bra. "You got any 'ludes?"

There was banging at the door. "Goddamn it, Andy!" It was Big Daddy Kane. "You working tonight or screwing tonight?" There was a roar of laughter in the background. "Get out here, or I ain't paying you."

"In my purse," Tina said. She leaned over and licked the end of his nose as she motioned to her bag on the floor. He leaned down and fumbled around inside it. "Be careful," she said offhandedly. "There's a loaded—"

A huge bang slammed into the room as the gun went off, shooting straight through Andy's right hand and into the refrigerator. His eyes were wide, and he saw Tina's hair fly upward as she threw her head back with a start. The pain was excruciating, and the last thing he remembered before he passed out was Tina somehow looking down at him and asking, "An-bee, honey, where'd you put the rest of these big bills?"

\*   \*   \*

Micelli, Neda and Otero sat on Mambo Taffy's screened back porch in Key Largo under the ceiling fan as it turned lazily. The wide, flat yard was filled with palm trees and greedy vines that climbed over and around everything. Brilliant bird of paradise plants and orchids peeked out from in between deep, lush ferns. Pascale had left the three of them with a cursory explanation about some of the contraband documents being "voodoo junk stuff," an idea he apparently found very funny before he left with a cursory "Be in touch."

Driving to Key Largo, they'd stopped at the vet's, where Anna was left in good care, and then the three of them went to Mambo Taffy's place at Neda's insistence. She refused to go back to her house and would be staying with Mambo, who was apparently also a good source of information as far as this Haitian magic went.

Neda was almost never surprised at the ignorance most folks dragged around their lives behind them. Agent Pascale would never understand the beauty and the grace of a woman like Mambo Taffy and the spirituality of the Vodou she practiced.

A hand-lettered plaque hung on the wall of the porch above a little table filled with candles.

*"Tout moun fet lib, egal eo pou diyite dou we swa. Nou gen la rezon ak la konsyans epi nou fet pou nou aji youn ak yon lespri fwantenite,"*

It was written in Creole, or Kreyol, depending on your place of reading, and Mambo Taffy translated:

*"All human beings are born free and equal in dignity and rights. They are endowed with reason and conscience and should act towards one another in a spirit of brotherhood."*

The text was from Article One of the Universal Declaration of Human Rights adopted by the United Nations in 1948. When Neda was a little girl, Mambo read it to her every night as they rocked in the big swinging chair hanging from the ceiling on the back porch, and they would talk about what it meant and how important it was. And when Mambo helped Neda learn to write, she would practice her letters by copying the words over and over again in crayon. It was a beautiful thought, and although Neda had grown in her later years to suspect it was never really true, she was still proud of Mambo Taffy. Not only for the type of life she lived, but also for the kind of human being she was.

*Many great ideas are like Santa Claus,* Neda thought. *They exist on the better side of our hopes.*

Aside from reading and talking about Haiti, Mambo also made sure to include Minnesota in her talks with the children, because that was where Andy was born. It seemed like an alien place to them, full of something called "cold" and "snow." The little house in the Keys became a wondrous combination of Haiti and Minnesota and Africa. Mambo cut pictures of snowdrifts and huge mountains out of magazines and hung them alongside pictures of brilliant orchids on the children's bedroom wall. As Neda and Andy held hands in their little bed at night, they would poke at each other and say, "You the Minnesota white one," or "You the Haiti brown one." Then they would turn it around and say, "No, you the Haiti white one," and so on until they giggled themselves to sleep. Each night, their dreams would take them on adventures at the tops of snow-capped mountains and into the deep, sweet, long-gone forests of a once-great Haiti.

Neda laughed as Mambo Taffy's cat jumped into Otero's lap.

"That's Zumbie," she said as she stroked the big orange cat under the chin. "Every Vodou priestess has a spirit."

How she loved the taste of African words on her tongue. The places were magical, and the people in them were alive in her imagination. The Ukuku of Corisco, the Yasi of the Ogowo, the Bweti and Njembe, the Egbo of the Niger Delta, the Shekani. To hear these names spoken filled her with such majesty, such history, and such pride. Her true roots may be lost, but her heart still searched for the road to find them. Listening to Mambo Taffy's stories, she could smell the sweet, sweet earth of her fathers, and she found comfort knowing it waited for her unwearyingly.

But for now, she was here. And the porch swing squeaked.

"Jesus!" Micelli jumped in his chair. "Good Christ! I will never get used to Florida cockroaches. Never."

A palmetto bug ran out from under his chair, across the wooden deck, and down through a small crack.

"That's not a real cockroach," Otero said, smiling. "That's a cockroach in training. They get so big around here that if you ask them to carry your suitcases, you can see the expression on their faces when they don't get tipped."

Neda rolled her eyes. It was a bug. People from up north were always like this.

Mambo Taffy placed a pitcher of sweet tea and lemon on the table for them and went back to the kitchen for some sweet potato pudding, a concoction she made by mashing bananas together with sweet potatoes and serving the whole lovely thing with rum syrup poured generously over the top.

"Mebbe he want de tea," chuckled Mambo, letting the screen door close with a slam behind her.

"No, he want de rum syrup," Neda answered, teasing her and laughing. She felt better here, today, than she'd felt in a long time. She missed Mambo and would be glad to spend some time with her.

"So, tell me about this priestess thing," said Otero, looking at Neda. "You gonna get a little Haitian doll made of me and stick it full of pins when I make you mad?"

"Have some respect," said Neda sharply. "And don't make statements when you don't know what you're talking about. Ignorance is hardly an excuse—even in your case."

"You are the one who loves the knife, yes?" Asked Mambo, returning with stacks of napkins. She looked at Otero. "Mwen kon pran'n Ou." *I understand you.* She let Zumbie come into her lap. "Vodou did not originate in Haiti, you know. It came to Haiti from Africa when the French plantation owners brought slaves to work in their fields."

Micelli's cell phone rang. He answered it as he got up from his chair, walked over to the corner of the porch, and looked out through the screen into a little vegetable garden. A copper rooster sat on top of a post near a chicken-wired square plot filled with lettuce, some end-of-season tomatoes, snow peas, and beets. Each row had a little Popsicle stick with a seed packet stapled to it. A basket with gloves and scissors sat just outside a little wire gate on a frame. *It's really nice here,* he thought, snapping the phone shut. *Like someplace in the movies.*

"That was the marina," he said. "Your captain has his boat ready. Let's go get that lobster pot."

Neda kissed Mambo on the cheek and shot Otero a warning glance as the group gathered themselves up and left the little porch.

Mambo was an understanding woman, and Otero's comment was not taken as a slight. She watched them as they got into the car and headed for the marina, and she said a prayer. She drew a circle in the dirt by her feet, and she stepped inside it, because she wanted the feet of her daughter to return. Besides, she knew some things they didn't. Despite her knowledge as a Vodou priestess, some of the ancient papers they would soon hold in their hands frightened even her.

"Live to transform," said she said in English, holding her hand out to Zumbie.

And the cat smiled.

# CHAPTER 17

## BAL HARBOR, MIAMI

Jean Alexander was surprised when she realized that Andy, the arsonist who was arrested in conjunction with the explosion at the mall, was Neda Mason's brother. That made too much sense for her to feel comfortable, and she hated it when there were too many connections. That was one reason she sent Seymour out with the bail money. Neda was Roy's housekeeper for about a year before Jean met him. Adding it up so far, she had Neda, a former employee, who had a brother, Andy, who caused an explosion in the mall, killing Roy. Continuing down this path, she had Neda, whose own husband, Wilson, was in business with Roy and was now also dead. Life's currents were swirling around Neda, and Jean didn't like that. But it told her where to look.

When she knocked on the door to Andy's room at the halfway house he was assigned to in Florida City, it was Tina who answered. She was holding a travel bag in her hand, and Jean could see stacks of clothes piled on the bed behind her. It looked like someone was packing.

Tina stood in the doorway looking at Jean, who couldn't quite think of what to say. That was the effect Tina often had on people. Today she was wearing a fluorescent lime-green bra and no shirt with red-and-white-striped skin-tight Capri pants. Her stiletto shoes were black and had clear resin heels with dice floating around in them.

"Is—um—is Andy here?" asked Jean after she finally snapped to.

"Andy?" said Tina, shaking her triple-hooped ears. "Don't know who you mean." She closed the door. Nobody looking like Jean Alexander had any business asking where Andy was. This could not be a good sign. She needed to pack faster.

The knock came again. Tina wasn't sure what to do. So she stood on the other side of the door and waited. Jean knocked again, harder. "My name is Jean Alexander," she said loudly through the door. "Maybe you've heard of me? The artist. Anyway, I was the one who posted bail for Andy, and I want to talk to him."

A minute went by. "Well, he's not here right now," Tina said through the door.

Jean leaned down so she was speaking near the doorknob. "When will he be back?" she said.

"Never, I don't think," said Tina. She opened the door and was eye-to-eye with Jean, who had leaned over to speak through the doorknob. "I'm just here to pick up his stuff. He was in a—a—occupational accident. He's moving down to Key Largo when he gets out of the hospital."

"Really?" said Jean, making a mental note to check with Jackson Memorial. "Look, if I give you my name and number, can you just ask him to call me?" She jotted her cell number on the back of a perfumed, personalized card, handing it to Tina. "It would be unfortunate for him if his bail got revoked." She paused for dramatic effect. "You know what I mean?"

"Nope," said Tina as she shut the door, leaving Jean standing in the hallway.

\*    \*    \*

The following morning, after a wildly exciting debut as "BlueJean, Artist of the Month" in the Schaftzberg Gallery on Biscayne Boulevard, Jean Alexander drove over to Jackson Memorial Hospital to try to talk with Andy. The critics were buzzing about her presentation the night before. At first, they'd been cautious if not caustic. "To seek to construct art without using a mechanism other than one's bare ass creates no artistic value at all—beyond acrylic voyeurism," said the *Miami Herald* Arts section. Perhaps her painting, *Bottoms and Tongues Perspective*, had been reaching too far. The *West Palm Beach Times* magazine had taken a different approach. They were calling her work "a juxtaposition of the absence of artistic aptitude flying in the face of commercial possibility."

It was, they said, "Anti-Art." And people loved it. Her phone was ringing off the hook by lunchtime, and Schaftzberg had already booked a showing of her "Noses and Toeses" portfolio. Pauley Trane, manager of the gallery and grandson of the owner, Mrs. M. Norris Schaftzberg, sat beside her at the reception table and placed his hand on her knee

under the long, white tablecloth. He smiled at her as his fingers played up the inside of her thigh.

She enjoyed art.

Now, walking down the long, slightly gray corridor of Jackson Memorial Hospital, looking for room 26B, she tried to refocus her thoughts back to Alexander's business dealings. Somehow, Andy and his sister, Neda, were involved with her dearly departed husband, and she wanted to find out just exactly how.

Passing the nurses' station, she pushed the door open to the next room and found Andy sitting up in bed, watching a rerun of *Walker, Texas Ranger*. He looked at her with a question on his face, and she walked over to him and said sweetly, "Hello. My name is Jean Alexander."

Andy had no idea who she was and thought perhaps the hospital had sent someone to talk to him about payment for the surgery to repair his right hand. A bullet spins around itself while traveling through the air, and as a result, Andy's hand had a clean little hole right through the soft tissue between the thumb and forefinger. He was lucky that it missed his fingers and tendons altogether.

"Hello there back," he said with his own sweet smile. "I guess I'm going to have to come up with some money."

She pulled a chair up beside his bed and looked at his heavily bandaged hand. Only the tip of his thumb was visible. It looked like a giant snowball.

"You owe more than you know," she said, leaning back against the fabric cushion of the overstuffed seat. "But we'll figure out a way for you to pay those debts."

Andy thought he might like this nice lady. She ran her fingers lightly down the heavy bandage. Then, still smiling, she slammed his wounded hand down as hard as she could against the bed railing. Andy was still shrieking as the nurse's station called on the intercom.

"Do you need assistance?"

"No, thank you," Jean calmly answered for him. "Andy accidentally bumped his hand. He's okay now."

Andy's eyes were filled with tears, and his lip trembled as she stroked the side of his face with the back of her cool hand. "Now let's talk about explosions, Andy," she said in a quiet voice. "After *that*, we'll talk about money."

# CHAPTER 18

## KEY LARGO, FLORIDA

The motor vessel *Seeker,* captained by Haitian Master Prosper Simeon, was moored at Key Largo and ran daily lobster-fishing trips for tourists. The boat departed at 5:00 a.m. every Tuesday through Sunday off the dock behind Gator Joe's Cousin's Place. She was a squared tug-looking boat, mostly white with blue trim—no canopy, with fish lockers filling the stern. Captain Prosper would motor out into the bay with his young deckhands, nephews Alais and Taber. Dressed finely in beige Bermuda shorts with knee-length white socks, the boys would lower gaffs to pick up buoys marking lobster pot locations. It was a fine way to make a living. *Bounty from the sea is a gift to the righteous man,* thought Prosper. The sea herself was a powerful spirit. After grabbing the line and hooking the buoy, the deckhands would use an electronic hauler to pull the traps out of the water. The wooden or wire traps were then surveyed for catch, re-baited, and set back into the water.

Tourists loved it—when the weather was good, they could help with cutting up bait, or just take pictures, or throw up over the side. Whatever they wanted to do. Once, he'd even married a couple from Indiana on the stern and then led a hokey-pokey line around the small deck well into the evening.

Lobster fishing was Prosper's life, and he was a hard worker. When his children were still very small, Mambo Taffy helped him get a working visa in the United States. Everyone called her "Mambo," which was not only an indication that she was a priestess, but also a title of great respect. Thanks to this friendship, Prosper's daughter was now graduating cum laude from the University of Miami with a degree in journalism. There was nothing—not a thing on the face of this Earth—Prosper would not do for his honored sister, Mambo Taffy.

So when Neda called and asked him if he could help her and Andy hide the lobster pot, he neither questioned nor hesitated to assist the children of his priestess.

"Kisa ou vie?" he asked softly on the telephone with Neda. *What do you need?*

"Kache," she had replied. *To hide.*

Today, it was very choppy out over the Atlantic shallows. Although the sun was shining, a strong wind was gusting in from the northeast, and the seas were fearful along the Key Largo coast. The water itself was deep green and grim. Possible strong showers were forecast, and Captain Prosper questioned Micelli's request for a trip to the lobster pots. A twenty-four-hour wait would seem more prudent, in his opinion, but the men with Mambo Taffy's daughter were impatient. This was a sign to Prosper that these men did not know how to look around them and see the world. They should listen to Agwe Tyowo, the spirit of the sea; it was there to show them the way, and impatient people, in his experience, were silly and made mistakes. How could you not look up into the sky and see what the spirits were telling you?

Next to the captain's chair in the wheelhouse, Prosper set a bowl with a tangerine in it and a small bottle of dry gin. In Vodou, when asking for something, you should give something first. Today, Prosper was asking the sea spirits for safety. He called to the boys, Alais and Taber, to stand by and cast off as the little boat braced her shoulders against the wind and left the dock.

Micelli was invigorated by the wind as spray from the water flew across the deck. He felt warm in the sunshine of the afternoon, although he made a mental note that the cloudy skies would bear watching. A sudden squall was more than a possibility, but hopefully the trip wouldn't take long, and they'd be back on shore soon. He asked Neda to stay behind but wasn't surprised when she refused. Although Captain Prosper knew the location of the lobster pot, Neda had every intention of being present when they pulled it to the surface.

The combination of the roll of the little boat and the smell of engine exhaust was having an effect on Otero. He hung his head over the side of *Seeker* almost as soon as they left the dock.

"Don't face into the wind when you throw up," Neda shouted, standing across the deck and out of his way. The roll of the boat required her to keep one hand on the starboard railing. She was wearing tennis shoes, and her feet kept slipping on the wet steel deck. She handed a bottle of water to Micelli and motioned for him to give it to Otero. There wasn't anyplace to lie down on the boat, and Neda knew how terrible seasickness could be. Otero was as white as a sheet.

Pulling lobster pots that belong to someone else is illegal, but nonetheless, it happens. Prosper had taken special precautions when hiding the pot by using his GPS to measure a spot equidistant from his own floats and then sinking the line. That way, there was no indication above water that a trap was located in that position. Only someone who knew the coordinates of the hiding spot would be able to retrieve the pot. After about forty-five minutes, he was able to maneuver the little boat into position and called for his nephews to lower the gaffs and retrieve the trap.

Watching as the electronic hauler began to pull the line to the surface, Prosper leaned over to an exhausted Otero, who was almost prostrate over the rail, "You have a spirit inside your head," he whispered to the sick man. "Why don't you listen to it?"

Otero, incredulous that someone would speak to him about spirits inside his head while he was dying, could not find the strength to talk. The squeal of the line tore through his ears, and he knew it would hurt much less if he were dead. It took all his might to cling to the railing as the little ship was tossed back and forth in increasingly rough seas. The skies were quickly becoming dark and cloudy, and it began to rain as the wind whipped his wet hair against his forehead. Most of the time, he kept his eyes open and tried to stare down into the water near the side of the ship. It helped with his nausea. If he closed his eyes, he found himself alone with his stomach. That was bad—very bad. If he stared at the water—not focusing on its movement, but rather focusing on the cool color of the froth on its surface and the way the fizzy spray burst forth into the air—then, well, that seemed to diffuse how truly life-threateningly awful he felt.

"Did you give him some water?" Neda shouted over the rain to Micelli. "I hate to see someone so sick."

"We won't be much longer," Micelli said. "The lobster pot is coming on board now—we can head back soon." He didn't like the weather either and anxiously looked up to the sky as the shrieking line from the electronic hauler stopped, and the pot was dropped onto the deck with a great thud. He looked over at Neda and then struggled to see through seaweed clinging to the sides of the pot. He could just make out the outline of a square box covered with layers of gray duct tape. Taber released the line, and Micelli wished the boat would stop lurching around so they could get a better look.

Otero had been throwing up almost as soon as the ship left the dock, and now that his stomach was empty, he continued to have one involuntary retch after the other. Closing his eyes briefly, he thought of Anna at the vet's. She'd be ready to come home tomorrow, and what if he didn't make it through this trip? A new dog toy was waiting for her in her bed. What would they do with her when he didn't pick her up?

*It's true,* he thought. *Your heart really can ache.* He said a small prayer then, and perhaps it was heard, perhaps not; but at that moment, the *Seeker* was hit squarely on the port side by a huge wave, sending water sweeping across the deck and carrying Otero out over the stern and into the bay.

He closed his eyes.

The amount of water was astonishing. Neda wanted to scream, but she couldn't. As the storm moved across them, it felt like a hand was knocking the little boat back and forth across the water—just like a toy in a bathtub. First she heard the wind howl, and then she saw a wave pick up Otero and carry him across the deck. Then she saw his feet go over the side, and only a second or two later, she felt the entire world burst with the explosion of a waterspout as it hit the *Seeker.*

There was no time to grab for a life ring, no time to see where the lobster pot went, and no time to pray for the safety of her dear friends. Certainly, she would have done all of these things if given the chance, though not necessarily in that order.

Waves crashed against ship with stomach-turning force, and when the *Seeker* went over on her side, all Neda could do was hold on to the rail. She closed her eyes tightly against the saltwater, and with sickening impact, she was kicked in the face by one of Prosper's boys as he was carried out of the boat by the water.

The sound of the wind and sea were eclipsed by a groan from the *Seeker.* The little boat retched fuel into the sea as her props came screaming out of the water and the vessel struggled to pull back from the waves.

Neda's mouth filled with blood and saltwater. The air around her was wet with sea and spray.

"Agwe! Shango! Yemanja!" Prosper was yelling now, calling to the Vodou spirits of the seas. "Baron Samedi!" he shouted to the Guardian of the Grave. "Stand en arrière!" *Stand back!*

His voice was piercing, and although she couldn't see him, she felt he was near to her in the boat. *At least there are two of us alive,* she thought. Disoriented, she was suddenly aware that she was standing up, not lying over the rail as she had been just moments ago. Another wave tore her hands away from the wooden cap rail, and her back was slammed up against the wheelhouse door. It knocked the wind out of her, and for a moment, she couldn't breathe; then she willed herself to try the knob, and the door flew open, crashing against the wall of the small deckhouse. Throwing herself inside and to the floor, she crawled into the cabin as water rushed in behind her from the flooded deck.

"Micelli!" she shouted after coughing up a froth of blood and foam. "Are you all right?"

"Alais! Taber!" Prosper was shrieking from the deck outside the broken cabin window. "Veuillez! ma famille!" *Please! My family!*

Inside the wheelhouse, she felt a leg against hers. Through the dark of the storm, Neda could just make out the form of a boy curled around the base of the captain's chair. She reached over and touched the figure, and a hand touched back. It was Taber. Her chest burned with joy. As she lay on the cold steel floor, staring up through a gaping hole left by the shattered window of the wheelhouse, she did not have the strength to lift her head.

"Poukisa?" she whispered in Creole to the sky. *Why?*

As the fury of the storm abated, Neda waited for the light.

# CHAPTER 19

## MIAMI, FLORIDA

The Religious Studies Building at the University of Miami is open on weekdays from 9:00 a.m. until 5:00 p.m., and Friar Bill had been there most of the day. Now, sitting on the edge of a long, wooden bench in the library, his lower back ached. The school had recently received a microfilmed collection of ancient religious manuscripts held by Princeton University. Like a rock star, the film was "on the road." The collection itself was called "Paroxysm of the Enigma," and its pages were extremely important because they comprised what was thought to be the first handwritten textual interpretation of a French religious montet. The interpretation was comprised of divine thought inspired by God through the music of his hymns. Eventually, these writings evolved into what became known as the "Second Section in the Canon of the Next World." Other Princeton papers fundamental to the anthology were the "First Canon of Thought" and the "Fourth Canon of Death." According to religious historians, it was an astonishing collection of information about the afterlife.

All of this was important to Friar Bill, because some of the papers he'd seen in his office—the ones sent to the Master, shook him to the core. At best, they were an antithesis to everything he believed in. At worst, they shook the foundations of the Church. He would have dismissed them out of hand, had he not been aware of the fact that the Master had been receiving this type of paperwork for some time now. Friar Bill felt it was his responsibility to find out why they were significant to his order.

He wanted to find out more about the documents that were delivered to His Holiness the Master from Mr. Alexander. The deliveries only started about eight months ago. They were fairly regular and occurred around the first of each month. For the last two months, the order received two deliveries—one on the first and one on the fifteenth. The Master received each delivery personally. Friar Bill only asked about them once, and after a curt response, he didn't inquire again. Such were the rules of the order, and that was fine with him—he knew what his personal mission was, and each day he was grateful to apply all of his energies toward accomplishing the tasks set out before him. He was worthy.

But then the Master, along with another member of the order, was killed in a horrible auto accident and there was an explosion at the mall where Mr. Alexander had his business and now three men were dead. It was tragic, and he was curious. That's why he spent an entire afternoon with Mr. Alexander's widow, who was found in a regrettable state on the floor of his office.

Privately, Friar Bill was becoming more and more concerned about the Master's business dealings, and instead of rising from his bed in the morning with love in his heart for the day, he began to rise with trepidation and a sense of urgency. He cut coffee out of his diet and convinced himself that he felt immediately better.

For a while, it worked.

Then a few days later, an indescribable thing happened. As he worked to pack Friar Nathan's personal belongings, he found a collection notice from a company called Soul Equity, LLC. The envelope was marked "CONFIDENTIAL" in red, and he noticed that it was addressed to the Master. He was horrified when he opened it, not only at the contents but at the position he'd put himself in. The notice was advising that full payment had been made on an equity contract for, of all things, a soul.

The name on the attached Equity Certificate was Royston Alexander.

"We'll be closing in a little over an hour," a young clerk said in a soft voice. "Do you need much more time?"

"Not too much, thanks," he answered. "I'll be finished by the time you close."

In frustration, he wandered over to a bank of computers and tried the Internet. Instantly, he found nearly twenty websites that guaranteed him an immediate full-price payment for his soul. He was also able to watch a video clip from a popular television show, as some cartoon character named Bart Simpson attempted to get top dollar for his. Whether or not Bart succeeded held no interest for Friar Bill.

Indeed, the more he surfed the Web and read about the whole process of soul-selling as it was intricately detailed on several sites, the more he was convinced that it was all just basically—well, crap. After a long day of researching the possibility of a material terminality to our very existence, he felt conflicted to be able to consider the probability of any assured immortality at all.

Walking back across the parking lot to his car, he felt strangely frustrated and let down. It was all so anticlimactic. Maybe he just watched too much television—maybe all of this was just best left alone. *"No, ladies and gentlemen,"* said an announcer's voice in Friar Bill's imagination just before the television show in his head cut to commercial. *"Our Friar Bill did not find any great secrets today in these hallowed halls."* His mind's eye watched as a camera panned back to show the library in fading shafts of sunlight against the long, empty tables. The announcer continued, *"Great prose will not be used to portray any enormous religious revelation, and there are no lost, secret interpretations of ancient text."* Fade. Cut to commercial.

Friar Bill sighed. He didn't want anyone in the order to know he had been to the library anyway; after all, he was supposed to be at the local coin laundry. At the end of the day, the only important new document in Friar Bill's life—and this could also be an interpretation of text—was to be a parking ticket. Fifty bucks. Payable within thirty days of the date it was issued, or a late penalty would be added

There were still a couple of hours before dusk, and it wouldn't take him very long to get back to the monastery. He wasn't in any particular hurry. Strangely, he found himself turning left as he drove out of the library parking lot onto Ninety-Fifth Street, rather than right toward the Interstate. Friar Bill believed in preordination; later, he'd say that he felt another hand had been driving.

He felt himself drawn deeper along the car-filled streets toward Biscayne Boulevard, then up Seventy-Sixth toward Second Avenue. It had rained heavily while he was in the library, and the streets were shining with water splashed across discarded Marlboro packets and empty amber bottles of Budweiser.

He passed the Saturday Market in Little Haiti and saw a thin crowd of people still milling around. The large gravel parking lot was filled with colorful stands laden with fresh fruit, candles, and incense; their canopies still dripping with small, shiny drops of rain. Milk crates served as seats for old women who chain-smoked Camel cigarettes as they sat next to wire pens filled with cackling chickens. In the corner of the gravel lot, a basketball hoop was the center of attention for a group of teens, playing around the edge of a large mud puddle.

Friar Bill pulled the car over and decided to follow his instincts. A stroll seemed interesting; something about Little Haiti always fascinated him. He walked along the street and crossed over to a small store. Haitian flags flapped red, white, and green along each storefront, as the raucous sound of gongs and drums shook the Gracious Gateway Botanica. Music blasted out over loudspeakers that were hung on either side of a front door plastered in colorful flyers. Inside, Mother Mary statuettes stood in abundance on purple-clothed tables.

"Bonswa," said a small woman as he entered the dark store. She was sitting on a plastic five-gallon bucket of paint in the corner of the room and peeling an orange.

"Bonswa," Friar Bill answered. That was the extent of his Creole. "How are you today?" he continued, smiling.

Her eyes narrowed slightly. She shrugged and returned to peeling the orange. Candles flickered on the table next to her, and flies crawled through the frosting of a stale cupcake set next to a rotting banana on a plate. She was wearing a white dress with a red scarf tied over her hair, knotted at the top.

Friar Bill walked along the dusty tables, slightly bothered by the sight of the rotting food. He understood the Vodou custom of offering the spirits something to eat, but after it sat there for a few days, it tended to nauseate him. He never did like flies.

It was when Friar Bill turned to leave the shop that he saw the boy. He looked to be about fourteen years old, and he was standing in the shadow of the doorway to the side of the front of the store. The friar couldn't see the boy's face, but somehow he could see his eyes, and they were locked to his own in a way that made Friar Bill feel uncomfortable. He paused and watched as the boy moved slowly toward him, walking along the wall and through the shadows, his gaze staying with Friar Bill. He was wearing beige Bermuda shorts with white knee-length socks—like a school uniform—and he was slight in build. Somehow he was mesmerizing, and Friar Bill only paid partial attention to the fact that he seemed to be gliding rather than walking. The air seemed sucked away, and the buzzing of flies grew louder; Friar Bill wanted to say something, but he couldn't think what.

"Are you okay?" he managed to croak in English. *Stupid,* he thought.

The boy had now passed him and was heading away when he slowed and glanced back over his shoulder at Friar Bill. A big smile burst across his face—an eager, youthful smile. Then the boy turned away, and everything seemed to move in slow motion as Friar Bill watched him walk with his head down, right through the solid concrete wall at the rear of the store.

The woman sitting on the paint bucket wept to the sound of the ceiling fan.

\* \* \*

Friar Bill couldn't remember leaving the little store or driving back to the monastery. All he could think about was the way the boy looked at him and smiled, and then—of all things—seemed to evaporate right through a solid wall. He couldn't tell anyone. Not anyone. Not ever. In a daze, he made himself a cup of black tea and collapsed at his desk. His hands were shaking so badly, he couldn't sign the stack of paperwork left for him, so he was just sitting there when his assistant gave a quick knock on the door and came into the room.

"I've looked through the last of the boxes the Master placed in storage," the young man said. He hefted an ornate wooden box covered with leather onto Friar Bill's desk and brushed a layer of dust off the top with his hand. "This one looks interesting, but it's locked, and I can't seem to find a key anywhere in his things. I thought you might have it."

"What?" stammered Friar Bill. "Oh! Thank you."

"Can I get you anything?" the young man asked. "Do you feel all right?"

"I've—yes, I'm fine. I mean no—I don't need anything. Because I'm fine."

"Right, well. I've got some errands to run—bank and such, so I'll be gone for a few hours," his assistant said, leaving the room.

Friar Bill turned the box around so it was facing him. It was fairly small in diameter, about the size of his laptop, but it was very heavy. Made from something that looked like polished Purple Heart, the box had inlaid carved leather panels on the top and sides, and it was unique, exotic, and singularly beautiful. He pulled a little cloth from his bottom desk drawer and used it to polish a small, silver plaque on the lower right edge of the box. Words appeared, in Latin script, that said, "Aula Animus."

He pushed the front of a small, silver lock and was surprised to see the box click open. His assistant said something about it being locked. Odd.

The box was filled with what looked like very old papers, rolled and tied with ribbons. He lifted one out and gingerly placed it in the middle of his desk, moving the box to the side. He switched on his desk light in order to see better and carefully removed a white ribbon.

The letters on the page were written by hand in some sort of red-looking ink. A lot of the text was in Latin. He could read some of it but not all. "Valde Maximus Concencio." *Very Important Agreement.*

He tried not to swear under his breath. Latin was his worst subject ever. He finished in the very last place in his class at school, even with tutoring. He could remember some of the words, but not many.

"Eo ire itum mortalitas," *Travel toward death.*

"Viaticus," *Money.*

"Plasmatis," *Ghost, or spirit.*

"Templum," *Church.*

Friar Bill noticed the scroll work on the front of the box, "Aula Animus." That could mean several things. "Aula," could mean a hall or a courtyard. "Animus," depending on the context of the sentence, could be a soul, consciousness, mind, or intellect. It could also mean bravery, courage, or character.

The friar sighed as he walked over to a large bookcase in his office and loaded his arms with Latin-to-English reference books and dictionaries. It was going to be a long night. He hated Latin.

The telephone rang. It was his assistant.

"Friar," said the young man, sounding excited., "I'm down at the bank, and we have a problem. That huge wedding we did for the Ramsey family? Well, Barbara Ramsey's check just bounced."

# CHAPTER 20

## KEY LARGO, FLORIDA

Captain Prosper took Taber into his arms and lifted him up into the captain's chair while Neda searched the cabin locker for the first aid kit. Out on deck, Micelli was badly shaken up, and his leg was throbbing, but he wasn't seriously hurt. The storm was over as fast as it had come; waterspouts were a real danger in this part of Florida.

Alais and Otero were gone. Tears rolled down Prosper's face. "We must find my boy," he kept saying to the sky. "Je vous prie, Je vous prie, ne le prend pas." *I beg you, I beg you, do not take him.*

Although the sea was still heaving, Neda could at least stagger across the deck as she looked out over the water and tried to see if she could see anything or anyone. She heard Micelli curse behind her and turned toward him.

The lobster pot had gone.

The two of them ran back and forth across the deck to peer over each side of the boat as Captain Prosper struggled to start the engines. The *Seeker* sputtered to life with only a slight bit of smoke, and Neda began calling out Alais's name as the ship trolled in a zigzag pattern. Although it made little sense, it made her feel better to shout. The three of them scanned the water, looking for clothing or floats or anything that might help them find the boy, Otero, or the lobster pot.

Micelli started to say something to her and then thought better of it.

Neda heard the ring of a cell phone, and Captain Prosper poked his head out of the wheelhouse door. He held a phone out toward Micelli.

"There is a woman on this phone who says she is your mother."

Micelli looked at his belt and saw the phone holster was empty. The phone must have been tossed around the deck and into the wheelhouse during the storm. *How on Earth could it still be working?*

"Mom?" he said into the phone. "I'm fine. I'm out in the bay off Key Largo on a boat. Yes, I'm having a nice day." He noticed Neda and Prosper were standing there, staring at him.

"You're having a nice *day?*" Neda was incredulous. "Two people are missing and most probably dead, you extreme idiot, and you're having a nice day?" She was shouting into his face and choking back tears.

"Mom, can I call you back? The weather has been a little bit rough. Yes, that woman is a friend of mine. No, I'm fine. She's—she doesn't like boats. Okay, me too. Bye. Yes. Bye. I will. Bye." He put the phone back on his belt. "There's no reason to upset her," he said.

They were interrupted by a scream from Prosper. He was pointing off the starboard side of the ship toward the sea. There was a man walking slowly across the top of the water toward them.

It was Otero.

The three of them stood together on the deck of the *Seeker* in silence and watched as the figure moved slowly across the water toward them. The seas were very quiet now, and the sun was just starting to peek through the clouds and brighten the day. There was almost no sound.

Neda reached over and took Micelli's hand.

Prosper crossed himself.

Otero walked to within about twenty feet of the boat and then stopped as the shadow of a cloud passed over the *Seeker*. He looked across at the three figures standing on deck.

"What are you lookin' at?" he said loudly. "What?"

"Mère Marie Mère de Dieu, protéger nous," whispered Prosper. *Mother Mary, Mother of God, protect us.*

"Hellooooo," said Otero. "You're in the channel. I'm not. It's shallow here. Look!" He kicked his right foot up in the air. He was standing in only about five inches of water. "This just looks deep, but it's not! Ha! How do I get back on the boat?"

Neda looked up quickly at Micelli and let go of his hand.

Prosper was shaking his head. The storm had pushed the boat into a channel running between the sandbars. There were many of these shallow sections in the bay, and it was tricky to navigate here. He went back into the wheelhouse and put the engines on slow ahead, nudging *Seeker* toward the shelf Otero was standing on. The shallow water was very clear near the edge, and he leaned as far out of the cabin window as possible in an effort to see the bottom of the bay. He didn't want to touch the bottom or go aground and damage his props.

As he chugged very carefully toward Otero, a flash of color beneath the water caught Prosper's eye. It was the bright-red float from the top of their lobster pot, and it was sitting on the sea bottom about twelve feet below the boat. He killed the engines and let the boat drift over to the pot as he called excitedly to Neda and Micelli.

"There is something on the bottom," he shouted. He did not realize that he had been holding his breath. "I see something."

They ran to the side and peered down into the water; it looked like the float connected to the lost lobster pot. Then, as the silt began to clear, something else came into their vision.

A tennis-shoe-clad foot and part of a boy's leg were visible underneath the pot.

They had found Alais.

Micelli and Captain Prosper hit the water at the same time. Otero joined them a few seconds later, and the three of them swam with all the strength they could muster. The boy's leg had become tangled with the rope from the float, and he was lying on the bottom, under the pot. Micelli used a pocketknife to cut the rope away from Alais, as Otero and Prosper lifted the pot away from the body.

Micelli thought that it should have been impossible to cry underwater, but it wasn't.

His leg was killing him as he swam to the surface, took a great breath of air, and went again to the bottom. Prosper and Otero were bringing Alais to the surface, each man supporting a lifeless arm. Micelli grabbed a long part of newly cut rope and tied the float to the top of the lobster pot so that it was visible on the top of the water and used the last of his strength to swim up to the boat.

*So where is your spirit of the sea now?* he thought grimly as he listened to Proper's wailing.

# CHAPTER 21

## KEY LARGO, FLORIDA

Under cloudy skies, Mambo Taffy stood on the long, wet grass in front of the Largo Interfaith Ascension Church and bowed her head. Shifting her weight from her left foot and back to her right, her black patent leather shoes were caked in mud from the parking lot. She wore a knit deep-purple two-piece suit with a black straw pillbox hat. Black jet stones decorated the brim, and a large hatpin was stuck through the front like a small baton. Over her shoulders, she wore her favorite church scarf, a brightly colored hand-painted silk made by her sister in Haiti. The scarf had brilliant flowers dancing around the edges in gold, purple, green, and red surrounding a bright sun background. In front of the sun in the center of the scarf was Our Mother Mary's visage. If Mambo Taffy folded the scarf just so, Our Mother's face could be centered squarely in the middle of her back, behind and beside her heart.

Cold-faced, Prosper stood next to her, wearing his dark-blue and white plaid short-sleeved shirt and black trousers. Mambo Taffy was grateful for Neda's safety but devastated at Prosper's loss. He looked resolute, she thought, glancing at him—he looked angry.

"Je n'ai plus aucune larme," he said to her before the short service started. "Je suis un homme vide." *I have no tears left. I am an empty man.*

She placed her hand against his arm and patted it gently as they listened to the speaker lead the group in prayer.

"We come together today to ask our God of mercy to help our community and our citizens heal. In the midst of our sadness, we ask for the help and the blessing of Mary our Mother. Grant this through Christ our Lord, and help us find the passage to enlightenment."

Scanning a little flyer handed out at the door, she read that three people were killed in the storm; two people died when a Walgreen's pharmacy sign broke loose in the wind, sending it flying straight across the street and through the front windshield of a Dodge station wagon, and the third person to die was a boy named Alais. He died when his leg became entangled in the float line from a lobster pot that was taken overboard by a wave. He was dragged to the bottom of the bay, and he drowned.

Members of the small community gathered for an impromptu prayer amid the chaos that was usually a tidy churchyard. During the storm, two large stained-glass windows were broken when the laurel oak in the rear corner of the lot snapped in half, taking a section of the hip roof with it. The churchyard was now speckled with shreds of torn black shingles and pieces of broken glass. Mambo Taffy thought that right here, the whole world looked like it was covered in God's confetti. *Even in the depths of loss,* she thought, *there remains great beauty in life. You just have to understand how to see the world.*

She walked back to the parking lot with Prosper, and they stopped next to a stone statuette of Mary with one hand broken off. She kissed the sides of his face and touched her cheek to the backs of both of his hands, wanting somehow to convey her profound respect and gratitude.

She would weep later.

A hand tapped her lightly on the shoulder, and she turned to see a young man standing there, dressed in dark slacks and a pullover sweatshirt. He smiled in an embarrassed flush and said, "Professor Taffy? Excuse me for interrupting, but may I speak with you? My name is Friar Bill."

Mambo Taffy looked up into his face, and she felt a strange personal sensation of being drawn into—*inside*—the person standing in front of her. It was an awareness that had happened to her only twice before in her life, and both times were significant in strengthening her Vodou faith. She felt an especially strong connection to this man and knew that something was moving between them. She allowed it to happen.

"You saw the boy pass through, didn't you?" she whispered after a moment, breathless. "You saw Alais." Her eyes were wide. "Who *are* you?"

# CHAPTER 22

---

## NORTH MIAMI, FLORIDA

At FBI headquarters in North Miami, Pascale was exasperated. "It's a commodity! Don't you get it?" he said, pushing his chair back against the wall and looking at Micelli over the top of his glasses. "This is going to be the biggest thing to hit today's designer financial market. This stock is going to be so big that you won't even recognize Wall Street after Soul Equity starts trading."

Micelli, for the most part, was too tired to object. *Whatever,* he thought. The table between them was piled with paperwork, including several scrolls rolled in white ribbons and some sheets of letterhead marked "Soul Equity."

"Look at it like this." Pascale stood up and started pacing around the table. "You got equity in your house, right? You can borrow against property that you own if you want to raise money. Well, what about if you wanted to take out an equity loan on your soul? What do you care what happens to it—you're going to be dead, right? Assuming you even believe in any of that stuff."

Micelli's leg hurt. "Initial public offering. You're talking about an IPO for a business that trades in the buying and selling of soul equity? This is a Halloween joke, right?" he asked. He never liked Pascale. He looked again at the papers spread all over the table. He was almost too tired to read.

"Can you listen to me?" Pascale said, annoyed. "The interesting part is that historians can document this type of activity, you know—selling your soul—going back centuries. But I think this equity twist is something that people today can really relate to, because it's like, well, like cyber-cashing-in, you know?" He sat down, leaned back, and put his feet up on the table. "Before it was just folklore for Chrissakes. This new company, Soul Equity, they have some interesting money behind them—some *real* interesting money. A lot of it." He was poking his index finger down on the stack of papers. "The FBI wants to know more."

Micelli was thinking about the moment when Neda reached over to him and took his hand on the deck of the *Seeker.*

"We want to know more about this Mambo woman," said Pascale. "She has connections that we need to learn about. Don't kid yourself, that brother of Neda Mason's—" He flipped through a stack of papers. "Andy. He's involved in this somehow, and so, possibly, is that guy, Friar Bill. Micelli, are you listening to me?"

Micelli was thinking that Neda had very soft, very smooth hands.

There was a knock at the door of the conference room. It was Micelli's assistant, Frances, and she entered the room carrying a box marked "Verizon." Plopping it in front of him on the conference table, she said, "Don't go swimming with this one. I downloaded your contact list, so it should be ready to go, and you have seven missed calls from your mother."

"Thanks," said Micelli. "Can you please get us some coffee?"

She smiled at them both and left the room.

"You know, she has nice teeth," said Pascale.

"Is tea okay?" said Frances, leaning around the door. "The FBI is out of coffee."

# CHAPTER 23

———⟫●⟪———

## KEY LARGO, FLORIDA

Tina was laughing so hard that she could hardly stand up. Andy could hear her in the next room, but he didn't want to stop counting the money just now. Every once in a while, it sounded like she was actually falling over, but he hated to stop counting, because then he would have to start all over again—not that that would be a bad thing, really, because he liked the way the money felt in his hand. He was still sporting a "snowball" bandage from surgery, but now, at least both his thumb and forefinger were able to slide his Xeroxed bills one by one into a nice, neat stack. *Maybe he should be writing all this counting down,* he thought. The copy machine in Big Daddy Kane's office jammed around 1:30 a.m., so Andy and Tina stuffed their night's work into a gym bag and brought it back to Mambo Taffy's house with them in the morning. He had a neat stack of $100s in front of him on her dining room table and was wrapping a band around them when he heard Tina burst into laughter again.

Andy walked to the doorway and looked into the bedroom.

Zumbie the cat was sitting on the bed, dressed in a bumblebee suit. Two black antennas with yellow bobs on them bounced back and forth on Zumbie's head as the cat growled softly. He guessed cats didn't like wearing bumblebee suits. It did look a little bit funny.

Tina, meanwhile, was choking with glee in between puffs on a joint and stamping her foot on the floor every time Zumbie moved his head.

"I bought him a cat Halloween costume, An-beeeee," she giggled, falling on the bed. "We're going to go to the party at the club, aren't we?" She dissolved into laughter again and rolled off the side of the bed, landing with a thump on the carpet. "Did I tell you?" she said, from the floor beside the nightstand. "I'm gonna be a mermaid."

He heard the back porch door squeak open and slam like all wooden porch doors do. Mambo Taffy's voice called, "Andy? Are you in this house?

"I know what I smell," she said from the kitchen, "and you know my rules."

"Sorry," said Andy, closing the bedroom door behind him and walking back to the dining room table. He quickly scooped the stacks of hundred-dollar bills into the duffel bag and set it on the floor just as the door swung open between the two rooms.

Mambo Taffy came through the door with a disapproving look on her face, but she still gathered Andy into her arms and gave him a kiss on his face. "This is Friar Bill," she said. A man wearing dark slacks and a blue sweatshirt stepped into the room. Andy remembered to stand up straight.

"Friar, this is my son, Andy."

"Nice to meet you," said the friar.

They were shaking hands when Andy glanced down and saw a cat in a bumblebee suit run past them and out into the kitchen. Mambo Taffy saw it too. As the three of them looked at each other, Friar Bill turned and beheld one of the most unusual individuals he had ever seen in his life. There, standing in the doorway to the bedroom, was a dwarf mermaid with the most enormous bare breasts he could have ever imagined, holding Poseidon's staff, and carrying an empty trick-or-treat bag with the words "Sea Witch" printed on it.

Everyone was quiet for a moment.

"Boo!" the little mermaid said, as she collapsed backward.

"Maybe we should talk on the porch," said Mambo Taffy, guiding Friar Bill back out through the kitchen. "Andy, help your friend find the rest of her—fish dress." She gave him a warning look.

"Okay," said Andy. He gave the friar a nod and a small smile. "Happy Halloween."

A car door slammed in the driveway, and Neda ran to the back porch. Andy was helping Tina get to her feet, and he heard Neda say to Mambo Taffy, "Where have you been? Where has everyone been? Why do people have cell phones if they don't answer them?"

Mambo Taffy said something back in muffled tones, and Andy heard Neda say, ". . . Micelli, but I can't reach him."

Andy moved closer to the kitchen door to listen just as it opened and Neda came into the room. The door missed Andy by inches.

"I got a call from Bluejean Alexander yesterday," she said to Andy. "Mrs.—Roy—Alexander." She was hissing now and stabbing her finger at him. "She said you gave her my cell number. Are you *insane?*" She looked across the room, through the door at Tina, who was now sitting on the edge of the bed, still holding Poseidon's staff. "Who—or *what*—is that?" she asked.

Andy walked over and shut the door. Turning to Neda, he said, "We're trying on Halloween costumes. I'm probably going to be a bear. A brown grizzly bear, you know, like I wanted to be last year."

"Last year at Halloween, you were in jail, remember?"

"Well, yeah, but I did want to be a bear. And I have it all figured out; I've got this bear suit with a big bear head and these big teeth—"

"Andy, I can't believe—number one, that you even talked to this woman, and number two, that you gave her my cell number. She called yesterday and I haven't talked to her, but she left several messages asking me all sorts of questions about Wilson and what kind of business he was working on with Roy. The woman is very pushy." Neda was almost breathless. "You can go to jail big time for that mall explosion, Andy, not just a few months like before." She took the flat part of her hand and smacked him hard in the middle of the chest.

The bedroom door opened and Tina stood there, dressed—sort of—in a white bathing suit cover-up that said "CHARM Will Only Get You So Far" and flip-flops. Without saying anything, she walked past them, into the dining room and over to the duffel bag Andy had placed under the table. She scooped it up into the crook of one arm and said calmly to Neda, "You know, I think you got problems. Some man called here earlier today looking for you. He said to tell you—here, let me get the paper." She walked over to the table and picked up a scrap and began reading, "Wilson's business at Big Daddy's is unfinished."

Neda could barely speak. Both she and Andy turned to look at Tina in amazement. But then, Tina was used to that.

"He said he'd call back, and he said something about a payment."

*"Payment?"* Neda finally stammered. "What kind of payment?"

"I dunno," said Tina. She turned the scrap of paper over and looked at the back. "I didn't write nothing else down."

The front door slammed as Andy and Tina walked down the porch steps, got into Tina's car, and drove down the street. Neda, shaken, took a deep breath and walked through the kitchen and out onto the back porch to join Mambo Taffy and Friar Bill. It might have been the end of October, but it was still humid. Neda could smell the rain coming.

"I did not feel that I would laugh today—or ever again," Mambo Taffy was saying. "But look—just look at Zumbie." It was with pure and utter annoyance that the cat sat at the bottom of the steps to the garden, looking up at them with bumblebee antennas flapping around wildly. "Goodness help me," she said chuckling. "It will take some time before this cat will talk to me again."

"Hello," said Neda, leaning over to take Friar Bill's hand, "I'm Neda."

"My daughter," said Mambo Taffy proudly. "The flower of my life."

"Don't worry, Zumbie will find his own way to pay us back," said Neda, leaning down and settling into the swinging chair. "We might need to light a candle or watch for something spooky."

Friar Bill was smiling. "Well, I guess that's appropriate. After all, it's Halloween."

They sat together in silence. Neda began to feel uncomfortable, and the squeak from her chair was starting to become annoying. Finally, Mambo Taffy broke the silence. "You do not know us, Friar Bill," she said, "but I know why you have come here."

They were quiet for a moment, and Friar Bill didn't offer any explanation.

"You have seen Alais two times now," she frowned. "You saw him in the newspaper, and you saw him in the Hallway of Souls."

"Ne vous inquiétez pas, *M*ère." Neda interrupted. *Don't worry yourself, Mother.*

Friar Bill had a somber look on his face. "I was shocked when I saw the boy's picture in the newspaper, and that's why I came to see you. Your name was mentioned in the article about his drowning." He cleared his throat. "I don't know about this hallway thing. But I need to understand how or why I saw him."

"Friar, it's not—" Neda started to interrupt.

"I saw him walk through a wall for God's sake!" He was shouting now. Crossing himself, he looked down at the floor. "I'm sorry." Neda started to get up, but Mambo Taffy motioned for her to sit down. He continued with his voice cracking.

"I saw him in Little Haiti when he was somewhere else—when he was on the boat in the storm." He looked like he was going to cry. "I compared the time between when I saw him and the time when the paper said he drowned—and I saw him right about the time of his death. I mean, he couldn't have been on the boat and in the shop at the same time, could he?" It was a rush of words, and suddenly he seemed exhausted.

Mambo Taffy looked relaxed, and watching her, Neda saw her as beautiful in a strong yet peaceful way. Neda also knew not to speak at this moment. Mambo was still wearing her mud-caked shoes from the churchyard. Her pillbox hat was gone now.

"I am going to go and change from these clothes," she said as she stood up from her chair. "When I come back, I will tell you about Papa Guede. If you are a true man of God, you will understand the passage of Alais, and you will know why you saw him." She held the screen door open with one hand and looked over her shoulder at Friar Bill. "If you are *not* a true man of God, but one who is seeking only fortune, then the Guede will visit you, and he will eat your soul with a spoon."

The wooden door slammed behind her, but Friar Bill could still see her looking at him through the top part of the screen. "C'est le prix de la connaissance," she said, but her mouth did not move. *This is the price of knowledge.*

# CHAPTER 24

———◆———

## KEY LARGO, FLORIDA

That evening, the sun was setting quickly into the bay as Otero carefully steered a battered dinghy out through the channel toward the place where the *Seeker* lost the lobster pot. He'd arranged to "borrow" a boat from the bored teenage attendant at the marina office. Twenty bucks was all it took. Instant captain's license.

As far as he knew, the pot had not yet been retrieved—so it might be a good idea to go on his own recovery mission. The papers Neda hid must be valuable to attract so much interest, and if they were in his possession—perhaps he could make a deal of sorts. As an enterprising individual and businessman, he liked to remember the old adage, "a bird in the hand is worth . . . something." He couldn't remember the rest of the saying *exactly* but considered that it was probably accurate.

Otero remembered the location of the pot because there was a cell tower to the northeast of where the wave washed him up on the sandbar. Lights from the Dead River Pub would be to the left of the tower. Still, Otero found himself meandering around the bay for quite a while, until it became almost too dark to see. Finally, when he was just about ready to give up, he spotted the red buoy, just below the surface of the water to the side of a fairly narrow channel. He shivered. It wasn't cold, but he never really liked the water—and it looked dark down there. Taking a deep breath, he told himself that this was all about nerves, and he had plenty of them. After all, it was really pretty shallow in the channel, only about twelve to fourteen feet. If he got into trouble, he reasoned, he could pop back up and grab the side of his boat. This was just like one great big swimming pool. He cut the little outboard motor and drifted over to the float.

Quickly, he removed his T-shirt, Bermuda shorts, and tennis shoes and lowered himself down into the bay in his underwear. Taking one last look across the water, he thought that everything seemed silver and ghostly. *Crap on Halloween,* he thought, *I'm not gonna start seeing spooks now.* The float was directly below him, and his feet could touch the line. He tried grabbing at it with his toes and then took a deep breath and willed himself to go under and down to the bottom.

The lobster pot was surprisingly light. It wasn't too large, but it was bulky, and someone had put several weights inside it to hold it down. Now they were shifting around, making it difficult to control the pot as he lifted it to the surface. It snagged almost immediately—he'd only lifted it about two feet. *Damn!* Swimming back to the surface, he inhaled half a mouthful of water before he was able to take a deep breath and swim back down again. With cold fingers, he felt around the edges of the pot; the outer layer of wire and wood were snagged against some sort of seaweed. He could hardly see now, so he tried to tear away the weeds and pull on the lobster pot at the same time. It began to come away from the bottom slowly. He needed another breath. When his face broke the surface of the water, he felt a rush of cold air and blinked to see the clear sky and the dark night.

He was alone in the bay. "I am not afraid," Otero said outloud and he swam to the bottom again and began to tear at the seaweed until his fingers hurt. All the air had left his lungs, and he tried not to think about breathing. His fingers tore against stiff, sharp pieces of seaweed and rock, and as his chest was about to burst, he gave the pot one last great tug, and it came away from the bottom. Swimming desperately toward the surface with the theme song to *Rocky* playing in his head, he pulled the wire lobster pot through the water up toward the boat.

He came out of the bay with water running out of his nose, and he threw the red float over the side and into the small boat and then awkwardly heaved the pot up behind it. With the very last of his strength gone, he hung on to the boat with one hand and let himself relax in the water. He was shivering now, and he was sick to his stomach. His right hand was bleeding, and he had a long gash down his thigh, where a sharp edge from the wire trap had sliced through his flesh.

Floating in the water, Otero tried not to panic.

After a few minutes, he placed both hands on the side of the boat and tried to pull himself up. He couldn't lift himself more than a few inches out of the water. He tried bobbing up and down, each time bobbing further up—but also bobbing further down. The effort was making him very tired, so he stopped. After a while, he tried putting one foot up on the side of the rail and pulling himself up that way. No luck.

*Of all the stupid things you've ever done*, he thought, *now you can't get your fat ass back into the freakin' boat. Jesus wept.*

Finally, he let go of the boat altogether, swam over to the bank of the channel, and tried to climb up onto a shallow island of sand. The sides of the waterway collapsed under his feet in the water, and he crawled furiously, trying to find some solid footing to help him step up to the surface. He saw a small bush, and he grabbed at it, but the whole thing came loose as he tried to pull himself up.

As Otero fell back once more into the water, he knew he would not come up again.

It was quiet, and he felt the dark water all around him, and he didn't feel cold anymore; he was just tired. He read somewhere that right before you're about to die, there are a lot of things that have been reported to happen. Some people have seen white lights, along with relatives standing in bright rooms with open arms. There were reports of all kinds of experiences, from pre-birth to out-of-body and tunnels of sorts. Some people have even said that they could see hell. Otero saw none of these things. What he saw were flashes of Anna in his arms, and in his mind's eye, he buried his face into the black fur around her neck. He saw his knife in his hand and smelled the sweet steel. For just a moment, he was back in the bowels of the federal penitentiary, and he felt truly, deeply sad. He saw the front of his empty house without any lights in the windows. And he felt alone.

So he made a wish to the wind—a prayer to the sea. *Please let me live. I will try to do good things. I will respect other people. I will be a better man, a better friend, a better human being.* In one of the only times in Otero's life that he could think of, he meant all of it from the bottom of his heart. *Let me live,* he said to the dark sky. *Please.*

It could have been hours or days or maybe just a few minutes; because after you are dead, time doesn't mean the same thing anymore. Still, the next time Otero opened his eyes, he was surprised to see that it was still night, and he was still in the water. He had expected to find himself somewhere else.

There was a rowboat next to his dinghy.

"Hey there," said a bear in the rowboat. A topless mermaid with enormous breasts sat next to him, smoking a cigarette.

"I don't wanna get wet," she said to the bear.

They were peering at him over the side of their boat.

"Come on then, cowboy," the bear said, extending a paw. "Take my hand, and we'll pull you on up."

Otero thought he would be too tired to move, but he just managed to raise one arm and then the other.

"Don't get any water on me," the mermaid squealed as the man rolled into the boat and then vomited back over the side. "I'm in a contest tonight, for Christ's sake."

The afterlife had never been described this way. But then Otero was too exhausted to care.

"We got the lobster pot from your dinghy," said the bear, picking up his oars and turning the rowboat back toward the shore.

"We're gonna be late." The mermaid lit another cigarette. "This is dumb. I don't care about that stupid pot."

"Well you prob'ly should—'cause lots of other folks do."

The boat creaked as the bear rowed. Otero lay in the bottom of the craft in his wet underwear and looked up at the stars in the sky. For some reason, he always thought that he would be able to fly when he was dead. Not with wings or anything like that, but he pretty much believed that wherever he ended up, he wouldn't be bogged down by his body anymore. But now, he found himself cold and shivering uncontrollably.

"You know, we shoulda brought a blanket," said the mermaid, frowning. "He looks really cold."

"Well, we didn't know he was going to be in the water, now, did we?"

*This must be a transition of some sort,* thought Otero, *some way of getting from one world to the next.* Where was his white light? It figured that whoever came to collect him would get it wrong—even in death, things weren't going to work out for him. He coughed and was working up the strength to say something when the bear leaned over him and took off its head.

Otero fainted.

"An-bee!" Tina was shrill, as Otero slumped sideways in the boat. "He don't look good at all!"

Andy placed the head of the bear costume beside him on the seat and peered closely at Otero. "I think he's just tired from swimming. He'll be okay." He reached out to grab a float tied to the side of the dock. "Whew!" he said, wiping his hand across the back of his neck. "It's hot in that head." Then he stepped out of the boat and tied it securely to a wooden post at the end of the jetty. Hopping up onto the dock, he held out his unbandaged hand to Tina. "Come on up then, little fishie," he said, helping her out of the boat. "Let's get moving. We got a busy night ahead." He reached down and grabbed the lobster pot, swinging it up and setting it down on the dock beside Tina.

"How we gonna get him out of the boat?" she said, as Andy lit a cigarette. "What are we gonna do with him?"

"Hey, do you know those guys in that black car over there?" he asked her, pointing toward the marina.

"What car?" She turned to look.

"Don't look!" he said in a quick whisper. "Act like you're thinking about something else."

"Yeah, well I *am* thinking about something else, you asshole," she said. "I'm thinking I'm late for the contest because we had to follow this dumb schmuck, and now I'm wet, and I'm standing on this stupid dock, and you don't want me to look at a car while we decide what to do with some passed-out guy in a boat that isn't ours." Her voice was getting louder. "And you know—I could catch a cold. In fact, that's exactly what I'm probably going to do."

"It's okay, the boat belongs to Big Daddy. He don't mind if I borrow it. Just sort of back away from that light post," he said. "Casually walk over to the boat."

"An-beeeeeee," she said in a stage whisper, looking over his shoulder as she took little steps toward the darker side of the dock. "One of those guys is getting out of the car."

\* \* \*

"Is it possible that I think I see what I'm seeing?" asked Pascale as he sat behind the wheel of his car in the marina parking lot.

"I don't think that's a sentence," answered Micelli. He reached over and opened the car door to get out. "In the Keys, anything is possible. I think that should be our motto or logo or whatever."

Micelli walked around the front of the car as Pascale turned the ignition off. He stood by the open driver's-side window. Neither of them spoke. There was a man on the dock wearing fuzzy clothing, some kind of brown suit, and he looked like he was doing a dance of sorts with a very short topless mermaid who was smoking a cigarette. Pascale had never seen breasts that size, even in his dreams.

"We're following these *people,* because we think they might try and retrieve a lobster pot containing valuable, possibly irreplaceable documents that have been submerged in a Scooby-Doo lunchbox sealed tightly—I hope—with duct tape," Pascale said, staring at the dancing couple. "Is this correct?"

"I think our motto in the Keys is something like, 'Sport fishing capital of the world,' or maybe it's 'dive capital of the world,'" said Micelli. "Sometimes I think it should be, 'nut job capital of the world.'"

"Oh, hell, it's Halloween, and the night is young. What happened to your sense of humor? I'll wait here—unless you think you need help."

"No," said Micelli, "I think I can handle this." He sighed as he walked toward a long, wooden pier and the dancing couple. It was a beautiful, clear night, and his feet made crunching sounds on the gravel parking surface. He was almost to the dock when he heard voices behind him and turned to look back. Pascale was standing outside the car, next to the driver's-side door, talking to a man, and their muffled voices sounded angry. Micelli was halfway between the car and the couple, and he paused, unsure what to do. In the dark, he couldn't see what the man talking to Pascale looked like—only the outline of a tall figure, but he heard the words "our property" and "stolen." The man was making pointing gestures toward the dock and seemed very animated. Micelli looked back toward the dancing couple, who had now stopped dancing and were looking in his direction and past him toward the argument. Weighing the two scenarios, he continued to walk toward the couple on the dock, while trying to listen to what was going on behind him back at the car. As he got closer to them, he could see the man was wearing the lower part of what looked like a bear suit.

"Hi there, sir," Andy said. The little mermaid stepped behind him.

Micelli cleared his throat. "Nice evening," he said. "Is this your boat?"

"Um . . . well, I—"

"Micelli!" A voice came from the other side of the dock, and Micelli turned in time to see a head poking up from a small boat tied across from them. He'd seen the boat tied there but didn't know that there was anyone in it. Walking over toward the voice, he looked down inside the boat, only to see an almost-naked Pete Otero.

For a minute, they just looked at each other.

"I know it's Halloween," said Micelli, "but Jesus, Cutter . . ."

"Am I dead?" asked Otero anxiously.

Micelli turned and looked at the couple standing behind him and then back at the shivering man. "No," all three of them said in unison.

"So none of you is dead either?"

"No," they said again.

Otero was feeling his chest.

"Serious? Wow. Then help me outta this boat, for Chrissakes!" He held up his hands.

The bear grabbed one hand, and Micelli grabbed the other, and they pulled him straight up into the air and onto the dock. The mermaid started laughing.

"Where's your underwear?" she said.

Otero looked down, surprised. It had come off when they pulled him up to the dock.

He looked up at Tina and smiled. She rolled her eyes. "I got some clothes in the other boat," he said, motioning over to the dinghy they towed in when they picked him up. "Back in a minute." His feet made slapping sounds across the dock. Soon, Otero was back on the dock, hastily dressed in a T-shirt, shorts, and sneakers.

"An-bee, come on, let's go," Tina was whining. "You did this guy a big favor here, but now, do me a favor, and let's go to the contest. We still got time to win the grand prize."

Micelli was staring back over into the parking lot. Otero looked, but all he could see was a parked car. No people.

"I feel better," said Otero. "Thanks, Mr. Bear." They shook hands.

Micelli walked over to the lobster pot and started to pick it up. "You know I have to take this," he said to Andy. "It's evidence in an ongoing investigation, right?"

"You want help carrying that thing?" Otero said to Micelli, pointing to the lobster pot. It was covered in weeds and grass. "I'll take one side and you take the other. Watch out—it's got sharp edges. See?" He pointed to a fresh cut on his leg. "I know."

The two of them carried the wire pot off the dock and up to the parking lot toward Pascale's car. The closer they got, the more concerned Micelli became. He still couldn't see any people, and the driver's-side door was slightly ajar. Light from an electric pole at the corner of the parking lot only partially illuminated the area. He stopped to look inside the car and could see the keys still in the ignition. There was no sign of Pascale. He was wondering if it would be very police-like to shout, and that was when he heard a sound from behind the car.

Setting the lobster pot down, he motioned to Otero to stand still and began to inch slowly toward the rear of the car. Looking down, he saw Pascale kneeling on the ground and vomiting everywhere.

"What is it?" Otero asked.

"I don't know. He's sick or something," Micelli answered, quickly moving around Pascale and putting his hand on his back. Pascale's body was shaking terribly, and he didn't turn toward Micelli or even seem to notice he was there. The sound and the smell were starting to make Micelli gag.

"Jesus, Pascale," he said, "what the hell? Are you all right? What happened?"

Pascale's face was perspiring, and he seemed to be gulping air in between being sick. For a second, Micelli thought he was going to say something, but then the retching continued, even though it had turned into a violent dry heave. Micelli had never seen anybody so sick.

Otero was now standing on the other side of the car, opposite Micelli. "Been there," he said. "You want me to call the paramedics or something?"

"I don't know," said Micelli. He knelt down and then sat next to the sick man. "Try and breathe slowly," he said. "Relax. You're going to be fine. Just slow down." He motioned to Otero. "I think there's a bottle of water in his car," he said. "Can you get it?"

Otero ran around and opened the driver's-side door and retrieved the bottle, quickly bringing it to Micelli.

"Try and drink some of this," Micelli said, offering the bottle to Pascale. The sick man could merely nod as he tried to lift the bottle to his lips. He sipped a little bit of water and then sank to his stomach on the ground. Turning onto his side with his legs in a fetal position, he looked up at Micelli. His eyes oozed tears out over his face from the effort of the stomach contractions. Micelli had seen some sick people before, but this had to be the worst. "You feel any better?" he asked.

Pascale nodded weakly and just lay there on the gravel, looking up into the sky. His hands were shaking, and there was puke everywhere.

Pacing back and forth, Otero looked over at Micelli. "Things like this piss me off," he said. "Something's not right." He touched the side of this nose with his index finger.

"You want us to call the paramedics?" Micelli asked Pascale. "Who was that guy you were talking to?"

"He said his name was Samedi, Baron-something freaking Samedi or something like that," said Pascale, almost whimpering. "I don't know where he came from." He took another drink from the bottle. "All of a sudden, this guy is standing beside the car, and he's telling me that if we find any papers in the lobster pot that they belong to him." Micelli helped Pascale stand up, and he leaned shakily against the car.

"So I asked him what his interest was in the papers and told him to file a report. He started to argue with me and then—" He took another drink from the bottle. Micelli could see his hands were still shaking. "Then he got angry, and he was smoking a cigarette, and he put it out against the side of the car." Pascale pointed to the passenger panel behind the driver's door, and Micelli could see an ash mark and a cigarette butt on the ground. "He was wearing sunglasses, and all of a sudden he took them off and looked at me really weird, and I started to feel sick." He took a bigger swig from the bottle.

"Listen," Pascale said. Micelli saw his face was wet with tears. "Once when I was a little kid, I was out in the yard, and I had this cat. I saw her run across the road, and this car hit her, and I saw her go under the tires." He wiped the back of his hand across his mouth.

"You want to try to sit up?" asked Micelli. He wasn't sure if Pascale was all right.

"No, I want you to listen to me, *okay?*" Pascale looked down at the ground. "So, I started to cry, because I was just a little *kid*, you know?" He was shaking his head. "I went to help her—my cat. But when I picked her up, I could feel something was different." His lips were trembling. "I can't explain it. I could feel it through my fingers, and it was the worst thing. I could feel her life fading away right there in my hands. Kinda like you can feel your teeth when it gets really cold, right? And then she started to feel really still. But the thing is, Micelli," he continued, his voice breaking, "she was still looking at me." His voice broke. "Then she—she left. She died. And vomit came out my nose."

The three men were quiet. Otero didn't say anything, because he knew that feeling too.

Pascale swallowed hard and continued. "When that Samedi guy got mad and he looked at me—I was back there again. Right back there in that street with my cat, holding her in my hands."

For the first time, Otero considered just forgetting this whole thing and driving down to Key West to fish for a week or three.

They helped Pascale back to the car. He was still shaking when Micelli opened the passenger-side door and said, "I'll drive. You rest." Walking around to get in the driver's seat, he saw Otero walking toward him, holding a card in his hand.

"Hey, I found this on the ground," Otero said, handing it to Micelli. It was a business card. Across the top in block, black print, it said, "Soul Equity, Inc."

They looked at each other, and for a second, Otero thought Micelli looked a lot older under the half-shadow of the electric light.

"Bada boom," he said.

# CHAPTER 25

## KEY LARGO, FLORIDA

Music from Muffy's Dive Club reverberated into the parking lot as Andy pulled Tina's Mustang into her reserved space next to the dumpster. *Ah, the sweet smell of garbage,* he thought. When Tina retired as a regular dancer at the club, Muffy, the owner, had given her a reserved parking place as a present. Whenever she chose to use it, she provided the clientele with a little entertainment. Muffy even painted her name on the yellow curb in front of the spot. *belina* it now said, because someone had been sick on part of it.

Halloween festivities were well underway as they entered via a side door to the dressing rooms. Moose, the bouncer, checked them in and waved them through. The final competition was just beginning, and there was a lot of talent in the house. Tina's friend Candee was dancing as "Candee Cane" with her naked body wrapped in red ribbon. Another girl, Amee, played to the house as "Naughty Nurse" and ran around the room taking people's temperatures using straws filled and capped with vodka. She collected stacks of dollar bills by sitting on them. While it was entertaining, it was pretty standard strip stuff, so when Tina brought her alter ego Thumbelina out onto the stage, the house really started to rock.

Muffy's was a small, one-pole club, with recessed black lighting above the raised stage and a swinging, multifaceted chandelier. When Manifesto, the bartender, flipped a light switch next to the blender, the chandelier was programmed to spin around, flashing alternating colored lights around the walls. The club interior was painted a very dark midnight blue, and the floor was covered in black linoleum, spiraled in deep blue and red swirls. The color was called "bruised." Tina thought that was stupid.

Most of the small tables dotting the room had been pushed to the sides to allow for more people, and it was shoulder to shoulder tonight.

As the song "Mermaid Queen" blasted out over the sound system, Tina strutted around the stage. Holding her shoulders back, she let her size-GG breasts speak for themselves. With almost an entire can of green spray glitter applied all over the upper half of her naked body, she leaned down from the stage directly over the head of the manager from Appliance Direct and rubbed her breasts against both sides of his face. When she stood up, the crowd cheered at the new color of his head.

> *Little girly fishy tail, little lovely mermaid scale,*
> *All the boys her sighs do hear, then one day she spies a mirror . . .*

The song blasted over the stage as Tina held on to the pole with both arms and lifted her mermaid tail straight up and out into a cross position. "That's hard to do," she heard somebody whisper from a stageside seat. Then she dropped down and did a little fishy crawl to the edge of the stage, where she wiggled a finger at a man to lay his money in his lap and then wriggled down to the floor and picked it up with her teeth.

"Haw, haw, haw," the man bellowed with laughter. "Good things come in small packages!"

> *All her long blonde curls do fall, she's a mermaid three feet tall,*
> *With her gift of pearls and gold, she won't let the truth be told.*

People were clapping to the tune, and Manifesto's blender was keeping time to the music, when Tina looked up and saw the man enter the club. True, it was Halloween, but he looked different, and after years in the business, Tina had an instinct. He was dressed in a black tuxedo with purple lining, and he was wearing a top hat and sunglasses and smoking a cigarette. Half of his face was painted white like a skeleton. The hat was tipped on his head in a jaunty manner, and he walked that way too. He was a black man—a very dark black man. So black, he was almost blue. *He's beautiful,* thought Tina. She had never seen skin so luminous.

> *Refrain!*
> *People in the town, town, town,*
> *Thought they heard she'd drowned, drowned, drowned.*

She looked over to Andy at the end of the bar and tried to motion to him, but he didn't see her. He was involved in a long, gesture-filled conversation with Manifesto's boyfriend, Floria.

> *Nestled in her arms at night,*
> *If you knew—well! Such a fright,*
> *For behind those eyes so green,*
> *Lives a real-life deep-sea queen.*

Tina was back on stage now, keeping one eye on the man as he walked toward the bar, and concentrating on making one breast bounce up while the other bounced down and then vice versa. She accomplished this by leaning one shoulder down as the other shoulder went up; then she rolled her shoulders even faster, making her breasts swing in a giant circle. Given her small stature, the effect was quite startling. Someone had once suggested that she paint a face on each breast and advertise that she had two whole additional people attached to her chest. Andy tried to glue some tiny arms onto the breasts, but they kept flying off with Tina's efforts to swing them around, and the result was more comical than sexy. She could actually slap herself in the forehead if she got too energized, so she and Andy decided that it was more important for her to concentrate on the art of the performance itself and not the distraction of special effects.

> *Refrain!*
> *People in the town, town, town,*
> *Thought they heard she'd drowned, drowned, drowned.*

Floria took the microphone to announce an open stage for local talent, while Tina collected handfuls of confetti that rained down from the ceiling and threw fists of it out into the audience. Piles of dollar bills lined the edges of the stage, and she stopped at each customer to give a personal thank-you. Customer service was an important part of business. Glancing through the crowd of people, Tina strained to see Andy. He was standing at the bar, talking to the man in the tuxedo.

Manifesto put on a CD by an aspiring local singer from Big Pine Key, and the soft sounds of "Voodoo Prayer" began to fill the room as puffs of smoke emitted from the floor of the stage. *Damn smoke machine is broken again,* thought Tina. Muffy needed to keep things running. It wasn't supposed to puff. Smoke was supposed to ooze eerily from the floor in a fluid, smoky motion. For almost a whole month now, Brian Peterman, a science teacher from Largo High School, sat under the stage on weekends and manually fed water into the pump to keep the thing running smoothly. He couldn't be here tonight, though, as his church was hosting an "Apple Bobbing Boo" in the big parking lot across the street from the school. *If this was my place,* thought Tina, *the damn smoke machine would work.*

"Tina, *darling,*" said Floria, pushing through the crowd toward her. "Honey, you are the *best.*" He put one hand on his hip and flapped the air with the other. "I've *missed* you, baby." They air kissed.

"Thanks, sweetie," said Tina. "Hey, do you know that guy standing over at the bar with Andy? I haven't seen him in here before."

"I know, he's *yummy,* isn't he?" said Floria. "I saw him the very *minute* he walked through the door. I like mysterious types, you know? I could just *lick* him till it hurts."

"Something about him I don't like," said Tina. She put her face into a pout.

"You think he's a cop?"

"No." Tina paused. "Nothing like that. I dunno; he makes me feel sort of creepy."

"Baby, I *know,*" said Floria, rolling his eyes. "My type."

They watched as the man made a motion toward the door to Andy, and the two of them stepped away from the bar. Andy took a big last swig from a bottle of Corona, and it looked like they might be leaving.

"I don't like what I see," said Tina. She put two fingers into her mouth and sent a shrill whistle across the dance floor.

Andy heard it and turned toward her mid-stride. She motioned him over; he waved back and continued walking toward the door, following the man in the tuxedo.

"You dumb git," she said under her breath. *Don't go outside the building.* Strip club rule number one.

She started to make her way through the crowd toward them and saw the front door open and close as they walked out into the night. *Andy could be so stupid sometimes.* She hoped this didn't have anything to do with drugs.

Passing the bar, she leaned behind it and said, "Pass me my sweater, will ya, Manifesto?"

"You know where Muffy is tonight?" he answered. "You call this handkerchief a sweater?"

"No, and yes," she said.

Floria was back up on stage introducing a young lady who was supposed to be some sort of flower. She was wearing giant pink petals in a circle around her neck and nothing else. "Don't you just *love* nature?" he was saying to the crowd. Tina walked out the front door and into the parking lot.

She was standing there as her lime-green Mustang sped past with Andy behind the wheel and the man in the tuxedo in the passenger seat.

"Son of a *bitch!*" she shouted, kicking gravel up into the air. "You son-of-a-stupid-effing *bitch!*" Andy had never pulled anything like this before. She let him drive most of the time, but that was because she was *in* the car. She was sure gonna make *that* clear when she got her hands on him. *Damn*, she was mad.

Feeling a hand on her shoulder, she turned to see Manifesto standing there.

"I forgot to give you this," he said, handing her a business card.

Andy had written "Back Soon" on it with a little smiley face.

She turned it over and read the large black, block print on the front.

"Soul Equity, Inc." was all it said. Nothing else.

*   *   *

Andy was flying, and the man sitting next to him in the Mustang was laughing wildly. *What a guy,* Andy thought, looking over at him. *What a funny guy.* The man told Andy his name was Sam-ee-di and suggested they go for a little ride. A ride to *paradise,* he called it, and then he had laughed and Andy thought, *Well, why not?* He had the keys to Tina's car in his pocket, and after four Coronas, he felt great. His new friend said he had something "special" in mind, and so now they were driving down the middle of the road, and the car was up over ninety. Sam-ee-di's head was tipped back, and he was looking up into the sky with the biggest smile Andy had ever seen. It was like he had never been in a convertible before.

Sam-ee-di raised his arms above his head, and his laugh turned into a loud whoop; then his mouth went wide with delight. "Plus vite, mon ami!" he screamed to Andy. *Faster, my friend.*

For fun, Andy ran the red light and put two wheels up on the curb as he turned left.

"La vie est courte," screamed Sam-ee-di. *Life is short. "Jouons!" Let's play!*

*Damn,* thought Andy, amazed, *I can understand French. Wait till Tina finds this out. You are some dude.* He reached down and flipped on the radio, cranking up the stereo to Dead Stone Drum's "Eat My Soul."

*Hold to hunger, wait for me, on toward eternity*

"It's bongo time!" laughed Andy, making a wolf howl and moving his head back and forth along with the drums in the song. He turned the music up louder until he could feel it inside his chest.

"Woo hoo hoo," said Sam-ee-di, laughing and hooting. He was slapping his knee and motioning to Andy to ask if he wanted a smoke. He held out what looked like a little packet of cigarettes with French writing on it.

*Hell, why not?* Andy thought. He'd been trying to quit smoking, but that wasn't working too well anyway. These funny cigarettes seemed interesting. He slowed the car and took one from his new friend. It looked self-rolled in dark paper, and when Sam-ee-di handed him one that was already lit, the smoke was sweet and nauseating at the same time. It burned good in his chest. It burned real good.

"Want to go to Miami?" Andy shouted to Sam-ee-di. "Want to go to the moon?"

They both laughed and laughed.

When Andy floored the car out onto the Overseas Highway and headed south toward the Seven Mile Bridge, he felt like a god.

*Hear the drum beat,*
*Watch the heart sleep,*
*Listen for the sound of death's feet.*

Sam-ee-di was drinking something from a little clear bottle now, and he handed it to Andy as the streetlights flashed past them faster and faster. Andy took a swig.

"Holy Mother!" he said, spitting the mixture out in a spray against the inside of the windshield. It was rum of sorts, laced with what tasted like hot peppers.

That made Sam-ee-di laugh even harder. He took the bottle back from Andy and drank a huge swallow. Then, wiping his mouth with the back of his hand, he let out a big belch.

"Ho, ho," said Andy, taking the bottle again. This time the mixture stayed down. He smacked his lips, cranked the stereo all the way up, and put his foot to the floor. He could hear Dead Stone Drums screaming into the night. What he didn't hear were the sirens in the distance.

There were only a few times in his life when Andy had felt so good. The night was beautiful and warm, there was a full moon, and there was just one bright star in the sky. The Mustang felt like it was part of him. He didn't even have to think about driving—it was just like the car could read his mind. Everything he did, Sam-ee-di thought was so *funny*. Andy imagined that the car could drive this way all by itself; he and his new friend could just sit back and enjoy themselves. To Andy's astonishment, Sam-ee-di was turning in his seat and trying to stand up. *What a funny guy.* Andy watched as the man turned, threw one leg over the rear of his seat and then the other, falling into the back seat of the car. A second later, Sam-ee-di was sitting there with his feet up on the center console, reclining and singing along to the song.

> *Death feet walking*
> *Death feet run*
> *Death feet stalking till it's done*

Andy looked at him in the rearview mirror and wondered for a second how he kept that top hat on his head. They were going almost ninety, and Andy's hair was flying all over the place, but Sam-ee-di looked like there was barely a breeze. He motioned to Andy to join him in the back. *Come on,* Andy heard him say without moving his mouth. *Come on and sit in the back with me. Let's just sit here and watch that star. This car will drive where I tell it to.*

All of a sudden, Andy *believed.*

When he took his hands off the steering wheel and turned to crawl into the back seat with Sam-ee-di, he felt himself flying toward something that had been waiting for him for a very, very long time.

*　　*　　*

Mambo Taffy's screened back porch flickered in soft candlelight. It was a very muggy, cloudy night, and shadows played against the screens as Mambo Taffy pulled aside a curtain to reveal a small altar built into a nook in the wall. After changing her clothes, she was now wearing a beautiful white, floor-length dress trimmed in silver. Her hair was gathered under a white scarf tied at the top of her head, and she wore layers of pearls around her neck. Her feet were bare, and in her right hand, she carried a gold cross, a sprig of herbs tied with a purple ribbon, and a small mirror.

Friar Bill and Neda were sitting together on the painted bench, and Mambo seated herself opposite them in a large, high-backed rattan chair.

"I invite you to share my faith with me, Friar," she began, speaking in a quiet voice. "I must ask, and you must accept."

There were fourteen candles burning around the edges of the porch, one for each of the years that Alais lived. Mambo would light them every evening for a month after his death, so that he'd be able to use the light as he traveled through the gates to his afterlife. She would pray to the escort spirit, Papa Babaco, to guide Alais and protect him. In the center of the altar, Mambo had placed a picture of Alais, along with a tall glass of water, an apple, a bottle of hot sauce, a pair of sunglasses, and a man's white top hat. These were gifts for the spirits; in Vodou, it always helped to have appreciative spirits. For Mambo, it was emotionally difficult when a child died, but she found comfort in knowing that Papa Babaco would never take a life before its time, and that he would carry the child in his arms.

"I'm a man of great personal faith," said Friar Bill, looking straight ahead. "It is within the context of my own beliefs that I accept."

"There is but one Creator," said Mambo as she closed her eyes, "and I serve him also."

Neda rose from her seat, took a match, and lit a small fire in a hibachi next to the altar. As the flames crackled to life, she retrieved a bag of potpourri from under the table, opened it, and spread its contents around them, creating a circle.

"My personal spirit, or *Iwa*, has something to tell you," she began. Her body swayed back and forth as she sang a song to the boy in French. "Mille mains vous portent," she sang. 'Prenez-vous la maison." *A thousand hands carry you. Take you home.* "Je vous reverrai. Vous faites partie de moi." *I will see you again. You are part of me.* "Mon enfant, mon enfant." *My child, my child.*

Neda had a wooden rattle in her hand, and she began to shake it along with Mambo's words, punctuating each phrase of the song. As if on cue, a lone barking dog began to howl. Friar Bill noticed the wind had picked up, and it was starting to rain lightly.

"Ten thousand years ago—eight thousand years before the birth of Christ, my Vodou God put his foot down on the dirt of his own earth and proclaimed that his children should go forth. He made many different spirits to help them. He made spirits of the water, of the forest, of the sun and wind, and most importantly, the spirit of the head."

She stood up and walked slowly around the outside of the circle.

"When the spark that is our life comes to this earth, we can be lonely and afraid. Our Creator saw that we needed guidance and protection, so he made many spirits to stay with us and give us counsel." She smiled over at Friar Bill. "*You* call these spirits 'guardian angels.'"

Her footsteps were rhythmic, and the sound of Neda's rattle seemed to melt back and forth like waves through the silence of the night.

"Vodou is a participatory faith," she said. "I have a personal relationship with my *Iwa*, or the spirit of my head; he has been my companion since I was eight years old. In life, his name was Rene Danto, and he was a slave on the Haitian plantation of Cap Gouget. He died when he was beaten unconscious and thrown onto an anthill by his owner—for the crime of singing after dinner. It was 1790, only one year before the great revolt of the slaves in Haiti."

Watching her, Friar Bill thought he noticed a change in her stance. She seemed to stiffen as she walked, and she began to carry herself in a straighter, taller fashion. He squinted into the light from the candles and tried to see her face. Glancing over at Neda, he could see her eyes were closed, and her head was gently bowed. Her legs were crossed in front of her, and her hands were on her knees, palms up. In one hand, she held the rattle that still punctuated Mambo Taffy's tale.

"Papa Gede!" Neda shouted.

Friar Bill jumped.

"We sing now to ask Papa Gede to open the gates," Mambo said quietly. She picked up a small bottle of oil from the table, removed the top, and dabbed some onto her right index finger. Then she leaned over and touched her finger once lightly on each side of Friar Bill's head at his temples.

She seated herself in a queen-backed rattan chair facing them as Neda rose and walked over to a table by the screen door. A tall glass bottle sat next to a fern and candle. Neda removed two long sticks from the bottle and lit the ends, releasing a shower of sparks. Red, blue, green, and gold pinpoints glistened and gleamed and burst like small rockets into the air. As the fire shot out in all directions, Friar Bill realized they were Fourth of July sparklers, and he watched as all sorts of colors danced in sparks as they flew around the small porch. Neda stood in the middle of the room with her arms raised above her head and began to twirl in circles. He watched as the ceiling fan stopped, paused, and began to turn slowly in the opposite direction. As the sparklers burnt to an end, Neda walked over to the altar and picked up a fairly large ceramic jar. Removing the top and tipping it, she scattered dozens and dozens of coins across the porch floor; copper and silver rained out over the wooden deck, rolling into corners and under the table, settling finally into piles of shimmering, shining coinage.

Returning to her seat, she began shaking the rattle again. Friar Bill thought he could hear music, but it was very faint—a low, moaning melody of voices along with a plaintive sound of bells tinkling.

Mambo Taffy's eyes were closed and her face relaxed. Without warning, she jumped to her feet and bent over the table between them with her mouth gaping wide and her tongue protruding. Making a loud "aaahhh," exhale, her mouth was only about an inch from Friar Bill's face. He tried to remain composed. Then her eyes rolled back in her head, and she began to sway along with the music and the rattle. Quickly she sat, looked directly at Friar Bill, and in a voice he had not heard before, said, "Ainsi soit-il." *So be it.*

"Amen," said Neda.

A burst of wind blew out all fourteen candles at once as the outside door of the patio blew open wildly, bounced against the screen, and then slammed shut. Violently, a ceramic flowerpot flew from the table by the door, crashing loudly and breaking against the floor, throwing dirt in all directions. It was raining harder outside now, and Friar Bill could see excitement on Mambo Taffy's face as a flash of nearby lightning lit the porch.

"Mon garcon cher," she whispered. *My darling boy.* "L'enfant est ici." *The child is here.*

Sitting there in the darkness, Friar Bill could feel something touching the side of his face; something like a small, cold hand ran unseen fingers across his cheek and along his ear. The hair on his arms stood up. Then he felt a cold sensation on the back of his neck and thought he could hear the quiet, soft sound of breathing very near to him. As he listened, the breathing began to get louder and louder, and then it turned into the sound of wings beating against air. He struggled with all his might to listen even more closely—to hear each little piece of sound, and even though his eyes were open, he saw nothing. Nothing at all. With every bit of effort he could summon, he listened as the sound of wings became louder and seemed to come closer with each beat. Like a metronome, the sound continued, and he could hear the wings pushing toward him, slower and deeper; the sound became hollow, and the air began to pulsate, until he could feel it pounding inside him. His chest began to throb along with the wings until the two sounds came together and became one unbearable heartbeat. And then, the sound itself passed right through him—through his chest, through his neck and face and arms and legs.

Suddenly, he felt his whole body lifted and thrown by unseen hands upward toward the glory of the black, rainy night. It was exhilarating, and he felt boundless, unimaginable joy. He was a child again—a boy, and in his heart, he knew the hopes of his future, and he saw anew the endless possibilities of life itself.

He could see his own face, and he was crying.

Then he felt strong hands shaking him, holding on to his shoulders and shaking him hard.

"Friar Bill," Neda was saying. She seemed very far away. "Friar Bill, are you all right?"

"Here, drink this," he heard Mambo Taffy say, and he felt a cold glass of water being placed into his hands.

With a blink, he looked around the porch and saw that it was brightly lit by the globe on an unmoving ceiling fan; the night sky outside was clear and quiet. There were no coins on the floor, and the flowerpot was unbroken and back on the table, sitting next to the fern. The altar was gone, covered by the curtain, and Mambo Taffy was sitting in front of him, wearing jeans and a black T-shirt that said "Profundity."

"Could I have something a little stronger?" he asked, with his heart racing in his chest. "I think I'm going to need it."

*   *   *

The cat-clock ticked its tail back and forth on the wall of Mambo Taffy's kitchen. The three of them had come inside for something to eat. "Always better to talk with food," Mambo said, opening the refrigerator and handing Neda a casserole dish. Friar Bill was sitting at the kitchen table in the middle of the room.

"I have a doctorate in education," she said. "I tell you this because I want you to know that I am a logical woman. I am not given to emotional hysterics or religious frenzy." She walked over to the sink and started washing her hands. "When most people see or hear the word 'v-o-o-d-o-o,' they can only picture things that the Hollywood scary-movie machine stereotyped back in the '30s and '40s. It's a shame people are so naive."

Neda was placing a casserole in the oven, and Friar Bill couldn't quite believe he was sitting in a room discussing Vodou in all sincerity.

"It helps if you know a little history, so I'm going to tell you about how Haiti came into existence," Mambo said with a slight smile. "You'll be able to tell I'm a teacher."

Neda pulled up a chair beside him at the table and handed him an unopened can of soda.

"Today Haiti is one of the poorest nations on the face of the Earth," Mambo Taffy started. "But this was not always the case. In 1607, Spain ceded the western half of the island of Hispaniola to France, who recognized the rich agricultural potential of the land. Unfortunately, the French quickly worked the native Arawak Indians into extinction. They were only cannibals, after all."

She stopped and smiled at Friar Bill before continuing. "Looking for labor, the French turned to the slave trade, and by the late 1700s they had almost five hundred thousand African souls working in the fields. Cocoa, coffee, sugar cane, and cotton brought great wealth to the people of the island, but also great misery, great inequity, and ultimately great and lasting sorrow." She was shaking her head.

"One day, some of the slaves escaped, and the group ran into the mountains, where they hid deep in the forest. Their leader was a man called Boukman, and he had a plan. Desperate measures, perhaps, but they were desperate people. Looking at the disparity of numbers in the country—there were, after all only some twenty-six thousand whites to seven hundred thousand blacks—his plan was an inevitable one. Some historic accounts mention his plan, and some do not; many people believe it to be a myth. I do not. I believe Boukman led his followers in a ceremony where they made a deal with the devil. They vowed to serve him—they gave up their souls and the souls of their children and their children's children—for a period of two hundred years. In exchange, they wanted freedom from the French.

His plan was this: scarcely one week after Boukman and his followers made their pact—on August 14, 1791—all the slaves in Haiti rose up *simultaneously* across the island and murdered their French overseers in their beds, in the streets, and in the fields themselves. Blood soaked each town. It was a massacre beyond comprehension. Think about this; in an era without the means of communication we have today, every person who was a slave in Haiti heard the same command at the same time in their heart. The struggle lasted until January 1, 1804, when France acknowledged defeat and finally gave the Haitians independence. The Africans were free at last, but they paid a terrible price."

"So, being enslaved by the devil is better than being enslaved by the French?" Friar Bill asked in attempted levity.

Neda shot him a sideways look.

"Apparently," Mambo said in a dry voice.

"Sorry, but what's Haitian history got to do with me?" he said.

"There are documents that still exist recording this event," she answered. "They are extremely valuable to certain, shall we call them, *collectors*. Many of them—but not all—are kept by your order. That was until the one you called 'the Master' was killed in that car accident, and then some of them went astray. I believe my daughter knows that I am speaking the truth." Mambo looked at Neda, who seemed shocked and surprised.

"You mean the papers that Wilson found in the extinguisher were from a deal with the devil in Haiti?" she gasped. "The papers I hid in the lobster pot?"

"I think so," said Mambo. "I can see them when I close my eyes, but I have only been able to see them since I met Friar Bill. The vision seems centered around him."

She stood up from the table and went over to the stove to remove the casserole. Setting it on the counter, she turned back to Neda.

"What you did was foolish," she said. "Those papers were being smuggled into the country, and there are a lot of people who want to possess them. Alais now wants them, and he has come to Friar Bill for help. Baron Samedi is trying to find them also." She looked at Friar Bill. "On Earth, we sometimes call him 'Death.' And there are others."

"Alais *was* the boy I saw in the store," said Friar Bill. "How did that happen?"

"He was in the 'Hallway of Souls,'" she answered. "You saw him as he moved between life and death. You will never see him again, because he no longer has a physical form, but you will know when he is near you. You felt him come to you a little while ago, didn't you?"

Friar Bill was quiet. He looked down at his hands. "What's this Hallway of Souls?"

"A place beyond explanation," Mambo said. "It's like this: We have a veil between us and this knowledge. In life, it cannot be lifted. Only at the moment our soul is released can we see what is both before and after us. The Hallway of Souls is the place we pass through at the moment of our death, and we become washed with grace and forgiveness, and we are given our final and lasting sovereignty. We have completed the great journey given to us by our Creator. The journey of life."

"So what does everyone want these papers for?" he asked, not really wanting to hear the answer.

"Well, you can't pass through the Hallway of Souls without a soul," Mambo said.

"You mean you can't die?" Neda interrupted.

"Oh, you can die—physically that is," Mambo answered, "but if you've given up your soul, there isn't anything to move forward. Or actually, I think the better word is 'change.'"

"So what happens to you?"

"You are nothing for all eternity. Christians call it 'hell.' For myself, I have always discounted the fire-and-brimstone theories; I tend to think of it as something empty. You were, and now you are not—or better said, *now you were never*. I really can't think of anything sadder. Or more wasteful."

"You mean the papers have something to do with people's souls?" Friar Bill was sitting up very straight in his chair.

"In Haiti, in 2004, when the two-hundred-year deal with the devil was over, some say there was an extension of the agreement. Another ceremony allegedly took place in exchange for an additional two hundred years. Your papers contain the signatures of several *hougans*, or witch doctors, along with the mark of the devil himself. If these papers are destroyed . . ."

Neda was standing now. "Maman," she said slowly, "are you saying that the fate of all those souls is contained by the signatures on those papers?"

It took a minute for Mambo Taffy to respond. "Yes, my daughter. I mean, it's possible," she said, standing up. "Anybody want casserole?"

# CHAPTER 26

## MIAMI, FLORIDA

It was Saturday morning, and Micelli, who had overslept, was just finishing a cup of Cuban coffee when he picked up the financial section. Startled by an article in the bottom corner of the front page, he almost missed the table when he set down his small cup.

(AP Miami) Soul Equity, Inc., newest darling of Wall Street's boutique financial industry, announced plans today for a worldwide rollout for its long-awaited initial public offering. The privately held company has operated in semi-secrecy during its history, and details of its operations have been kept confidential for over 50 years. The company offers to purchase equity shares in personal souls, a practice seen by some as questionably legal. But Soul Equity's position remains that it is not trafficking in body parts, but rather in "personal spiritual property."

President and CEO, Rix Roman, maintains the company acts more like a charity than anything else. "There's a need for our offer," he said yesterday in a press conference held on the steps of the Federal Hall National Memorial Building in New York's financial district. "After all, if you're not using your soul, why not let it work for you? People have a great asset that can make money for them. We're just here to help."

And Roman also points out that taking out an equity loan against your soul does not mean that you can't pay it off at a later date. "It's up to you," he says. "It's your property after all. If you pay the money back, we are glad to return the rights to your soul."

In one minor incident, police arrested Rev. Isadore Conklin, who attempted to interrupt the interview by driving a Unified Church of Freedom van back and forth with the horn blaring.

"It's nothing but the devil's work," he reportedly shouted as the truck hit a fire hydrant. "This financial offering stuff is only a cover up. Don't be fooled."

Analysts are predicting the valuation of the company will be much higher than expected when the IPO was first reported in May, with the range more than tripling its initial base of 20.3 billion dollars.

"Shit!" said Micelli, remembering his conversation with Pascale. Rummaging around his kitchen junk drawer unsuccessfully for some scissors, he finally tore the article carefully from the newspaper. Folding it, he glanced at his watch and jumped from the table with a snort; he needed to get going. Rinsing the coffee cup in the sink, he wondered how much equity his soul had. *How would somebody find that out?* he wondered, making a mental note to look at the Soul Equity business card Otero found. After all, what could be wrong with getting money for signing a piece of paper?

\*     \*     \*

Otero spent the day practicing being invisible.

He'd been pretty busy lately and had neglected this practice. Invisibility was a skill you had to work at, to stay in top form. One slip and—well, there was a big difference between being invisible and not. After all, it wasn't like you could measure it in degrees or anything like that; you couldn't be "sort of" invisible. Also, sometimes it was difficult to tell if people couldn't see you, because you couldn't actually stop and *ask* them. You just sort of had to watch what people were doing when you were around. In a crowd, indifference and invisibility were close cousins.

The first rule was to never, ever look anyone in the eye. Once you did that—boom—visible. This was the part that took practice. You had to watch what people were doing without actually looking at them. Well, directly at them in the face anyway. Otero practiced by watching the lower halves of people's bodies as he moved past them. He had been doing this since he was a kid.

For today's invisibility practice, he went into a busy supermarket and waited around until there were long lines at several checkout registers. Then he walked over and stood behind one of the vacant tills. If he was visible, he figured one of two things would happen. Either people would line up to have their groceries checked, or some manager would ask him what he was doing.

He was careful not to look directly at anyone. No one lined up.

*You still got it,* he thought to himself after ten minutes had gone by.

Whistling, he walked around the till to the outside aisle and ran directly into the store manager. "Good afternoon," said Otero, looking straight at the man.

"Uh, what? Oh! Good afternoon," the manager said, flustered. He seemed about to say something else, but Otero's second rule was this: once people start talking to you—they could see you—so keep moving. He walked past the manager and out of the store.

Down the street, he paused in front of Tech City. Something caught his eye on a bank of flat-screen television sets flashing the early evening news out toward the sidewalk. It was that lady—BlueJean, the artist with the good legs. Why was she on the news? He hurried inside just in time to hear, ". . . investigators still have no suspects in the gruesome attack last night, and Alexander, also known in the art world as 'BlueJean,' remains hospitalized in Miami's Jackson Memorial Hospital. The family is not releasing any information about her injuries other than to confirm that she suffered a stroke shortly after she was admitted."

*This can't be good,* thought Otero as he picked up his cell phone to call Micelli. *I bet it's got something to do with those Soul Equity people.* He reached inside his pocket and pulled out the card he palmed from Pascale's car. This time the card had a phone number printed on it.

# CHAPTER 27

## KEY LARGO, FLORIDA

After an open-casket viewing in a simple morning ceremony, Alais was laid to rest at the True Church of Saint-Domingue Ayti. The first hour of the viewing was reserved for immediate family, and then a tour bus hired for the occasion brought cousins from Miami along with a percussion band from Little Haiti called *Chantez à un Dieu,* Sing to God. As the mournful cacophony skittered sound throughout the cemetery, cymbals and rattles accompanied by a lone bird whistle attempted to make a joyful noise unto the Lord. The entire class from the boy's school walked behind the hearse. Final prayers were said after four hours, as three stone masons sealed up the opening of the family tomb with mortar. Then there was singing and much crying, followed by Mass and a meal at the home of Prosper's sister. After Mambo Taffy said a long prayer, each person at the gathering gave Captain Prosper and his sister an extended hug and left, dropping a coin or three into a glass bowl by the front door as payment to the family spirit, thus ensuring a safe journey for the boy.

Micelli slowed his car beside Neda as she walked home from the gathering along the shaded side of a Key Largo street.

"It's hot," he remarked, looking at her through the open passenger window. Crickets screamed to the sun. "How come we keep meeting at funerals?"

She rolled her eyes and stopped walking, so he stopped the car. She turned her back to him, saying nothing, and she leaned against the car, looking up into the sky. *Well, there's actually very little to say,* thought Micelli, and so he waited. *Everything in its own time.* He looked at his watch; she had been standing there now for almost ten minutes.

Finally, she took a tissue out of her purse, blew her nose, and got into the car. They drove away together in silence.

His cell phone rang when they were almost at her house. "Micelli," he said, answering it. *"What?"* He listened for a long time. "No, it won't take me long. Did you call an ambulance? Look, don't give the media anything on this, okay? I'm serious." He listened for a minute longer and then clipped the phone shut.

"You want to come with me?" he asked. "Someone broke into Royston Alexander's house late last night." He pulled the car into a U-turn without waiting for her to answer and began to speed toward the Interstate. "They turned the place and—" He rubbed his lips together, swallowing hard. "Well, Mrs. Alexander—*Bluejean* . . . she's not in such good shape."

"What do you mean, 'not in such good shape'?" said Neda. "Was she hurt?"

Micelli was quiet for a minute and then decided to get it all out at once. He took a deep breath. "They roughed her up. Then they tied her up and left her with a freakin' hollowed-out goat's head over her face."

"They *what?*" said Neda. She was Haitian, and she had seen plenty of goats' heads at the markets. But to think someone would scoop one out and stick it over somebody's head, well, that was—"Jesus, Micelli. How could she breathe?"

"Well, that's part of the problem," answered Micelli. "She couldn't. Whoever stuck that thing on her wasn't particularly interested in whether she could breathe or not. The EMTs got her to come around, but they said she's hysterical. Maybe you can help—I don't know."

Neda exhaled deeply. "Maybe I should have called her back."

"Another thing I need to tell you," he said. "We picked up the lobster pot last night."

"You *what?*" She sounded startled. "For—Jesus, do you have any other bombshells, or is this it?"

"No. That's enough, isn't it? We were following Cutter last night. We watched him take a small boat out of the harbor toward where *Seeker* lost the pot, and so we waited at the marina for him to come back. We were surprised to see your brother along for the ride. He and that girlfriend of his were following Cutter too."

"I asked Andy to keep an eye out for Pete," she said. "I had a feeling he might try and make the trip. So where's the pot? What happened?"

"Well, technically it's still your property—for now anyway. We've got it locked in the safe at the station, but I think it would be smarter for you to open it there than to take it home. Unless you want to end up like Bluejean, that is."

124

"I already told you what's in it, Micelli. Just creepy papers. Nothing's in English, so if you want to make any sense out of them, you're going to need help with translation."

"Yeah, well there *is* more to tell you," he said. "Bluejean keeps talking about this company called Soul Equity. And Pascale says Soul Equity is a bombshell all by itself. Apparently, they deal in equity payments for people's souls—or something like that. I saw an article in the *Miami Herald* about them this morning. Their corporate logo was stamped all over some papers Bluejean had that were stolen when she was attacked. We think they're tied to the papers in your lobster pot."

"How the hell would you do that?" she asked after a minute. "How do you buy equity in a soul?"

"I'm not really sure myself. The FBI says it could violate interstate commerce laws. But the fact that Soul Equity is *giving* money rather than taking it seems to have everyone confused. You know—where's the fraud? Basically, they're exchanging money for a signature on a piece of paper giving away rights to their soul. Kind of like buying futures, I guess. I never was very good at this stock market stuff."

"Well, that's a stupid idea," Neda said.

"Is it?" he asked, weaving in and out of traffic. "Would you do it?"

"Would I take a loan out against my soul? Hell no, I wouldn't."

"Well then, it's not that stupid, is it?" said Micelli. He had the car up over eighty-five miles per hour when his cell phone rang.

"Don't kill us," Neda said. "Do me a favor and slow down." She picked up the phone from its dashboard carrier and handed it to him. Micelli only said a few words and then backed the car off to sixty-five.

"We don't have to hurry," he said with a grim look on his face. "Bluejean had a stroke about fifteen minutes ago."

Neda slumped in her seat. "My karma is going to be crap." She rubbed her eyes with the palms of her hands. "How bad was it? Is she going to be all right?"

"They don't know. Pascale said they were trying to give her something to calm her down when it happened. Apparently whoever did this really, really wanted to send a message."

"What do you mean, *message?* Message for whom?"

"Well," Micelli said and then paused, "they wanted some blueprints that Bluejean had."

"Yeah? And . . . ?"

"They told her the goat's head was a warning."

"Message—warning." Neda was irritated now. "Get to the point—before I have a stroke myself."

"When they took the blueprints, they told her they wanted the rest of the papers. I think that's what you have in the lobster pot. They said to tell you that the 'fun part starts here.'"

He pulled the car into a parking place in front of the hospital and turned off the ignition. Turning toward her, he thought she had the most beautiful face in the whole world. He didn't want her to be frightened, but he couldn't think of any other way to tell her. "The whole thing with the goat's head and all that, Neda. It was a warning for you."

# CHAPTER 28

## MIAMI, FLORIDA

Pascale met them in the lobby of the hospital and steered them toward an elevator that took them up the sixth floor. From there, they went to a private waiting room. There were reporters outside, but so far they hadn't been aggressive enough to actually troop through the halls, and the hospital staff was turning everyone away with a "no comment" order issued by the family. Except there wasn't any—family, that is. BlueJean's two young boys were still staying with her mother-in-law. Without them—and they were just children—she was alone. Neda thought that was sad. And so she made a mental note to offer her support when Mrs. Alexander woke up.

Micelli saw piles of paperwork on a desk-sized corner table when they entered the small room. Manila folders and printed stacks of papers and what looked like little flyers were strewn across one whole side of the small space. There were four comfortable, cloth-covered blue chairs; a television set; and two small end tables with lamps. Empty soda cans filled a wire trash bin. Although there were "No Smoking" signs everywhere in the hospital, a cigarette butt floated in a half-empty coffee cup.

"Pascale, you've been in this room for less than twenty-four hours, and it looks like an army of secretarial bandits pillaged it," Neda remarked as they entered.

"Yeah, what's going on?" Micelli remarked. "It looks like a command center here or something."

"We've been gathering information on Soul Equity, and my office sent the files over so I could review them. There is some very interesting stuff here. Come on in and sit down." Pascale motioned Neda over to one of the chairs. He winked at her. "It's really comfortable in here; I've already fallen asleep twice."

She smiled, and then she was serious. "First, I want to know the extent of Mrs. Alexander's injuries, and I want to know her prognosis."

Pascale picked up a piece of paper from the table and began reading. "In medical speak, it was a transient ischemic attack caused by atrial fibrillation." He looked up from the paper. "In English, it was a mini-stroke caused by a blood clot."

"What's her outlook?" Micelli asked.

"They're doing an MRI now," said Pascale. "Things got screwed up with her insurance and all. Nobody was here to do the admitting paperwork. They're still trying to contact her family. You know. All that stuff gets in the way."

"So if you're a single mother with no immediate relatives in the area, you should just walk around with a note pinned to your collar with all your health-insurance information on it, right?" Neda was annoyed. "Don't even get me started about medical care in this country." She stared at the wall. For a minute, she was back in her husband Wilson's hospital room, and they were telling him he would never walk again. She remembered how his tears tasted on his face. God, how she missed that face.

Neda sighed deeply. Then was then. Now was now.

Micelli's cell phone rang again. He answered quickly. "Cutter, yeah. Television? Yeah, we're here at the hospital now. No, we don't know anything yet. The card? *What?* No, I don't want you to call the number. I want you to bring the card down here. Yes, bring it here—sixth floor. Hang on, wait a minute. No, we'll come to you. Are you going to be at the dealership in Little Haiti? Yes? Okay, we'll see you this afternoon." He started to hang up. "Wait," he said. "How's Anna—how's your dog?"

Neda looked at him. *He is such a nice man,* she thought. *Such a really nice man.*

"What did the vet say?" he was asking. "Good—that's real good. She *did?* I'm glad. Yeah. Bye." He put the cell phone back in his jacket pocket.

Neda reached over and touched his arm. "Thanks, Micelli," she said.

"For what?"

Neda thought for a minute. "Wherever this road is leading us, well—I like the people who are on it with me."

"You know what?" Micelli said. "So do I." Neda smelled pretty good, and he wanted to say it again, so he did. "So do I."

# CHAPTER 29

---

## NORTH MIAMI BEACH, FLORIDA

The monastery had been Friar Bill's home for the past eighteen months. Unlike monks, who take a vow called "stability," making them a member of one monastery for the rest of their lives, Francescans often move to other monasteries in different communities as they follow their spiritual mission or ministry.

When he was twenty-three years old, Friar Bill became a member of the specialized lesser order of *Mot Garde,* a religious group identifying with the movement of New Monasticism taking place in the Canadian province of Quebec. Their purpose was to fulfill a need in the church for cataloging and preserving religious documents. As such, the friars searched throughout the world, seeking to obtain written history of the Gospel, preserving documents relating to religious events. There were currently eleven friars from *Mot Garde* living at the monastery. They relied entirely on the charity of the order.

Located about thirty minutes from the Miami International Airport, the order found the location perfect in maintaining connections throughout the world. They operated freely in the Caribbean and South America, as well as Europe and beyond. Certainly, there was also much to be said for Miami weather. Winters were significantly milder than those found in locations further north, and the climate year-round was much more conducive to healthy and active lifestyles. Discounting hurricane season, of course.

Their senior friar, a term given to brothers with over forty-five years of dedication, had been a man named Friar Rene Ferrer—commonly known as "the Master" by members of his order. He was an exceptional teacher and mentor; unfortunately, his death in an automobile accident off Card Sound Road left the order stunned and disorganized. Slowly, however, the brothers were regaining their zeal for the work at hand and had already begun to contemplate the task of selecting a new respected senior.

From the beginning, Friar Bill had found himself overwhelmed with the joy he experienced working in this order. He loved the written word. He loved the power of a sentence, and he believed with all his heart that historic religious documents needed to be found, carefully catalogued, and protected at all cost.

If there was one thing that made his hours of contemplation less than satisfactory, it was that he tended to dwell on the sad fact that he was born into a century dominated by copy machines and computer screens, rather than quill pens and candlelight. As the pace of technology increased, he felt personal despair watching the exquisite gifts of reading and writing degrade into a process of blips and beeps. Indeed, often when he was inspecting documents or translating, he would work only by candlelight, finding that it seemed to soothe this need in him.

For a man involved in the translation of the written word, he was extremely poor at languages, being fluent in only two, English and French. And if he had any personal weakness, it would be that he was ashamed of his ability and of his education. Many of his brothers were fluent in up to ten languages; one, Friar Rambert, could be counted on to know at least twenty-three languages. He had spent an entire year learning how to converse in the clicking dialect of the Great Namaqua in central Africa. Friar Bill was never convinced that this skill was entirely worthwhile in its application to written documents, and he noticed that Brother Rambert had a tendency to lapse into clicking whenever he was frustrated or being slightly temperamental. It was irritating.

Friar Bill was not too forthcoming about his abbreviated language abilities and made every effort to hide a personally acknowledged inclination toward anxiety and defensiveness. However, because he was extraordinarily bright, he found ways to cover any deficiency in his qualification. Most of the time, he did specific research, concentrating on only one important detail or passage in a document. Eventually, he developed a reputation of sorts—the "go-to detail guy" in the world of religious translation—and that suited him and kept him very busy. Additionally, he had an exceptional ability to relate to people, and fortunately for him, most if not all of his brothers preferred to be contemplative rather than to interact with the public. As such, he more naturally fell into the role of spokesman and public intermediary for the order. Conveniently, this left him with less time to contribute to the often arduous task of translation.

This is why he was struggling now, sitting late at night with rolls of mysterious parchment tied in purple-and-white ribbon, strewn across the desk in front of him. *Things are starting to knit themselves together,* he thought. His experience with Mambo Taffy and her story about Haitian souls was unsettling, and now—well, nothing could have prepared him for the realization that his order was the collector and steward of documents such as these. He struggled with the fact that they existed at all, let alone the fact that the Master, his good friend, Father Ferrer, was actively involved in their collection. The discovery of the Master's leather-bound box was unsettling. He had to keep reminding himself that as a historian, his role was to preserve and not to judge.

Fortunately, many of the texts he was translating were written in French, with only a few references in Latin, so he was able to make some headway. After Mambo Taffy told him the story about Haiti's deal with the devil, Friar Bill had felt a great, almost emotional sense of purpose. Haiti, it seemed, was not the first deal the devil made involving such a magnitude of people. There were other agreements witnessed and signed during periods of war, such as the WWI Battle of Verdun between Germany and France, and the Battle of El Alamein in North Africa in WWII. Friar Bill remembered Churchill's famous quote, "Before Alamein, we never won a battle; after Alamein, we never lost one." War, it seemed, could be quite lucrative if one collected souls. References to these battles and others were made in notes he found in the strange leather box along with the Haitian agreement—by far the largest in terms of souls.

There were many, many agreements in the box; one, signed on the deck of a pirate ship in 1697, agreed to fly the "Banner of Death" in Madagascar's Ranter Bay in exchange for "gold for life." Another, written on a napkin in a Welsh pub called the Rat and Carrot, agreed to exchange two adult souls for the health of one desperately ill baby. The cancer would go away. All manner of documents were contained in the box kept so secret by the Master.

And a few of the very old papers were, in fact, written and signed in blood.

In the case of some of them—well, he was not even sure that the paper itself was indeed paper. In fact, some of the pages looked like they had follicles, complete with hair and occasionally other matter attached to them. His only thought was that these documents were grotesque. Sometimes when he handled them, he felt drawn back to when they were first created. Reading them slowly, he gagged on the strong taste of mucus in the back of his throat. *Such times that men create,* he thought, shaking his head. *Such times.*

Page after ghastly page chronicled personal struggle, heartbreak, and desperate circumstance, along with jealousy, greed, debauchery, and even murder.

This night, as he worked intently on his ghoulish translation, he was struck to his heart that he could almost *hear* the words on the sheets. Perhaps he was tired. But he felt that if he really listened, he could hear some of the pages sobbing.

He had so much work to do. So much work.

At the very bottom of the leather box, Friar Bill found a thick, sealed, white envelope. He hesitated, trying to decide what to do. There was nothing fancy about it. No writing on the outside, no ribbon. In fact, it appeared to be very new—certainly not anything historic, so he made the conclusion that it would not matter if he opened it.

Inside the first one, he found two sheets of paper. The first had "DRAFT" written across the top.

PRESS RELEASE
Contact: Angela Reading
Truveska Marketing

(AP) Mary's Grin, Florida

The investment firm of Soul Equity, Inc. announced plans today for a massive initial public offering of stock. Privately owned by Sulfur Products for People, LLC. (SPP LLC), the edgy spinoff is rumored to have the backing of several global venture capitalists. While maintaining a certain amount of secrecy regarding details of the offering, Senior Vice President and Comptroller Candice Brickman said an in-house estimate placed the market value of the IPO to be almost 86 billion dollars, eclipsing corporate giants General Electric and Hong Kong Shanghai Bank of China.

Twenty-five million shares will be offered in the range of $210 to $270 each, and at least one regulatory filing placed the anticipated date for the IPO sometime during the coming summer. Industry estimates are forecasting an approximate cash input of 15.22 billion dollars to be funded to the company within six months of the initial offering date, placing it in the top 10 of IPO history. Planning is underway for the offering to be truly global and positioned in every exchange around the world at precisely the same time.

Parent company Sulfur Products for People has been privately held for over 125 years and only recently acted to incorporate Soul Equity, formerly a non-profit entity operated as a hobby by its founder, Rix Roman. SPP, a leader in the worldwide agricultural and industrial sulfur markets, was one of the first Western companies to be provided with a business license to trade in mainland China and has recently finalized exclusive agreements with Venezuela and North Korea.

"I think it's the right time to take my hobby public," said Roman, 62. "Finance is morphing, just like technology did. You've heard of Silicon Valley? Here comes Sulfur Valley."

Friar Bill reached over and pushed the button on his telephone. "Brian," he said, "would you bring me large scotch? Yes, I know what time it is. Two cubes."

He read the press release again and was reaching for the second page as a young man entered the room.

"I brought you a ginger ale instead," he said, setting a glass on the table and putting his hands in his pockets. "I figured you were kidding."

Friar Bill flipped through his Rolodex and pulled out a card. "Can you get this woman on the phone for me?" he said, handing it to the young man. "Yes, I was kidding. Ginger ale will be fine."

"Ha!" There was an exhale from the man. "Thought so." Smiling, he looked at the card. "Who's this?"

"She's a professor at the University of Miami and a well-known Haitian Vodou priestess," said Friar Bill. "Recently, she was able to explain to me just exactly how—and why—I saw a young boy at the very moment of his death." He paused. "Now I need to speak with her about a company that is selling equity positions in personal souls."

"Right," said the young man, turning to leave the room, "scotch it is."

"Thank you," said Friar Bill. "Brian?"

The young man stopped and looked back at the desk. Before Friar Bill could speak, he made a zipping motion with his fingers across his mouth.

"Yes," said Friar Bill. "Most definitely, yes."

He waited a moment and then, taking a deep breath, he flipped over the first page and laid it carefully on the desk. Immediately, he recognized MVD stationery, and a feeling of disappointment was followed by curiosity. Why would there be a letter from the monastery in the box? He read the following:

To Whom It Many Concern:

As you are reading this letter and I am not present, I will conclude that you have come upon the contents of my leather box on the event of my death.

I am leaving these instructions:

The documents in this box are part of a larger collection kept by the company mentioned in the attached press release. Today, the company is called Soul Equity, but they have been in possession of papers like these for centuries—who knows what other names they have gone by.

Recently, I've been the target of some vandalism, and I believe I'm being followed. I'm certain this is being done by people who are employed by Soul Equity. They have been (unsuccessfully) trying to purchase some of the documents in our collection. Imagine—they sincerely believe that our order can be swayed from its purpose. Under no circumstances should any of the documents in this box be delivered to them. Keep the box under lock and key and on the grounds of the monastery at all times.

I despair that this offering of stock throughout the world will only serve to bring untold souls to Satan's plate. There must be a way to stop this from happening.

God help me and absolve me from my sins in the name of the Father, and of the Son, and of the Holy Spirit.

Signed,
Friar Rene Ferrer, Master

Friar Bill got up from the desk and crossed over to the door. "Brian?" he said, leaning out into the hallway. "I did say I was serious about the scotch, didn't I? Hello? Can you make that a double?"

# CHAPTER 30

## MIAMI, FLORIDA

When Pascale walked into BlueJean's private room at Miami's Jackson Memorial Hospital, she was sitting up in the bed, talking to a nurse. She looked terrible. Her hair was sticking out all over the place, and her face was haggard. Her eye makeup was badly smeared down the front of her face, and Pascale thought the least the hospital could do would be to clean her up.

"First, all I remember is I felt dizzy for a minute," she was saying. "Then my face was sort of numb. Are you my doctor?" she said, turning to him. "Where's my purse?" she asked, ignoring Pascale and returning to the nurse. "I have appointments."

"No, I'm not your doctor," said Pascale. "I—"

*"Precious!"* There was a squeal from the doorway. "I came as *soon* as I heard." A man with spiked white-blond hair, wearing purple corduroy slacks and an orange silk shirt, minced into the room. "I saw you on television, and the picture was *ghastly*—really. Sorry. Remember, I told you to have some publicity shots on file at the station? Well, now—we—know—why. *Hmmmmm?*"

He was punctuating his words with one hand on his hip as he turned toward Pascale, "Who are you?" he said, turning to BlueJean. "Who is he?"

"Uh, I—" Pascale started.

"Bruno, thank *God!*" BlueJean was whimpering now as she motioned to the man. "*Look* at me. I look like something in a Tim Burton film."

He stepped past Pascale and took her hand. "Honey, I *know*. Remember, I was in here last year at Easter when I had those warts removed. You, know, *those* warts? Who knew you could get warts *there?*"

Pascale cleared his throat. "Excuse me, but I—"

The door closed behind them as the nurse went out.

"Sorry," said BlueJean, looking at Pascale, "you were—you are—who?"

The door opened again, and an aide entered pushing a blood-pressure monitor.

"S'cuse," she said, "Blood pressure time." She placed the cart directly behind Pascale. "Can you move?"

He stepped to one side and watched as she pulled out the cuff and began pressing buttons on the face of the machine.

"Is there a cafeteria here?" Bruno asked no one in particular. "I really need a hamburger. Do you want me to get you a hamburger, BJ?"

"No," BlueJean answered with a sigh. She leaned back against her pillow and looked at the ceiling. "What I'd really like is a nice, chilled glass of champagne and some shrimp."

"No alcohol in the rooms," the aide said, looking at the monitor. She pulled a Velcro strip loose and flipped a thermometer around in the air several times.

BlueJean rolled her eyes. "Please get me out of here," she said to Bruno. "You—whoever you are." She was looking at Pascale now. "Can you get me out of here?"

The nurse stuck the thermometer in BlueJean's mouth and looked at her watch.

"Thank you," Pascale said looking at the nurse. He took a small notepad out of his pocket, flipped it open, and made a note with his pen. "Mrs. Alexander, I'm Special Agent Pascale with the FBI. I need to ask you a few questions if you feel up to it."

"Are there any press outside?" she asked him, rolling the thermometer to one side of her mouth.

"What? Well, there were, but—we're trying to—"

"For God's *sake,* Bruno," she said, sitting straight up in the bed, "what have you been *doing?* This could be the opportunity we've been waiting for. I've just been through a horrible ordeal. As an artist, I'm *suffering.*"

"Right, well I just *rushed* right over here," Bruno said petulantly. "I didn't even *change.* I wasn't thinking about *myself.*" Pascale wondered how he got his hair to stick straight up like that. "I suppose I could make some phone calls . . ."

"This is what happens when your hairdresser is also your publicist," BlueJean said to Pascale. She fell back again—a bit dramatically—against her pillows. "What sort of questions do you have? I don't owe you any money, do I?"

Pascale pulled a chair up next to the hospital bed and sat down. This woman irritated him. He opened the top button of his shirt, leaned forward in the chair, and began to speak very quietly. He was fed up.

"Let me be very clear," he said. "I have questions—but I also have answers. And both of them add up to a lot of money—possibly billions. I'm with the FBI, and we want to talk to you about a company called Soul Equity. We want to talk about your husband's death and about the smuggling of illegal documents and artifacts into the United States."

He let the air leave the room. His face was very close to hers now.

"You're lucky you're alive, Mrs. Alexander, because it's entirely possible that you were visited by the closest thing you can imagine to the devil himself."

The nurse put down the thermometer and walked out of the room, leaving the blood-pressure equipment behind.

BlueJean's eyes narrowed.

"Well, *that's rich*—" Bruno started, rolling his eyes.

"Get out, Bruno," she said quietly without moving her eyes from Pascale's face. "Go get your hamburger. I'm going to be busy for a while."

*Yup. You still got it,* Pascale thought to himself. *Yup.*

They waited while Bruno left in a huff. And then she turned to him.

"What do you mean . . . I was visited by the devil? What kind of talk is that? The men who did this to me were thugs—nothing more. Pure trash." She was resolute. "If I wasn't a lady, I'd spit."

"Did you recognize any of them?" asked Pascale.

"No. There were three that pushed their way into the house and a couple more outside. God!" She was squirming. "I can't get comfortable in this bed." She closed her eyes and squeezed them tightly. "They kept talking on their phone to somebody. Calling him *Sir.*"

"No names?"

"No."

"What did they say to you?"

"Well, they got right to the point," she snorted. "That would be this bruise right here." She ran her hand across her left cheek, where the skin had turned different shades of purple and green. "They wanted some papers my late husband had in his office when he was killed. They were in a briefcase. Some blueprints."

"I know about those," Pascale said. "We—"

"Did you see that thing they stuck on my face?" Her voice went up an octave, and he noticed that her hand was shaking as she brushed her hair away from her forehead. "All I can say is it's a good thing my boys weren't at home. Did those assholes think about the fact that my kids might have been in the house? Christ almighty!" She was flushed.

"That's one reason I'm here to talk to you," said Pascale. "We need to find out who's behind all this. Was there anything you noticed about the men that can help us identify—"

"Am I being charged with anything?" she interrupted.

"Well—no," he said. "I'm sorry. I guess I—"

"Well then, are you here to see me because you're investigating this attack? Because I find it a little unusual for the FBI to be involved in a home invasion."

"You and I both know this wasn't a random attack," said Pascale. "Your husband was involved in the smuggling of drugs—among other things—along with Wilson Mason. The blueprints you mentioned are important, and I need to know more about them."

"Yes, well, I need to know more about them too," she answered. "There was a stamp in the corner of each page that I remember. It said 'Soul Equity,' and one of the men said the same thing over the cell phone. Can you find me a mirror? Look in that table over by the window. Please?"

Pascale got up and walked over to the table. He opened the center drawer and pulled out a medium-sized hand mirror. Walking back to the bed, he handed it to her, saying, "Mirror, mirror on the wall."

She held it up, looked at herself, and flinched. "Shit!" she said. "Look, I'm sorry, but can you get me a washcloth?"

"If you want me to call the nurse, I can do that," he said, "but right now, I need some answers more than you need to wash your face."

"I respectfully disagree," she said. "Look. I'll spend all day with you. I'll answer whatever questions you want; just give me a few minutes to get myself together first. I'm a girl." She smiled for the first time. "It comes with the territory." She was pulling herself up and awkwardly trying to swing one leg out of the bed.

"Okay, whatever, fine," Pascale said. He helped her out of the bed and over to the bathroom door. "I'll call the nurse, and I'll be right outside the room. Let me know when you're ready."

"Sometime Thursday," he heard her reply from inside the bathroom.

Pascale walked down the hallway to the private room. He was holding the back of his neck with his hand, and his shoulder felt very stiff. *Might as well finish reading the files,* he thought to himself.

What he couldn't hear was BlueJean talking on her cell phone from the hospital bathroom.

"Bruno?" she was saying. "Get that hamburger out of your mouth and get back up here. Oh! And call *every* member of *every* press outlet in town, and bring them too. I'm going to splash this attack across every front page in the country. Bastards. It all has something to do with a company called Soul Equity. Listen, hire me a bodyguard—not that guy we used last time, and get somebody up here to clean me up. Now. I need hair, nails, and clothes."

Brushing her teeth, she took slow stock of the bruises on her body. *You want to play, boys? You picked the wrong girl. And by tomorrow, everyone in the country is going to know it.*

Pascale made himself comfortable in the private waiting room while BlueJean "put herself back together." He poked through the stack of files sent over by his office and pulled out one labeled "Sulfur Products for People." This was Soul Equity's parent company. Reading the stock prospectus, he was astonished at what a large company it was. Who ever heard of sulfur products? He never had. But according to the reference pamphlets in the file, they had a lot of uses. Agriculturally, sulfur products could be added to the soil to improve air and water penetration, act as an organic fungicide, or be used as an additive in fertilizers. Industrially, sulfur products were used to make circuit boards, were part of the production of cement and concrete, as well as an important ingredient in photographic processes and coatings. Apparently, there was also a lucrative recycling program of sorts for liquid sulfur products that the plant obtained from oil refineries, in compliance with environmental regulation. Oil refineries produced contaminated sulfuric acid as a byproduct, and Sulfur Products for People collected it and reprocessed it back into merchant-grade sulfuric acid that was, in turn, delivered back to the refinery to be reused.

*Nice little business,* he thought. The references to oil caught Pascale's attention, so he read the prospectus again. The company had an impressive history:

1941 Sulfur Products for People, LLC enters the fertilizer business.
1945 Idaho Phosphates, Inc. mine acquired and company purchased.
1962 Canada Fertilizer Services (CFS) acquired.
1967 Alberta, Canada, Potash Operation location begins production.
1972 Ontario, Canada, Phosphate Mine location begins production.
1973 All Canadian Oil (ACO) acquired along with 17 refinery sites.
1973 SPP opens Industrial Sulfur Products plant in Eustis, Florida.
1977 USA Fertilizer Technology in Benton, Arkansas acquired.
1987 Russia's largest production plant in Novorossijsk, Black Sea Sulfur purchased.
1992 SPP establishes an international presence with the trade name "World Sulfur."
1994 SPP purchases 23.7% equity position in China's Zhuhai Nitrogen.
1995 North Korea offers SPP an exclusive partnership to build and operate sulfur products manufacturing plants in the country.
1999 Petro-Venezuela acquired along with two refineries and three Phosphorite plants.
2006 SPP begins construction of Dubai Center for "World Sulfur" Operations with completion set for 2012.

*Soul Equity's parent company is certainly well connected,* he thought. With interests around the world and a factory near Russia's only deep-water port, as well as connections in South America, Canada, and in the Arab world, Sulfur Products for People had undoubtedly deep pockets, both in money and in political influence. An enclosed list of members of the board of directors included two names from Parliament in the United Kingdom and at least one member of the Japanese royal family.

Noise from the hallway interrupted him, so Pascale got up and shut the door. He needed to concentrate.

Going back to the files, he found little information about Soul Equity specifically. A copy of a press release announcing a pending initial public offering of stock was in one file, attached to a short newspaper clip about some charitable work being done by the company in Africa.

Looking through more files, he came across an article in the *Miami Herald* business section written just a few months ago.

FINAL FINANCING

(AP) Miami, FL

Ever wonder what your soul is worth? Soul Equity, Inc., with national headquarters located in Mary's Grin, about 40 miles west of Miami, can tell you.

The secretive company declined an interview for this article but said through a spokesperson that the company "makes personal recommendations" and "private agreements" with people who are interested in taking out loans against their souls or selling them outright.

"You can make a lot of money from something that you're probably not using," said Thomas Findlay of Miami Beach law firm, Arturo, Masters and Diaz, hired by Soul Equity to manage public relations.

"Our recent announcement of an IPO is extremely exciting," said Findlay. "Worldwide, people will have an opportunity to invest in this lucrative market."

Not everybody is happy about that prospect.

"It's heresy," said Pastor Nathan Smithson of the South Kendall Non-denominational Congregation for Truth in Life Church. "I feel sad and sorry for the person who would use their soul for personal gain."

Specific client information is not released by Soul Equity. Individuals interested in finding out more about available services may contact the law firm for a referral or send a query through the Soul Equity website.

One piece of information that still didn't seem to fit was the blueprint that Jean Alexander had. How could it be related to Soul Equity? And just what was Wilson Mason's connection to the whole thing? Why was he shot? It all seemed like it happened such a long time ago now, but it had only been seven or eight months since the issue had come to the FBI's attention. *Put the pieces together,* he told himself. *What purpose did the explosion at the mall serve?* Andy Taffy had been arrested, and BlueJean involved herself by posting his bail. The department had pretty much ruled Andy out now. They found a complex detonating device hidden in the wall of the jewelry store, and it was far too intricate for Andy to have constructed it. His homemade firecracker might have sparked a fire or broken a few windows, but it wasn't behind the utter destruction that eventually occurred.

Certainly, the question that haunted him the most was his encounter in the parking lot on Halloween night at the marina. Who was the man that, with one look, brought his childhood memory back in such a visceral way? Pascale would never forget him, and closing his eyes, even now, he could still see the man's dark face, framed by a top hat and purple-trimmed tuxedo. Such a calm face, hiding such horror. He felt sick all over again, just thinking about it.

More noise in the hallway irritated him. There was a thump and then a heavy scrape against the door, and he heard the muffled sound of footsteps running. *Sick people are trying to sleep in here,* he thought to himself as he got up and crossed the room to the door. A little authority might be needed; probably just some kids.

He was completely unprepared for the sight that greeted him. The door to BlueJean's hospital room across the hall was open, and the corridor itself was filled with people and cameras and microphones and cables. Standing on a small platform next to her bed, BlueJean was visible throughout the room and out into the hallway. *Damn!* he thought—*She looked pretty good. How do women do that?*

"Thank you all for coming today," she was saying. Her voice was steady, and she looked straight into each face of each person in the crowd. Bruno stood slightly behind her, holding a comb in one hand and a towel in the other.

"I've chosen to speak directly to the press, rather than let rumors go out about my attack. You will hear the truth today right from me." Bruno handed her a small, folded piece of paper.

Reading, she continued. "Last night, I was brutally attacked in my home by three men. I now know, after in-depth conversations with law-enforcement personnel, that the FBI is actively involved in the case and believes that the men may have direct ties to a satanic organization called Soul Equity. The purpose of their attack was to steal some papers that belonged to my husband. As you can see by my condition and appearance, these men were desperate and ruthless in their determination."

Pens were scribbling wildly across pads, and the television camera lights were very hot.

Pascale winced when she mentioned the FBI. *I never said satanic organization,* he thought. *And what condition is she referring to? She looks like she just stepped out of a perfume ad in a magazine. Apparently her attackers were so desperate, they left every bobby pin still in her upturned hair.*

"As a member of this community and a fighter against crime, I do not worry for myself," she was saying. "I worry for our children. If Soul Equity can send its people into our homes and do things like this—well, it undermines the very fabric, the very core of the safety of our families!"

Pascale was leaning against the doorframe, thinking that she must have been a suffragette in another life as she continued.

"I literally fought for my life." There was a dramatic pause. "Now, I have a special announcement to make—and I hope those satanic equity bastards, sorry, are listening. I still have the papers you wanted. I kept them. All you have are the blueprints to my house, you cruel, stupid idiots. The other blueprints you wanted are safely hidden, and I shall turn them over to the FBI as soon as this afternoon."

Pascale couldn't believe what he was hearing. He'd talked to her about the blueprints all along, and he just never thought to ask her whether or not they were actually taken. He'd just assumed that they were. Standing in the doorway, he had his hand over his face when she introduced him.

"Now, a word from Special Investigator Pascale from the Miami office of the Federal Bureau of Investigation." She swept her hand across the hall toward him, and a sea of faces, not to mention cameras, turned and followed her gesture.

Stunned, he could do nothing but clear his throat. It was going to be a very long day. A very, very long day.

\*     \*     \*

"Well, thanks," said Pascale to BlueJean as she stood in the empty corridor and blew her nose. She'd been weeping about the terror of the "satanic attack" to any journalist who would listen, and although they had all gone now, her act wouldn't go away. "You could have given me a little bit of notice."

He was standing against the doorframe with his arms crossed, as a young woman in an austere business suit came striding up the corridor toward them. She looked annoyed and got straight to the point.

"Mrs. Alexander, you have shown *no regard* for the other patients in this wing. Your idea to hold a press conference here is *unforgivable*. There are some very sick people in this ward, Mrs. Alexander, and you have shown them—and the staff of this hospital—complete disregard."

"And you are . . . ?" said BlueJean coolly.

"My name is Valerie Peters," the woman said. "I'm the director of admissions."

"Yes, dear. Well, I think you'll find that I'm admitted."

BlueJean turned to walk back into her room. "Bruno," she said, ignoring anyone else standing there, "call the *Herald,* and see if they're planning on using the story for the metro section or for the front page. The B section is good, but this is an A-section story. And of course, I want to be above the fold."

"You don't understand," said the woman angrily. "Jackson Memorial *will not* be used as a publicity gimmick for your fading art career. If one word of this ridiculous press conference ends up in print—we *will* take measures."

"You'll *take measures?*" said BlueJean sarcastically. "And I have a *fading* art career?"

Pascale didn't like what he was seeing and considered that maybe this might be a good time to get out of the hallway.

"Look," he said to the two of them, "let's just calm down a little . . ."

Bruno stepped to BlueJean's side and started using the comb to quickly touch up the top of her hair. Then he turned and looked down—literally—on the shorter Valerie Peters. Tapping the comb on the tip of her nose, he said, "Listen, Miss Peepers, this hospital is paid for by taxpayer dollars, and I'm a taxpayer. A celebrity like BlueJean doesn't hold *ridiculous* press conferences. She's gone through a terrible ordeal, and her concern is that the public has a right to know." He was still tapping the comb on her nose when she grabbed it in one fist and jabbed it into the side of BlueJean's hair.

"*Ow!*" shrieked BlueJean. "Why, you—"

"Just let me—" said Bruno, trying to remove the comb. "Darling, *please.*"

BlueJean was flailing away with both hands, trying to push Bruno back and slap Miss Peters at the same time.

"Get—stop!" She was turning bright red and spitting. "I had a *goat's head* stuck on my face," she shrieked at the woman, placing their faces nose to nose. "That's *newsworthy.*" She gave Bruno a final shove, and he backed into a foodservice cart, sending the contents crashing to the floor.

"*Security!*" screamed Peters.

"You can't—"

Picking lettuce off the front of his shirt, Bruno joined in. "I think you should apologize for pushing me," he huffed to BlueJean. "That wasn't really necessary."

"Shut *up!*" she shrieked, as two men came running up the hallway toward them.

"Mrs. Alexander is having a nervous breakdown," Peters said to the men, "or a possible adverse reaction to her medication. It could be life-threatening, and I authorize you to restrain her."

"*What?* You can't possibly—" BlueJean was shouting as the men took her by the arms and started to lead her into her room.

"No, not that way," said Peters. "She could be a danger to herself. I think Psych would be a better place."

"I—will—not . . ." BlueJean pushed at the men with her elbows. "Bruno—*do* something."

"*You* do something," he sniffed, looking at the back of his thumbnail. "I'm waiting for an apology."

Pascale stepped forward and spoke to the woman. "Excuse me, I'm Special Agent Pascale with the FBI, and—"

"I know who you are," Peters snapped. "This isn't a federal matter. This is a hospital matter."

BlueJean was kicking one security guard as the other stood behind her, holding on to her shoulders. "You stupid, inept, *fat*—poof!" she shrieked at Bruno, still flailing both arms.

*"Fat?"* he was incredulous. Turning to Peters with wide eyes and an open mouth, he stuttered, "Why, I think you're *right*. As her *dear* friend, I *urge* you to protect this magnificent woman from herself."

Another man from security joined them. "Psych," said Peters with a nod toward BlueJean. "Now."

"You think I'm magnificent?" BlueJean asked Bruno sweetly as the three men carried her horizontally, past him and down the hallway to the other ward. "Darling, bring my makeup!"

Bruno turned to Pascale with a pinched face. "She just *loves* to flog me." He sighed and went into her room, collecting combs and the small mirror, along with cosmetics and a few pieces of clothing.

As Peters turned to follow the group down the hall, Pascale saw her flip open her cell phone and heard her say, "Call another press conference. We'll be announcing a nervous breakdown and suicide attempt by Jean Alexander. Yeah, the artist. Really! Completely delusional. She attacked several staff members. Oh, and advise the *Herald* that if they print anything she said earlier in the day, they're going to look pretty stupid."

Bruno huffed past Pascale, carrying a load of clothes and jewelry in his arms.

"I've *got* to go to her," he said. "I'm leaving that bag on the bed for you. It has a blueprint in it or something. BlueJean, *bless her,* said it was important, and she was going to give it to you this afternoon. So there." He hurried down the hall.

Amazed, Pascale went quickly to the bed and opened the bag. There, placed in between a push-up bra and a bottle of vodka, rolled tightly and secured by several large rubber bands, was the blueprint everyone had been looking for. *Things you need in the hospital,* thought Pascale as he carefully removed the roll of paper. *Damn it, BlueJean, you are pretty magnificent.*

Down the hall, Valerie Peters was making one last call on her cell phone.

"It's all taken care of, sir," she was saying. "No problem. The *Herald* won't be printing any announcements made by a mentally deficient BlueJean Alexander. But the FBI was here. Name? Pascale. P-a-s-c-a-l-e." She paused, listening. "Why, thank you, Mr. Rix. That's really appreciated. Thank you very much."

# CHAPTER 31

## LITTLE HAITI, MIAMI

When Otero arrived at the car lot in the morning, he found a dead rooster placed on the ground in front of the office door. Its neck had been broken, and it stunk. And that made him angry, because seeing something senseless like that could possibly cause new customers to have understandable distress. Now, more than ever, he felt that his decision to sell the lot had been a good one; any future misfortune would soon be somebody else's problem. More and more, Otero's daydreams were beginning to take place in the Keys, featuring a margarita in one hand and a fishing pole in the other.

Cursing, he found a large, black trash sack and bagged the bird for garbage day. As he walked around to the side of the building to put it in the dumpster, he noticed a group of men standing in the alley next to the back door of the Krak Krak Haiti Bar. It wasn't quite noon, but they all held cans of Prestige Lager and seemed to be in a festive mood. Three of them were smoking cigarettes as one held up a newspaper and was pointing at it and laughing loudly.

"Hey, guys," Otero said, "I'm gonna open up in a few minutes. You want to take your party inside?" He motioned toward the bar.

"Can't smoke in there now," one man said. "Got to stand outside." He dropped the cigarette in the dirt and stepped on the butt.

The group was still giggling. Otero raised the dumpster lid and heaved the rooster inside. As he closed it, he heard one of the men say, "Flying cluck," and they roared with laughter. He closed the lid and as was turning around when one of the men tossed the folded paper toward the top of the dumpster. It missed, landing in the dust by Otero's feet. Chuckling, the men opened the back door of the bar and went inside. *Trash just made the whole place look worse,* Otero thought to himself. *I got to clean up after everyone.* He picked up the paper, shook the dirt off, and looked at the headline.

"Airborne through Intersection," it read, and there was a picture of a lime-green Mustang taken by a traffic camera. The car looked like it had been shot off a ramp or something, as a fairly large photograph showed the car in the apparent act of flying through an intersection without touching the ground. Three people in the background of the picture were standing there, looking skyward with their mouths open. The article continued:

(AP) *Miami Herald*

Miami-Dade Police confirmed that a man wearing a bear suit drove at high speeds through downtown Homestead on Halloween night, sending his vehicle the full length of a busy intersection without touching the ground. Andrew Taffy, 39, of North Miami was not wearing a seat belt and was thrown from the vehicle. A resident of Key Largo, Taffy was the only occupant of the car and was found unconscious and badly bruised after he landed in a large canopy over the entry to a Holiday Inn, and bounced out and into an adjacent swimming pool.

The car continued, driverless, for almost a quarter of a mile through town, finally crashing into the glass storefront of a Publix supermarket on NE 8th Street.

"I never seen nothing like that," said Muriel Fastback of Coral Gables. "We was here to visit my sister and we saw this man looking like a bear just fly in the air, go through that there awning and hit the water. Made one hell of a splash."

Police spokesman Sgt. William Black provided the *Herald* with a prepared statement reminding people that Halloween pranks can result in damage to property and loss of life, and the fact that no one was injured does not make the incident any less serious. In addition to speeding, Taffy faces charges of reckless endangerment, and his driver's license is subject to suspension. Blood tests showed he had not been drinking.

Otero walked slowly around to the front of the building and was still holding the paper when he saw he had problems of his own. Tina was striding up the walk to the building with a resolute look on her face.

"So," she said, noting the paper in his hand, "you saw it, huh?" She had a sour look on her face.

He could only nod. She was wearing red hot pants with a tight, white T-shirt that said, "Lick Here" printed across the front in the design of two large mostly misshapen postage stamps, and the words, "US Male Carrier." Her white-blonde hair was tied back into a ponytail, and her wooden platform heels made a clacking sound as she crossed the pavement in front of him.

"Dumb bastard," she said, her lower lip sticking out. "Wait till I get my hands on him."

Otero couldn't think of anything to say.

"You look different with your clothes on," she said, squinting and looking up at him. "I wonder if people say that about me." Then she walked past him, opening the door to his office. "You got any coffee?" He followed her, and she turned and took the paper out of his hands.

"I want you to tell me about this lobster pot," she said, looking at the picture of her car. "I been thinking about why everybody wants it. Andy said there was just papers in it, but, well, I think I oughta know what's on 'em." She sat down on a small leather couch. "And there's another i-tem," she said, clicking her bright-red thumbnail against her index finger. Her eyes narrowed. "I know about your thing with the razor. They call you Cutter, right?"

He was amazed and wary at the same time. She looked at him intently, with her head cocked to the side, and continued. "There's a guy looking for you. He was in the club the other night. Says he owes you for something you did to his brother. The guy is the size of a house. Scary."

Otero walked over to a brewing pot of coffee, poured a cup, and handed it to her. Guys had always been looking for him. So what? This was just another reason he needed to practice being invisible.

"Got cream?" she said with a smile. "And I mean that in a nice way."

"No," he said. "I need to go to the store."

"Fine. Su-*gar?*"

He reached into a basket on the counter, grabbed a couple of packets, and tossed them in her direction.

"So what I told him was this—"

They were interrupted by a knock on the front door; through the glass, they could see Micelli and Neda.

"Come on in," Otero shouted. He sat down in his chair, squared both elbows on the desktop, and put his head in his hands. "Party's just getting started."

*    *    *

Gathered around Otero's desk, the group was listening to the speakerphone in the middle of the office. Micelli and Neda had pulled two chairs over from next to the door, Otero was behind the desk, and Tina was sprawled across a leather loveseat against the wall under a picture of Niagara Falls. It was free, explained Otero.

On the seventh ring, a woman answered and said, "Good afternoon, Soul Equity, can I help you?"

The business card was lying on the desk in front of Otero, so they all looked at him.

Only then did it dawn on Micelli that they hadn't discussed what to say.

"Um, yeah," started Otero.

"Thank you," the woman's voice cut in. "One moment."

Otero mouthed the word, *What?* to Micelli and shrugged his shoulders. There was a long silence on the line. Then an audible click was followed by a man's deep voice. "Good afternoon, Mr. Otero. Nice to have you present also, Captain Micelli," said the voice.

"Oh, hello," said Otero.

Micelli didn't say anything.

The voice continued. "Don't think I've forgotten *you,* Mrs. Mason."

Bewildered, Neda looked at Micelli and then over at Tina, who was flapping her hands wildly in the air like someone trying to dry wet nail polish.

"Last but never least, hello to our talented friend, Miss Tina-Thumbelina."

"Shit!" Tina said loudly.

Micelli would have given her a warning look, had he been able to take his eyes off the telephone.

"I've been expecting your call, and I'm delighted to be able to speak with all of you today."

"So, can I ask," interrupted Micelli, "just who exactly is it are we talking with?"

"Of course," the voice boomed cheerfully over the speaker. "My name is Rix Roman. Just call me Rix—everybody does. I'm the owner and founder of Soul Equity, and I'm excited about our services—as I know you will be. We should be able to get down to the bottom line quickly. That's what this is all about, right? Money?"

His deep laugh filled the room. It made a sound that Micelli didn't like, and by the looks on the faces around the desk, no one else did either.

"Sure," said Tina. "Well, he's right," she said in a stage whisper to the others. "Most things *are* about money."

"*Everything*, my dear Tina," said the voice, "is about money. Every single thing in the world today boils down to just one thing: money. Too much of it, too little of it, the wrong kind of it . . . believe me, I've got terrific speeches about money—terrific. Some of it's kind of sad, actually, but it's all very pertinent and motivating. Yes, money can be very motivating."

"I'd like to ask you a few questions," said Micelli, recovering, "if you don't mind." He pulled a notepad out of his trouser pocket.

"Certainly," said the voice. "However, wouldn't it be better if we met in person? I never liked speakerphones."

They all looked at each other. This time it was Neda who spoke. Micelli thought she looked very serious.

"Do we have your address, Mr. Rix?"

"Ah!" said the voice. "You've been very quiet lately, Mrs. Mason. By the way, please accept my sincere condolences on the loss of your young friend, Alais."

Neda looked at Micelli.

"Your address?" said Micelli, with his pencil poised over the pad.

"Why don't you take our bus?" said Rix. "It will be easier, and you see, Mary's Grin—our corporate headquarters location—is out of town a little way. We have a direct bus departing from the corner of North Miami Avenue and Second Street at 8:30 a.m. and 12:30 p.m. daily. That's not too far from your office, is it, Mr. Otero? What an odd coincidence."

Otero seemed startled; apparently he had been thinking about something else.

"Yes," he answered quickly. "I mean no. A bus?"

"We have quite a number of employees living in the city. Call it a benefit, if you will. All right, this is great! I invite you all for a late lunch," said Rix. "On me, of course. You still have time to catch that 12:30 p.m. The driver is expecting you."

Micelli looked at his watch; they had about twenty minutes to get to the bus stop.

"Until then," Rix said cheerfully and hung up.

The group sat in silence until at last Tina jumped up and said, "Well, I know *I'm* hungry. How 'bout you guys?" She started toward the door.

"Where's this Mary's Glen place?" asked Otero, standing up from his chair.

"It's *Grin*," said Tina. "Mary's Grin. Like Mother Mary's laughin' atcha," she giggled, sticking her chin out and showing all her teeth.

"I've never heard of it," said Neda, "and I've lived here most of my life."

"It's out in sinkhole country." Tina fished around in her purse for a stick of gum.

"It used to be an old fish camp. When I was a kid, we would go out there and shrimp. Buggy, sticky place."

"Sinkholes?" asked Micelli.

"You don't have 'em in Jersey," sniffed Tina. "We got a whole bunch that caved in and made some big lakes out past the Everglades on the way to the gulf. You know, it's like when water runs underground, and then the land on top falls in. You don't hear about 'em much unless there's a house on top or somethin'."

"Great," said Micelli. "So we're going to get on a bus that will take us to the edge of where the land might fall in under us?"

"I would've thought that a big company like this would at least have private transportation," said Otero. He flipped out the lights in the office and turned the "Closed" sign over on the door. "Bus, my ass."

"At least they could have an address," added Neda.

"Well, we're about to see it for ourselves," said Micelli as they trooped into the parking lot. "Take a right at the corner."

# CHAPTER 32

---

## KEY LARGO, FLORIDA

Andy was taking a nap on the couch at Mambo Taffy's house when the phone rang. In his dreams, he was flying through the night again in the Mustang, but this time it was Tina in the car with him. She was laughing and saying, "Did I ever tell you that my real name is Ramona?" and he kissed her and said, "No it isn't." And she kissed him back and said, "No. It isn't." Then there was this ringing and ringing, and suddenly he was lying on the couch and not flying at all. *Bummer.*

He stumbled over to the side table and answered it. "-Lo?"

"Is Professor Taffy at home?" said a man's voice. "I'm calling from Friar Bill's office at the monastery."

"I'm—I dunno." His head hurt. "Let me check."

He hung up the phone and walked into the kitchen and over to the refrigerator. Opening the freezer-side door, he stuck his head as far inside as possible and let the cold air blow against his face.

Mambo Taffy stood up from the chair she was sitting in on the back porch and looked through the open screen door. "Andy, get your head out of the freezer," she said. "Did I hear the phone?"

Andy didn't move, answering her from somewhere next to the ice tray. "Yeah, some guy from the monastery."

She sighed, set her book down in the chair, and pushed open the screen door. "*Andy!* I said get out of the freezer! Right—this—minute."

She walked past him and into the dining room in time for the phone to ring again.

"Professor Taffy?" said a voice as she answered. "Friar Bill's office calling. One moment."

"Yes, hello," she said finally.

Friar Bill came on the line, and after wishing her a good morning and asking about her family, got to the point. "Are you available to come over here?" He sounded tired. "One of our brothers was going through some paperwork in the Master's possession, and what we've found is very disturbing. I really don't want to talk about it over the phone."

Mambo Taffy wasn't surprised. For the past few days, she'd been seeing flashes of things that bothered her—things that bothered her very much. Sometimes it was just a face—part of a face even, or just a sound like a cry, or a burst of color. Sometimes it was a smell. It was as if a giant jigsaw puzzle was beginning to show itself to her one piece at a time. She hadn't slept well the past two nights. Then, too, there was Andy. In the middle of the night, the police called after he was in some bizarre car accident in Tina's car. She couldn't get any sense out of him and didn't know where Tina was, although there was a message on the answering machine that *sounded* like Tina, saying something about how Andy should consider moving to Mexico. God only knew what *that* could be about.

"This afternoon?" she said into the phone. "Well, I have a lecture to attend at 2:00 p.m. . . . . I won't be available until after 4:00 p.m. That's good? All right, I'll see you then."

She hung up the phone and walked back into the kitchen. Grabbing Andy by the back of the shirt, she pulled him away from the freezer and shut the door.

"I have to go out this afternoon," she said. "If you could manage to not burn down the house while I'm gone, I'd appreciate it."

He leaned down and gave her a kiss on the cheek.

"Goodness!" she laughed. "Your face is cold!"

The phone rang again in the other room; turning to answer it, she muttered under her breath, "Probably froze the rest of those brain cells that still function. Not too many of 'em . . .

"Hello?" she said, answering it. "Yes, this is Professor Taffy. Yes, he does. No, I don't know anything about a boat. Andy doesn't own a boat. Really? No, I can't help you. *How much?* Dear, no. I'll have to call you back. Yes."

She walked as calmly as possible into the kitchen to find Andy standing at the sink, pouring a glass of cold water.

"That was the police on the phone, Andy." She had learned years ago not to yell. "They said they found a gym bag in the boat you borrowed last night. They said it had money in it."

After a long pause, Andy said, "Money?"

"Yes, Andy. A lot of money. They want to know if you know anything about the money. Do you, Andy?"

"Do I know about the money?" he repeated. *Think,* he thought to himself. If only his head didn't hurt so *bad.*

"That's Tina's money," he said. It was partly true.

"One hundred thousand dollars?" she said. "Why would—*how* could Tina have *one hundred thousand dollars* in a gym bag?"

"We—I was counting it," he stammered. "I put it in the bag."

"Why were you counting it?" This was going nowhere.

"So I could know how much was there."

He was so frustrating—still, he had the look of an angel on his face. To her, at that moment, he was six years old again. She wanted to hug him; he was always so sweet, so innocent, and now she had the awful, helpless feeling he was caught up in something beyond his control. There were things she liked about Tina and things she didn't like about Tina. "I have to call the police back this afternoon," she said sternly. "You think some more about this, and we'll talk about it when I get home."

He followed her into the living room and sat on the edge of the couch, feeling sick and sorry for himself while she picked up her purse and car keys.

The first thing he needed to do was make up with Tina. He didn't want to have to go live in Mexico. He liked it right here. He couldn't talk Mexico either.

Mambo Taffy was opening the front door and turning to say something to him at the same time. She looked at him and said he should take a shower or something; her back was to the open door, and her hand was on the doorknob.

Behind her, standing on the front porch, with his face pressed up against the screen, was Andy's new friend, Samedi. He was still wearing that black tuxedo with the purple lining and top hat.

Andy shrieked.

"What on Earth?" she said, slamming the door. "What's the matter with you?"

Andy jumped up from the couch and ran past her, opening the front door to an empty front step.

"Maman," he said earnestly, turning to her with wide eyes, "I'm seeing things that are sometimes there—and sometimes not there."

"Happens to me all the time," she said in a flat voice. "I'll be home around dinner. I'll cook. Don't play with the stove."

# CHAPTER 33

## NORTH MIAMI BEACH, FLORIDA

It was four thirty on the button when Mambo Taffy's Ford Taurus crunched across the driveway to the monastery. Once, years ago, she had been there to attend a reception held by the university. Now the grounds were even more beautiful than she remembered. Although it was early November, the weather was still quite warm, and carriage lights were beginning to supplement the sun's glow as they sparkled across outdoor fountains and brilliant bromeliads. Miami, in the lushness of a tropical fall, could be lovely and peaceful. She took a deep breath as she stepped out of her car. *Such perfect quiet.*

The gift shop was just closing as she walked into the building, and a pleasant young man asked if he could help her.

"I'm here for an appointment with Friar Bill," she said. "I'm Professor Taffy from the University of Miami."

"Ah! Hello," a voice boomed behind her, and she turned to see him walking down the hall. "Thank you for coming. Thank you so much." He looked tired, and after touching his cheek once quickly against hers, he took her by the elbow, leading her toward his office.

"What's the mystery, my friend?" she asked, feeling suddenly and strangely old.

"Quite frankly, I don't know where to start," he said, ushering her through the heavy, wooden doors and into his small office. There were several candles lit on his desk, and a small reading lamp was turned down toward a stack of odd-sized papers. Rolls of parchment tied with purple ribbons were strewn around the desktop; some of the papers looked very, very old. An ornate box sat open on his desk, with still more papers inside, as well as several small leather-bound books. The box had a dusty, uncomfortable smell. Friar Bill pulled a heavy wing chair away from the window and pushed it over next to his desk.

"Sit here," he said. "Would you like something to eat? A small snack?"

"No, I'm fine," she answered. "Watching this waist." She patted her stomach. "Holidays coming, you know."

"Yes," he said absently. He hadn't thought about the holidays.

"I see you've been doing some reading," she gestured toward the papers. "A lot of reading." She picked up the dictionary on the corner of his desk. "Greek? My goodness. How can I help? Unless some of this is written in French . . ." She shrugged and smiled at the same time.

"Well—some of it is," he said. "At least I think it is." He was almost wringing his hands. "I'm trying so hard to figure out how to say this without sounding like a complete lunatic."

"Just blurt," she said. "Sometimes I think that works best."

"Right." He took a deep breath. "As you may already know, our task here at the monastery is to find historic, religious papers, with the goal of preserving them and keeping them for antiquity. We are collectors and restorers, keepers of some truly fabulous treasurers of human insight. Many of our historic documents pertain to the actual life of Jesus Christ. Our varied collection of early church records—some over a thousand years old—is quite comprehensive. In fact, outside of the Vatican and one or two religious libraries in Egypt, we maintain the largest private collection of this type in the world."

He collected his thoughts for a minute and then continued. "The great fire that supposedly burned nearly all of the scrolls at the Library of Alexandria in Egypt? It was set to hide a scandalous theft of those scrolls. They're dated from the third century before Christ, and we have most of them here. Our members travel the world, searching for rare, sometimes controversial manuscripts. As an example, recently, we obtained a copy of the Secret Gospel of Mark, parts of which were not included in the Bible. It's a spectacular version and very valuable."

He motioned toward the heavy leather box on his desk. "This box, or trunk, or whatever, belonged to a senior member of our order. He was killed in a car accident earlier this year. Some of its contents were found in a tomb in El Minya, Egypt, along with papyrus telling us another story about Daniel—remember Daniel and the lions? It's a different version again. Quite fascinating."

Mambo pointed toward the dictionaries on his desk, one Latin, one Greek, with a question in her eyes.

"Yes, I'm trying to translate on my own," he said with a smile. "I'm not very good at it—weakest subject and all."

"I'm impressed," she said. "But other than the obvious, what's the mystery?"

He took his reading glasses off and wiped the palm of his hand across his eyes wearily. Then he reached into the box, removing a stiff, cardboard-like stack of pages, and handed them to her. "Well, here you go," he said. "Jump on in."

She turned the reading lamp down further so that it poured light on the documents and frowned as she looked at them.

"What is this material?" she asked, turning a page over and looking at the back side. "Leather?"

"Of sorts. I mean it could be," he sighed. "Well—I think it might be human skin."

They looked at each other, and for just a moment, Mambo Taffy felt the connection again with Friar Bill. She concentrated to make it last longer, accepting a razor-sharp feeling of such sweet pain that she felt wounded and vulnerable. *Help me,* she thought to herself. It was difficult to look away from him.

Squinting at the text and fighting a metallic taste in her mouth, she looked closely at the pages. "Most of this is written in French," she said. "There are some other words here I don't know, but they could have African origin." She laid the page down on the top of the desk and looked at him earnestly. "The title says *'Un accord de vente.'* An agreement of sale." She looked at the bottom of the page, and he saw her eyes go wide.

"It is the story of Mbwento." She was whispering now. "The most monstrous being ever to walk the face of the Earth." She rubbed her temples with her fingertips. "No wonder I've been getting headaches."

"M—who?"

"There is an old African legend that tells us about a being that collects and eats souls to obtain eternal life. To those who practice Vodou, the Mbwento is kind of like your American boogeyman."

"Souls again. Why would anyone want to give up their soul?"

"Money. Hard times. Who knows? Sometimes people are in desperate circumstances." She read further and then looked at him with sadness in her face. "The Mbwento is a person who makes a contract with the devil to collect souls. For each soul he takes, the devil grants the Mbwento one additional lifetime on Earth. So, mathematically anyway, living for eternity suddenly becomes feasible."

"You're not serious. You think this thing is real?"

"I'll tell you what I know. Firstly, most superstition has some basis in reality." She shifted in her chair, trying to make herself comfortable. "A person who gives his soul to the Mbwento must acknowledge, or give permission, for this to occur. The transaction itself must be concrete in nature, such as a written instrument. It cannot be verbal; once the promise is made and signed or sealed or whatever, it cannot be retracted. The only way to break the agreement is for the document itself to be destroyed. Thus, the soul can be released back to its owner."

"So the actual instrument, or paper, or whatever is important," the friar interjected.

"Extremely," she answered. "Once the Mbwento has lived his lifetimes, he, along with the souls he has already eaten, are 'absorbed' into the body of the devil himself."

"I ask that question for a reason," he said, handing her a piece of paper from the corner of his desk. "Wilson Mason—the man who was killed in the Keys, your son-in-law? He approached our order about a blueprint. It's outlined here. Read what it says."

She looked at the letter. "It's talking about Dutty Boukman and the Haitian Revolution. Those documents were never recovered. The signature!" She was whispering again. "It says, 'For Dutty Boukman on 14 August.' See this mark here?" She pointed at a circle of sorts near the edge of the paper. "As a slave, Bookman would not have learned to write his name. This is incredible!" Her face was flushed. "His mark," she whispered, running her finger lightly over the page. "This is the mark that started the revolt of the slaves and resulted in the Haitian Revolution. You know the location of the original document! Boukman sold the souls of the Haitian people in exchange for their freedom. This is incredible—absolutely incredible. Whoever has that blueprint has the souls of those people in their hands."

"I know." He felt like crying all of a sudden, overwhelmed with the human cost on the pages in front of him. "I found those shortly after we met at your home. It's almost too coincidental. I've never believed in coincidence."

"What do you mean?" she asked. "Of course it's not coincidental. It's your Iwa guiding you. There is work you—we—must do."

Friar Bill nodded. "Wilson got his hands on a very special collection. The blueprint shows us where the original documents are hidden. We have ourselves a box of souls. Agreements for the sale of souls."

"These?" she said, waving her hand toward the leather box. "Daniel too? He had some help with the lions?"

"As did many other individuals whose names you would probably recognize."

"Fascinating," she said. "I simply don't know what to say. This collection must be extremely significant."

"One thing is amazing above all," he answered, leaning forward in his chair toward her. "And I have been unable to sleep since I noticed it."

"What?"

"Look closely at each agreement—take your time." He leaned back heavily into the chair. "There are many languages represented here, languages spoken throughout the whole of the world, and some of these pages are very, very old indeed. Hundreds and hundreds of years. Look at the signatures on each."

She spent several minutes carefully reviewing the pages, then got up and walked over to the box, lifting documents out quickly and searching each for signatures. Returning to her chair, she looked stricken.

"How—" she was stammering. "I know what I see, but my heart is racing to understand. All our lives, we are taught the biblical stories of good and evil. Now you have handed me proof of the existence of both. I never thought with my own eyes that I would actually see Satan—but now I see his hand on each page. These documents span hundreds and hundreds of years—yet the signature is the very same on each one!"

"It's written in Hebrew," he said. "It says *Satanael*."

"Satanael?"

"A Hebrew name used in reference to the devil. It's first used around the time of the Apocrypha."

"The Apo—what?"

"The Apocrypha. It means 'hidden things' in Greek. These are religious writings that date back two or three centuries before Christ was born. It's kind of a 'supplement' to the Bible, if you will. Fascinating stuff; it includes the Gospel of Mary. Sayings of Jesus written by his twin brother, Thomas. That kind of thing."

"Jesus had a brother? A twin?"

"Well," he smiled weakly, "in the Apocrypha, he did. I guess it depends on which stack of books you believe in. But I *can* tell you one thing: they exist, I can tell you that much—we have many of the volumes here. Anyway, they tell us about Satanael, a soul cast away from the presence of God. Interestingly, one of our members recently located a cache of documents in Vercelli, Italy, containing a very old collection of papyrus titled 'Speeches of Satan.' Apparently he was quite an orator."

"Unbelievable." She was still looking at the signatures and shaking her head. "Not Lucifer?"

"No, he doesn't get called that until Virgil writes some poems in Rome."

"I see." She felt exhausted yet exhilarated at the same time. "You said there was a mystery?"

"The 'Speeches of Satan' contain many references to one last great deal—one cataclysmic movement to collect the souls of the children of God. I think the mystery has always been where this movement would take place and when. Until now." He handed her the clipping about Soul Equity's intention to sell stock in the company. "Satan has also—apparently—got a day job on Wall Street."

She read the clipping and shook her head. "I don't know anything about these stock and IPO things. What do they have to do with selling souls? This company—Soul Equity—what does this have to do with us?"

"Well, if this company begins trading on the New York Stock Exchange, not to mention on other exchanges throughout the world—in effect, you will see a way for each and every transaction to be a barter on the soul. Can you imagine? Worldwide public trading on the sale of souls? Not to mention the very idea of equity on your soul. I've never heard anything like this before. People can borrow against their own souls! Good God in heaven! The ramifications are enormous."

"This company—it's like a giant corporate Mbwento. I know how silly this all sounds. Well then, there is our task," she said matter-of-factly. "This can't happen. We can't let Soul Equity have Dutty Boukman's papers, and we have to stop this IPO."

Friar Bill smiled. "I feel like this *can't* be something that I'm seriously considering as possible."

Mambo Taffy smiled. "I've had a lot of days in my life like that."

# CHAPTER 34

## LITTLE HAITI, MIAMI

It had been a long time since Neda had waited for a bus. Standing on the corner of the street, she thought back to her years of part-time work while studying for her teaching degree. It seemed like she took buses and cleaned houses forever during that time. Then she met Wilson, and there was the thrill of marriage, and then—out of nowhere—his accident. They'd only been married for one year when Wilson fell off the roof trying to fix a stubborn leak over the master bedroom. The joy at her graduation was overshadowed by the grief of his slow recovery. She shook her head. The memory of it all could still be so strong. Sixteen years of struggle and pain in a wheelchair for her beautiful husband had finally ended that night in the parking lot. She felt lonely and wistful, and a little bit cold. *Life was just a road,* Mambo always said. *Be sure to look around you and see the scenery.* Then she would laugh and say, "Unless things start to get too bumpy—then just try to watch where you're going." Neda decided that she was spending too much time looking at that road ahead; for once, she just wanted to watch the scenery. She was tired of bumpy roads.

There were no other people at the bus stop. "So, what do ya think?" said Tina to the group as they stood on the corner. "We're just gonna get on this bus? I mean, what do we know about this guy? He could be taking us anywhere."

"Doubtful," said Micelli. "Who would make something like 'Mary's Grin' up? That's a real place, right? You've been there." He was looking up and down the street.

"Yea, well—" she started, only to be interrupted by Otero.

"Who makes these names up?" he said. "Who ever heard of a place bein' called something like 'Mary's Grin'?"

"I think if you discover somethin' or build it or whatever, you get to call it what you want," Tina answered. She sounded matter-of-fact as she looked for cigarettes in her purse. "You know, like that hamburger place—Wendy's—right? This guy builds a hamburger place, and he names it after his daughter, Wendy. Wendy's hamburgers."

"How's that work with 'Mary's Grin'?" said Neda. "Mary was somebody's daughter?"

"Yeah, it's kind of a cute story," said Tina. "Some guy in the late 1800s has this really sick little girl—they lived in Ohio or somewhere—and so he buys this fish camp in Florida, for her health and whatever, and he moves her and her mother down here, and the kid loves the place. And she gets well right away. In fact, it's the happiest he's ever seen the kid. Of course, her name is Mary, and whenever he sees her running around and whatever, she's got this big grin on her face. So the whole place makes her happy. So he names it Mary's Grin."

"Well, that's heartwarming," said Neda. *I could use some heartwarming,* she thought.

"Not really," said Tina. "Kid drowned the first summer they were there. Fish camps have a lot of water around 'em."

They heard Otero give a low whistle. Down the road, coming toward them, was a bus like none of them had ever seen before. It was a luxury coach, huge and black and sleek like one of those rock-star tour buses on television. Trimmed in broad bands of polished silver, a huge starburst was lettered on the side, emanating out from a red circle. Inside the circle on a deep blue background, were the letters SE. A silver, intricately detailed crown topped the whole side panel. Every part of the bus gleamed with the shiny reflection of sunlight as it slowed to a stop in front of them. Even the black paint on the side seemed to have dimension, as if you could reach your hand deep down inside the color. There was no noise at all as the door opened.

Unlike a conventional coach, the driver's position was not visible through the open door. The stairs onto the bus curved a little like a small circular staircase. Each step was black and trimmed with several small pinpoint lights. Otero, who was standing closest to the door, motioned to Neda and Tina. "Ladies first," he said.

"Politeness aside," responded Neda, "I think we'll follow you."

That was when Micelli's cell phone rang. Looking down at the caller ID, Otero watched him take a deep breath. "Go ahead," Micelli said. "I got your back." He waved Neda forward. "Mom," they heard him say. "Yes, I'm fine, just fine."

So Otero was first on the bus, followed by Neda and Tina. Micelli, talking on his cell phone, stood at the curb as the others climbed aboard.

The driver, a bald white man with a large diamond earring, dressed smartly in all black, nodded as Otero entered the coach and said, "Nonstop to Mary's Grin."

"Uh," Otero looked behind him for Micelli. "We're having lunch with Mr. Rix . . ."

"Please—make yourselves comfortable," answered the driver, motioning to a door behind him. The whole interior around the driver was covered in black leather, tufted in silver studs. "Just press the disk beside the door."

Otero touched the disk, and the door slid smoothly open, revealing a plush compartment, even more elegant than what they had seen so far. Rather than bench seats, several black leather couches lined the sides of the coach, and there were glass-topped coffee tables where the center aisle should be. Sparkling chandeliers hung from the ceiling, and the floor was covered in what looked like black marble. Otero whistled again and stepped into the space, closely followed by Neda.

"My Gosh," she said, "will you look at this?"

As Tina passed the driver, he nodded toward her and said slowly, "Hello there, golden girl."

"Hello yourself," she answered.

As the three of them began to move farther inside the bus, they failed to hear an exchange between the driver and Micelli. Finishing his call, Micelli went to step up into the bus, and the driver shut the doors. "I'm sorry, sir," he was saying as the doors closed and the bus began to move. "I only have seats for three."

It took everybody a second or two to figure out that one of them had been left behind. But by then, the door between their passenger section and the driver had been closed and locked. Mortified, they watched the bus pull away from the curb as Micelli jumped up and down and tried to run partway down the block behind them. Neda winced as she watched the pain in his face. He was holding the back of his leg with his hand and dragging it behind him. Tina pushed again and again on the disk beside the door to the driver, to no avail.

"Mother!" she was saying every time she hit it. "Piece of—. Mother!"

Neda opened her purse and fished around for her cell; finding it, she tried to call Micelli, but she had no service. "What?" she said. "Try your cell." Looking doubtful, both Tina and Otero each tried a call.

"I got nothing," said Otero, holding the small phone in front of him with a sour look on his face.

"Zip," said Tina. "I'm tryin' not to get creeped out here."

As the luxury coach proceeded to glide through traffic, the three of them sat inside, glumly watching as the already-tinted windows began to darken. Like sunglasses adapting to bright light, the windows changed, until they could no longer see outside.

They rode on in silence.

"Why can't we see outside?" asked Tina. "Why do you think that is?"

"Must come in handy on some trips," said Otero. He stood up and walked to the rear of the coach. Opening a small under-counter refrigerator, he peered inside and said, "Hey, look—food." He reached inside it and pulled out a silver tray filled with small pastries.

"Ooh, I like those little cakes," said Tina. "Those are those French ones, right? The petit fors. Cool."

"We got that, and we got some olives," said Otero, holding up a glass jar of green olives stuffed with almonds. "And there's some cheese too."

"How 'bout something to drink?" said Tina.

"I think you guys should put that stuff back and concentrate on how we're going to keep a cool head here," said Neda.

Otero and Tina looked at each other. Otero, chastised, put the pastry back into the refrigerator but popped an olive into his mouth. "I always got a cool head," he replied, sitting back down on the couch. "Neda, listen, we're gonna have lunch at this place, find out who these Soul Equity people are, and go from there. The guy we talked to on the phone sounded like a businessman. Don't worry about it."

"I hate it when men are condescending," Neda snapped. "Don't tell me what to worry about and when to do it." She sat stiffly back against the leather couch with both her arms and legs crossed.

"You prob'ly can't think real good, all crossed up like that," said Tina with a nod toward Neda. "I, myself—I try not to think too far ahead. I'm more spontaneous."

"What about Micelli?" Neda blurted out.

Otero got up and walked slowly around the perimeter of the couch. "That bothers me too," he said, looking carefully at the ceiling. "Not gonna obsess about it." He was running his hand around the tops of the windows and then under the countertops in the rear. Opening a

165

cupboard above the refrigerator, he found an intercom panel. "Woo," he said, pushing a button. "Hello?"

"Yes, sir," came a voice. It was the driver. "How can I help you?"

"What happened to our friend?" said Otero into little speaker. "The other man who was with us?"

There was a pause, and then the driver said, "Other man? The gentleman on the cell phone? I heard him say something about an emergency. He told me to go ahead."

Tina was shaking her head and mouthing the words, *I don't think so.*

"Why can't we get service on our cell phones back here?" asked Otero.

"We've got a passive jammer. The coach is equipped with the latest in security," the driver answered. "Some very—*very* important people have ridden to Mary's Grin. Heads of state." They felt the coach make a right turn and then accelerate up a ramp. "With the jammer, there's no worry about a bomb being detonated by a cell phone signal. Right now, you're in what we call our 'security bubble.'"

"What's up with the windows?" asked Otero

"It's all about precaution," answered the driver. "Look, folks, relax and have a good ride. We'll be at Mary's Grin in about an hour."

"Feel better?" Otero asked Neda as he closed the cabinet door. "We gotta stop seein' spooks where there aren't any." He walked over and sat down next to her.

Neda was quiet for a minute. "Is that what you think?" she asked finally.

"What?"

"That there aren't any spooks?" He looked at her face, and saw that she really wanted to have an answer.

"Hey! Where are those little cakes?" said Tina, poking her head inside the refrigerator. "Look," she squeaked, turning toward them, holding a small bottle in her hand. "Champagne splits."

\* \* \*

When the bus pulled away from the curb, Micelli was still on the cell phone with his mother. She was talking as he slipped the phone into his pocket and took three or four large strides along the sidewalk, trying to keep up with the coach. He slapped the flat part of his left hand against the door until it became obvious that the driver had no intention of slowing down. Then, sprinting—or trying to—he ran the block and a half back to Otero's office and fumbled for his car keys as he tried to catch his breath. *Shit,* he thought, *my leg is killing me. I've got to see the doctor.* As he started the engine, it occurred to him that he had no idea which direction to drive, so he just sat there. "Dammit!" he shouted, hitting the steering wheel. Then, remembering the cell phone, he shouted again, "Shit!" as he fished in his pocket for the phone.

"Hello?" he waited. "Yes," he said finally. "We sort of broke up there for a minute, but I'm back now. No, I didn't swear. That wasn't me—can I call you later? Okay, what? Toast? No, I don't think toast is a good thing to serve for dinner. You're having a dinner guest, and you're serving toast? Mom, put something *on* the toast at least. Yeah, on top of it. I gotta go. Really. Yes, later. You have this thing about food, you know. We need talk about this. I will. Bye."

His next call was to Frances, his assistant.

"Hey," he said. "Can you look up the directions to Mary's Grin on the Internet and call me back? Grin. G-R-I-N. Like smile. Yeah. I'm in Little Haiti. Thanks." He was sitting there in his car when something caught his eye. It was a quick movement in the shop window across the street. A face or a bit of color or something, but it caught his attention, and he felt a strange pull—a strong desire to walk over to the shop. *Why not?* he thought. *I have a few minutes before Frances figures out which direction I need to drive.*

This part of town always fascinated him. Once, he read that Miami had the largest community of Haitian people outside of Haiti itself; and although the area was notoriously poor, the people who lived there carried themselves with pride. Often he would see women wearing long, flowing dresses with head wraps of brilliant color, followed down the streets by skipping children wearing clean pinafores and little suits on their way to church. Downtown, storefronts were painted in a juxtaposition of wild colors, and each was like a book with a unique story inside. Dodging a few cars, he walked across the street toward a low, one-story cement-block building painted in parrot-yellow with peeling deep-blue trim. The shop's green front door was festooned with flyers. Cheerful colors were visible through large plate-glass windows covered in several hand-painted signs that said in English, "Little Haiti Dress." Bright scarves and big pieces of colored glass and beads lay on tables placed in the sunlight of the front window. An upturned milk crate created a seat next to the front door—*not a bad place to sit and watch the world,* he thought, as he went back to looking in the window. Leaning his forehead against the glass, Micelli could see the place was jammed with clothing piled high on tables and hanging along the walls. A decorative rope of sorts was hung from the ceiling, and brightly colored skirts and blouses hung from wire coat hangers placed one above the other.

Turning, he saw an old Haitian woman sitting on the milk crate. Dressed in a long black-and-red flowing skirt trimmed in white, she wore a skinny black tank top along with a necklace of red and green glass beads with a wooden cross at the bottom. The strap on one side of her black bra had fallen down her arm, and her face was framed by a shock of very white hair. She smiled at him, and he saw that she had almost no teeth.

*"Sa va?"* she said.

"Sorry," Micelli answered, feeling slightly embarrassed. "I don't speak—"

"Bread is the body of Christ," she said in a thick Creole accent.

"What?—I don't—"

"And fire. There is fire, too." She used a match to light a cigarette and held the little flame toward him until it burned down to her fingers.

He started to back away. Better to go back and wait in the car, perhaps.

"Pay me, and I'll tell you about your mother," she said quickly. There was something mesmerizing about her in an unsettling way. Looking at her reminded Micelli of road kill. You couldn't always take your eyes away from it.

"My—mother?"

"Jackyyyyy," she said in a singsong voice, holding her chin down and looking up at him coquettishly.

Almost in slow motion, he felt in his pants pocket for a wad of bills and pulled out a few of them, holding them at arm's length toward her. She took them and puffed again on the cigarette. Blowing the smoke toward him in a big puff, she said, "She is in the smoke, Jacky-Jack. Surrounded by smoke. There is a fire. Jackyyyyyyyy," her voice was wailing now, louder, and her eyes were squinted shut. She began make huffing sounds with her breath.

"Stop it," he said, disturbed.

"In the kitchen with the smoke, Jack-Jack-Jack-Jack . . . she lays on the floor." The old woman was screaming now. "Burnt body of Christ, Jackyyyyyyyyyy." There were tears on her face.

Alarmed, he backed away and could still hear her moaning as he quickly crossed through traffic, almost stumbling to get to the other side of the street and his car. *Crazy people,* he thought. *Damn, stupid, crazy people. She was probably drunk or something.* He flipped open the cell phone and with shaking hands called his mother, but there was no answer. He listened as it rang six times, and then the call went to voicemail.

*"Shit!"* He took a deep breath and tried again, this time more slowly. Stupid small buttons. Listening to the phone ring, he glanced over to the dress shop. The milk carton had gone, and there was no sign of the old woman. He looked up and down both sides of the street and then slammed his hand against the dashboard. Starting the engine, he pulled the car out of the lot. It didn't matter what direction he was driving in; any direction away from the dress shop would be fine. The sun was just starting to set, and the colors of the storefronts began to run together as he drove past them; *like the whole place is melting,* he thought.

He jumped as the cell rang, and he answered it quickly. Caller ID said it was Frances.

"Text me the information," he said without letting her speak; then he clipped the phone shut and pulled into a gas station to fill up. Leaving the car, he walked slowly to the men's room, where he threw cold water from the sink over his face and washed his hands twice—once before, once after. Then he cruised through the little convenience store and threw a couple of bags of chips and peanuts on the counter along with a large bottle of orange juice and an apple. *Nice touch,* he thought. *Fresh fruit at a gas station. Health and all that.*

The text from Frances provided step-by-step directions to the fish camp at Mary's Grin, and he read them three times. A new map helped—the Everglades wasn't a place where he spent much time, so he was uncertain how far away everything was. A quick Mapquest link confirmed the distance—seventy-three miles; one hour and forty-five minutes.

*Head west, young man,* he said to himself as he pushed the car toward the highway. He hit the onramp to I-95 and drove south toward US Highway 41; Alligator Alley would take too long. The text said to turn north off 41 at Monroe Station and watch for an unpaved road 3.6 miles west from town. Turn right at the Pickup Paradise Pub. Pulling the cell out of his pocket, he called his mother again, with the same result as before. *I'm not superstitious,* he thought, crossing himself—*no I'm not. One crazy old lady isn't going to get to me. But Jesus wept, how did she know my name was Jack?*

# CHAPTER 35

## KEY LARGO, FLORIDA

Andy felt better after a nap and decided to walk down to Big Daddy's and have a beer and some fries. Nothing like fat for a headache. *Some of the hair that bit you,* he liked to say to himself; although he was never sure why people said that, because it didn't make too much sense. In any event, it was late afternoon, and Daddy might need some extra help for the evening shift. More importantly, if Daddy wasn't around, he should be able to slip into the back office and make some more copies of money. Although the police had apparently found the gym bag, it wouldn't take him too long to make more. He'd been thinking all day long about how he could get back on good terms with Tina, and he had come up with a plan. Once, Tina had said something to him about trading his copied money for real money and that had given him an idea. That same afternoon, he'd made a stack of fives and tens and then taken them to several gas stations and convenience stores and purchased money orders with them. He never made hundred-dollar bills, because he had seen people at the bank check them with little gold pens to see if they were fake. But most folks didn't look twice at small bills. So far, at least.

Once at the bar, he was greeted by the day girl, Penny.

"Hey there, Pretty Penny," he said with a slow smile. "Daddy around?" He sat down on a bar stool and put both elbows on the counter. The place was empty.

She rolled her eyes. "He was. Now he's not." Wiping the top of the counter with a dank-smelling rag, she wiped around his arms and then squeezed the cloth into a bucket on the floor. "I heard you was in a car crash or somethin'—you okay?"

"Well, I have some headaches," he said, "but yeah."

"If you want a beer, you know Daddy said you have to pay for it."

"I always do," he said. "How 'bout if I just do your afternoon shift for you? You can take off early for one beer and some fries."

"Yeah?" She thought about it, snapped her gum, and shrugged. "That's good by me." Swinging her purse over her shoulder, she glanced back at him from the door. "You gotta make the fries. Don't shoot yourself again or anything like that."

Andy smiled at her and looked down at his hand once she was gone, wiggling his thumb and forefinger. Sometimes it still ached. Waiting only a minute after he heard her car pull away, he poured a draft and then walked down the long bar to the kitchen to get some fries. Penny had some prepped for the lunch crowd, and they were still left over, so he turned on the gas at the fryer to heat up the oil. He was emptying the fries into a wire basket on the aluminum work counter when he heard Big Daddy's stuffed rooster mascot start crowing at the front door. "Cock-a, cock-a," it was saying. Some college kids down on spring break had figured out how to shut off the "Doodle-doo" part. That was a fun night.

He poked his head out the kitchen door but didn't see anyone in the bar. Sometimes the motion sensor on the bird went off with a change of light instead of motion. Whatever.

He lowered the basket carefully into the hot oil and set the timer. An empty glass reminded him that there was more beer in the bar, so he went back in to pour himself another. *I won't forget to write this beer down,* he promised himself. *Gotta pay my way.*

As soon as he went back to the bar area, he felt there was something different about the space. The hair stood up on his arms. Andy squinted toward a darker space against a black wall between the pool table and the front door. He couldn't see the man exactly, but the outline of a figure was muted by light coming in around the door. He was just standing there, so Andy walked back to the center of the bar, flipped on the Christmas lights running along the tiki-top, and said, "Help you?"

The figure started forward, and after one step, Andy could see the outline of a top hat. His heart went to his throat.

"Is that you, Mr. Samedi?" *Please don't let it be. Please, please don't let it be.*

A deep chuckle filtered toward the bar. The figure took another halting step. Andy felt as if the air had been sucked out of the room, and he had to concentrate to breathe. The chuckle turned into a laugh, and the laugh into a bellow. The figure rocked back and forth in glee and suddenly leapt toward the bar and slammed down a gloved hand onto the bar with a whoop.

"Whoo—we had a ride, mon, what a grrrrreat ride!"

Andy saw a glint on the bar top and looked down to see that the man had placed a set of keys there on a fob topped by a pair of dice.

"Wha—what's this?" he said with a stammer. He picked up the keys and looked at them. Even in the darkness of the bar, they seemed to shine. He turned them over in his hand, and a warm feeling ran up his arm.

Samedi sat down on a bar stool, lifted his feet up, and twirled himself in a circle.

"Ha! Hee-hee, ha! *Un cadeau pour un ami*," he said as he circled again in the chair.

"Is that English?" said Andy. "Did you say a gift for a friend?" *How do I know what he's saying?* Andy thought. *Somehow I hear it in my head.*

"I can speak any language, and you will understand me," said the man. "Ich habe nicht viele Freunde." *I don't have many friends.*

"This is way cool," Andy said. "I didn't know that I could speak so many languages. Maybe—am I a—one of those—savant people? You know, like those people who've never seen a piano before and then they can play, like with one hand behind their backs and stuff?

"Well then, you must be special," said Samedi, smiling broadly. "Because I like you very much."

"Well, wow!" said Andy, beaming. "Thanks. Hey, would you like a beer?"

"No. Not now. I just came to give you my gift."

"Yeah!" Andy remembered the keys. "Is this it? They're pretty. Thanks." He picked up the keys and shook them, thinking for a moment that he could see a shower of very tiny sparks fly across the room.

The man gave another great chuckle. "You are so funny," he said, holding his sides. "My gift is outside."

Andy practically ran to the door. There, parked directly in front of the bar, was absolutely the most beautiful Mustang GT he'd ever seen. The thing was practically steaming, just sitting there. In fact, it was humming. Andy was certain he could *hear* it—a jet-black monster, oozing luminescence and power.

"What—" Andy couldn't speak, so he just stood there with his mouth open. "It's so *beautiful*," he whispered. Looking back at Samedi, he remembered that he liked him a lot. "*That* is my gift?"

"Well, I feel responsible for our ride the other night. So I fixed the car," Samedi said, stepping through the door past Andy and running his fingers lightly along the arch above the wheel well. Watching him, Andy thought that for just a second, his hand dipped below the paint.

"You fixed—how? It was only a few days ago," said Andy.

"It was easy," Samedi said with a smile. He had really big teeth. "I have my own shop."

"*Really?*" Andy was thrilled. His *own* shop! How cool was *this?*

"Maybe I will have a beer," said Samedi. He winked as Andy went to open the car door. "I have a favor to ask you."

A Chevy van pulled into the parking lot and parked next to the Mustang. When a small man opened the car door to get out, Andy shouted, "Closed." The man looked at Andy, over at Samedi, and back again to Andy. "Closed," Andy said again. "Fire in the kitchen. Smoke damage." The man frowned, and then nodding, shut his car door and began to back out of the lot.

"Holy shit!" said Andy, looking at Samedi. "I forgot the fries!" And he broke into a run back toward the bar.

Bursting through the front door, Andy could see a billow of smoke rolling out from under the door to the kitchen.

"No," he was saying as he ran to open the kitchen door. "No. Oh, no!"

He felt a strong hand on his shoulder.

"Don't touch the handle," said Samedi sharply. "Stand back, *mon ami.*"

Andy could see a red glow around the bottom of the door, and it seemed to be bulging outward toward him. He could smell smoke, and his eyes were starting to burn.

"Please, what are we gonna do?" Andy asked, whimpering. Big Daddy was going to be *so* mad.

"About what?" said Samedi, stepping past him and reaching toward the handle to open the door. Andy's eyes went wide, and he winced, turning away and bracing himself against the heat. Instead, a burst of cool air and light from the kitchen windows greeted them. Everything in the next room looked fine, and the fries were sitting in the deep fryer in cold oil.

"What did you—" Andy couldn't believe what he was seeing. "What? Did you do this?" he asked in wonder. "Did you make that fire go away?"

"Andy," said Samedi, laughing, "you only see what you think you see." He was leading Andy back toward the bar. "Things are like that in life as well. Now, let's talk about that favor I need. And then you can take your new car home."

*   *   *

It was very simple, Samedi was explaining to Andy as they sat at the bar. Some papers that belonged to him were stolen, and Samedi needed Andy's help to get them back. These papers were very important, and there was this bet, see, so Samedi couldn't go and get the papers himself because of this bet.

Andy listened very carefully. He understood about bets. Once, a long time ago, he remembered that he'd made a bet with his friend James in school. *I bet I can swallow more Elmer's glue than you can,* Andy had said. *No you can't,* said James. *No way.* So on arts-and-crafts day, they sat in the back of the class, and between the two of them, drank over seven large bottles of the stuff. They had started on bottle number eight, when James said his stomach hurt and projectile vomited all over the back of Heidi Bassett's hair. She stood up, and when she realized what had happened, she took an Xacto knife and stabbed James in the back of his hand. So when the teacher came back from the supply cabinet, there was James, running around the room, bleeding and vomiting, and Heidi Bassett sitting on the floor, crying, with her hair covered in some God-awful white, gooey, smelly paste with peas or something in it.

Andy won that bet, and James got kicked out of class for the rest of the week. That was a fun bet.

Samedi said this would be a fun bet too.

Actually, Andy already had the papers once. *How about that?* They were in that Scooby-Doo lunchbox that Neda had given him to hide. *Dang!* If he'd only known about this bet, he could have given them to Samedi then. Well, there would be another chance soon, because although the papers were in the safe at the police station, the police would have to give them back to Neda pretty soon. After all, they belonged to her, didn't they? No! They belonged to Samedi.

Andy said he understood.

*But you have to say yes or no*, Samedi said. *And you have to say it out loud—it's part of the bet. Will you help me get my papers back, Andy?*

Suddenly, there was a slam as the front door to the bar flew open and Big Daddy stood there with sunlight streaming in all around him.

"What's goin' on around here?" he bellowed. "I send a plumber over to fix the damn bathroom sink, and he comes back and tells me the place is closed because you had a fire in the kitchen?" Daddy stomped through the bar and over to the kitchen door. "What's *wrong* with you?" he was saying as he brushed past Andy.

"Nuh—nuh, nuh, nuh—" was the best Andy could come up with as he ran after him.

"Where's Penny?" Daddy was standing in the kitchen, looking around with his hands on his hips. He was wearing a white undershirt and blue plaid Bermuda shorts with flip-flops. "The place looks fine." Shaking his head, he stepped quickly to the side and down hard on a cockroach.

"She—I don't know, right now—exactly."

"Boy—you got *nothin'* between those ears." Daddy put his finger up to the side of his head and tapped it. "I been tryin' to get that plumber here for *weeks*. Shit!" He stomped back into the bar. "Weeks."

Following him, Andy looked around but didn't see Samedi. Maybe he left. Andy sort of hoped he left, because he was still wearing that funny Halloween costume, and Big Daddy probably wouldn't get the joke.

Daddy rang out the till and opened the drawer to take out the bills. Counting them, he stood behind the bar for a minute and then flipped on the lights to the liquor shelves and started the popcorn machine. "These yours?" he asked, pushing a set of keys and a napkin over toward Andy.

Andy looked at the napkin. In ink, Samedi had drawn a question mark. Squeezing the car keys tightly in his left hand and looking at the napkin, Andy said out loud, "Yes, I will," up into the air.

"Huh?" Daddy said.

"It's a bet," said Andy.

Daddy was taking wine glasses out of the under-counter dishwasher. "Did you win or lose?"

"My friend and I plan on winning."

"Well, if you plan on *working*, then I might plan on paying you."

"Yes, sir. Anything special you need me to do?"

"Yeah, can you clear that paper jam out of the copy machine in the office? I don't know what the deal is with that machine; it's always broke, and I hardly ever use it."

"Sure," said Andy, walking behind the bar and past Daddy. "I hardly ever use it either—usually."

He opened the door to the office and flipped on the light. Samedi was sitting on the couch.

"What are you *doing* in here?" Andy whispered, closing the door quickly.

"Waiting for you," said Samedi. "Why?"

"Well—oh," said Andy, walking around to the back of the copy machine.

Samedi got up and took a few steps into a small bathroom off the office. Andy heard the water start running in the sink. "There is no paper jam in that machine," he told Andy. "It needs a fuse."

The door to the office opened, and Daddy poked his head around it. "I'm takin' off," he said to Andy. "I'll be back in a couple of hours." He made a face. "You smoking in here? Why is the water running in the bathroom?"

"Sometimes I smoke," said Andy, stammering. "Right now, I'm—I'm looking at that leak—testing it—sort of—and smoking. But not currently."

Daddy opened his mouth to say something and then just shook his head and closed the door.

Samedi came out of the bathroom and leaned against the doorframe. Water slowly began to trickle out from the room and pool around his feet on the floor. "My friend," he said, "there's a very bad leak in that sink."

*I need to get some more money orders,* thought Andy, sighing. *Working for a living is just getting too complicated.*

# CHAPTER 36

---

## MARY'S GRIN, FLORIDA

It actually took less than an hour—about fifty minutes—before the Soul Equity coach pulled to a smooth stop in the small Florida fish camp called Mary's Grin.

"I'm still hungry," said Tina, looking at the empty plate of small cakes and tucking an unopened champagne split into her purse. "What a nice ride."

The door to the passenger section slid open quietly, and the group shuffled past the driver. He handed them a piece of paper, smiled broadly, and said, "Present this in the post office. And have a great day!"

"Smart ass," said Tina as she walked by him.

"Sweet one," the driver answered, flicking his tongue at her like a snake.

"You know, you got a way with people," said Otero to Tina as they stepped down onto the dirt road.

"Yeah," she answered, shrugging, "maybe I could be a ambassador or something."

"Will you guys stop it?" asked Neda. "Let's figure out what's going on here." She flipped open her cell phone and saw that she had service; but trying to reach Micelli, she went to voicemail. She left a message. "It's Neda," she said. "We're here at Mary's Grin. Give me a call and let me know what's going on. Bye—I hate these things. Bye."

The road in front of them was lined on each side by towering and very old live oak trees. Long strings of dense, swaying Spanish moss hung down from gnarled branches, licking the tops of shingled, dank cabin roofs and acting as a picture frame for two neat rows of one-bedroom cabins. Tucked deep in the midst of heavy foliage, the faded pastel houses welcomed weekend fishermen and down-on-their-luck families. Two steps up to each wooden porch led to a rocking chair with a worn seat—each placed next the front door, under a single paned window that gazed blankly into the street. Pine trees dropped needles, filling up mud puddles, and small lizards darted over and under each set of front steps.

"Damn!" said Tina as they walked down the street. "You can *hear* the South."

"Isn't this place pretty?" said Neda, pointing to two leather work boots placed beside a set of steps. Filled with dirt, the shoes created flowerpots, and multi-colored blooms burst out from between gaps in the laces and grew down and out over the sides. A rusted bicycle with training wheels leaned against the porch railing.

"Can we find the post office?" Tina was saying. "I ain't got all day."

The place wasn't completely deserted; there were cars parked here and there. Otero heard a baby crying in the distance, and an older woman appeared in one cabin door carrying a basket of laundry from one room to another. All in all, it just looked like an off-season tourist trap for low-budget fishing families.

Ahead, a small, one-story wooden building sat hugging the pier next to the lake. They walked down the street and up onto its wide wooden porch. "Lake Laundry," said a sign painted in the front window. "Open 7am till midnight. No alcohol, no dogs." They peered into the window. It was closed. A flyer stuck on the front door advertised "Slappy's Tavern. Donnie-Ray Neal performs live *AND* in person this Saturday."

"Well, I don't see a post office," said Otero. "Wait a second, what's this?" A small sticker on the very bottom of the front window said, "U.S. Post Office, 50 yards north."

"What?" said Neda. "North? That's in the lake."

"I think there's a building out there," said Tina. "It's on stilts. Look."

The three of them walked to the end of the pier and stood there, looking out across the lake at a small structure in the middle of the water.

"I think there's a handicapped rule against that," said Tina.

They looked at her.

"No, really," she said. "Trust me, I occasionally speak on behalf of the disabled—though I myself—are not one."

"Am not," said Neda.

"What?"

"I, myself, am not disabled."

"No, of course you're not," said Tina. "How ridiculous."

"There's a sign here, look," said Otero, pointing at a small, hand-lettered notice stuck to the wooden railing.

FOR STAMPS, PRESS BUTTON ONCE.
TO SEE THE POSTMASTER, PRESS BUTTON TWICE.

"Fine," said Neda, looking at the piece of paper the driver had given to them. "This says POSTMASTER on it. Press twice."

Tina started giggling. "Wait!" she said, touching his arm. "Do Morse code for SOS—dit, dit, dit—dah, dah, dah—dit, dit, dit."

"Stop being so stupid," said Neda, annoyed.

"You know who's stupid?" said Tina. "These people, or persons or whatever, *want* us here. We are not here to *benefit* us, right?" She looked at both of them. "Am I right?"

"Well, maybe you have a point—but I seem to remember somebody talking about money," said Otero.

"They want us, more than we want them," Tina said resolutely. "I know these things about people."

"So your point is?"

"Don't make it too easy," she answered.

"Point taken," said Otero. Tina rolled her eyes. "No," he said. "Really. But for right now, we start this chess game from square one." Reaching over, he pressed the button hard twice. Two slow tones rolled out over the water.

Then, nothing.

"Aw, I shoulda put some sandwiches in my purse," said Tina, after a minute or two had passed.

As the group turned to walk back to the land side of the pier, they felt a very, very slight shudder—almost a shift, rather than an actual movement. In any case, it was enough that Neda reached out to touch Otero's arm before she looked back at the water. To her amazement, there was an entire building sitting there. They were standing in front of a huge building—at least five stories high—and it was sitting right at the water's edge. The end of the pier they were standing on was replaced by an awning-covered paved walkway leading into a two-story glass foyer filled with artwork and huge palm trees.

"What the—" said Neda. "My God."

The sight was incredible. Otero could barely breathe.

"There's a clock, look," said Tina. Next to the front door, suspended in the air, was a silver digital clock counting down from sixty seconds. It was at thirty-two before anyone could move.

"Get in the door before the clock gets to zero," said Otero. "Just do it."

"I don't think—" Neda started.

"Shut up," said Tina. "Now, this is what I'm talking about. Move your legs, girly." She gave Neda a little push. "People prob'ly felt this way the first time they saw electricity. I ain't scared. I like this ride."

They walked into the foyer, and when the clock hit zero, the building vanished.

\* \* \*

The three of them were standing in the lobby of the post office, and Tina was amazed. It looked like a place straight out of her dreams; a two-story spacious atrium, with the entire front section made out of lightly tinted, shimmering blue glass. Truly, she thought that she had never been in a place so beautiful in her entire life. Closing her eyes, she took a deep breath in through her nose, blowing it out slowly through her mouth. This was better than the movies.

"Goodness, me," she whispered, for the first time in her life feeling small. "And I left my tiara at home."

It was cool and airy and brilliantly spotless, with a stainless-steel baseboard running around the edges of a shimmering white marble floor. Textured white paper with little squares of silver thread ran vertically all the way up the walls to a recessed ceiling that she could swear was open to the sky above; yet there were lights floating around the perimeter of it somehow, evenly spaced every few feet. In the very center of the wall facing the front door was a huge painting that looked like a color-wheel in a paint store, with lines of bright, bold color bursting out from a center point. It looked like a giant, round rainbow, and Tina found herself mesmerized by it as white lines turned into yellow lines and pink lines morphed into deep blood red; sky blue graduated into the deepest of midnight colors, and spring greens changed into earthen hues only lush forests know. The whole painting almost seemed to be a moving thing.

"I feel like I'm in *The Wizard of Oz,*" she said, looking away from the painting and straight up into the sky.

"Yeah, said Otero after a minute, "I'm agreeing with you."

Neda was looking out behind them through the huge windows and back over to the wooden pier. "How come we couldn't see this building?" she asked the others.

"I dunno; touch something," Otero said. "Are we really here?"

Tina took a few steps away from the others and poked her finger at the painting.

"Yeah, and?" she said, slapping her hand against the wall. "We're here all right."

"Hey," they heard Neda gasp behind them. "Look." Turning, they could see the entire room begin to rise, like an elevator, with the pier falling away below. They could hear no mechanical sound, just a slight hum, as the atrium slowly began to move toward the very top of the building.

"Woo, hoo," said Tina, looking down onto the water. "We're goin' *up*town!"

After a short pause, the motion ceased, and the rainbow painting on the opposite wall split open in the middle, with each half moving sideways to provide an opening into a small waiting area. Again, the room was exquisitely decorated in different shades of blue, with rounded velvet chairs suspended horizontally from poles in the wall so that they didn't touch the floor. Light was projected from beneath them up through the floor giving the effect that it was the light that held up the chairs. Neda marveled at how clever it was; Otero considered the expense.

The women sat, while Otero paced, running his fingers lightly over the razor in his pocket.

"Look, we're obviously sitting here in a real room in a real building," said Neda. "I still want to know why we didn't see it when we were standing on the dock."

"Maybe it's—*ma*-gic," said Tina, holding her fingers together across her face to make a Batman mask.

"It could be some kind of an optical illusion," said Otero as Neda rolled her eyes. "No, really—I saw this magic show once—"

"Optical camouflage," said a man's deep voice. There was a push of air against them as the group turned and saw a tall man standing near the edge of the room; his shoulder-length blond hair was tied back neatly into a ponytail, and his arms were folded across his chest. *Nice looking,* thought Tina. *Very nice looking.* Wearing crisp, black slacks with a white mock turtleneck sweater, he appeared to be professional and relaxed.

"Welcome to Soul Equity," he said, stepping forward and extending a hand to Otero. "It's always the first question people ask," he shrugged. "And the answer is 'optical camouflage'; a simple premise that can produce an amazing effect."

"Optical—what?" said Otero.

"A special photographic covering is applied to a surface—in this case, the walls of the building. Then, a camera projects an image of the background against the surface and—well, look—what's behind the building?"

"Water."

"A lake."

"That's right. It's simple to reproduce that on film and then project it onto the *front* of the building. It's all about two things: surface reflectivity and people's expectation of what they're going to see. Optical camouflage. The British Ministry of Defense is using this technology on tanks right now." The man smiled. He had big, square, very white teeth. "Can you imagine standing in an empty field and then suddenly looking down the barrel of a tank gun?"

"Are you serious?" said Neda. "That's just amazing. I really, truly couldn't see the building."

"Yes, we're quite proud of it, really; it's our patent, you see. But—" He paused and looked around. "Sorry, I should introduce myself. I'm Rix; we spoke on the telephone. Again, welcome to Soul Equity."

"I got another question," said Otero warily. "When we talked on the speakerphone in my office, you knew who was in the room. How?"

"Another little parlor trick," he said with a laugh. "I like to play games, I guess. We just cyber-tapped into a communications satellite in your area and took a thermal reading of the room you were in. It was your office, Mr. Otero, so we figured that you would be there, and you, Miss Tina." He nodded toward her. "You look slightly smaller thermally than the rest of the group. We watched Mrs. Mason and Captain Micelli arrive by car."

"So you were watching before we called?" Neda asked in a quiet voice.

The man laughed loudly. "This is going to be fun. Let's continue our talk over some lunch, shall we? I promise you answers to all your questions." He motioned toward the blue chairs. "Mr. Otero, the ladies have already been identified, can I ask you to sit in one of the chairs for a moment?"

"Sit?" Otero said. "Why?"

"Your core temperature and heart rate will be identified by the chair. It's added to our database."

Hesitantly, Otero sat down. "I don't think communications satellites can track thermal images."

"That's because most of them aren't communications satellites," said Rix. "Really—I'm surprised you would be so naïve. Just because they're called that doesn't mean that's what they *are*."

He walked to the middle of the room and said, "Missy? Are you here?"

A woman's voice coming from nowhere except all around them said, "Yes, sir. How can I help?"

"Lunch for four."

"Thank you, sir. Menu?"

"What would you folks like to eat?" he asked.

They looked at each other. Tina shrugged. Finally, Neda spoke. "Anything is fine. We're not picky."

"Where's the fun in *that?*" said Rix. "Come on, give Missy a challenge." In a stage whisper, he added as an aside, "It's new software. Be creative."

"Ah—New Jersey dog," Otero said loudly to the ceiling.

"I said *new* software," said Rix. "As in alpha version." Then, talking to the room again, he said, "Missy, that's not a biological dog—that's a hot dog cooked a special way."

"Thank you, sir," the woman's voice said. "Deep fried."

"Sushi for me," said Tina, also looking at the ceiling, "and two glasses of white wine. Chardonnay."

"Thank you," said the woman. "Is California acceptable?"

Tina sighed. "Bo-ring. Stateside, I prefer Oregon."

They all looked at Neda, who said, "Salad," to the floor.

"The usual for me," said Rix cheerfully.

"Well, where's the challenge in *that?*" mocked Otero.

"She hasn't been able to get it right yet," said Rix. He shook his head. "Well, you know, learning is just the ongoing process of failing." He smiled. "Follow me."

Leading them out of the room and down a long, carpeted hallway, Rix brought the group into a rotunda in the center of the building, with corridors running outward like spokes from a wheel. Everywhere they looked, the building was splashed in brilliant flashes of paint. Bold shades festooned the walls like spattered confetti, and the marble floor swirled in color beneath their feet as they passed. The rotunda was open all the way through the building and filled with a lush, tropical haze of beautiful palm trees draped in sparkling droplets of dew—like diamonds. From far below, the soothing sound of rushing waterfalls could be heard, accompanied by the songs of cockatiel and parrot.

As they walked, Neda peered down each corridor and saw a surprising amount of activity. Many of the offices were full of people, and she heard several conversations in foreign languages. Everyone seemed to be bustling about, and the energy was almost palpable.

Rix saw her looking and made a comment. "This is a busy time for us. We're getting ready to go public," he said. "Soul Equity only has a few more deadlines to meet for the SEC, and we're on our way."

"Let me get this straight," said Neda slowly. "You're going to sell stock in a company that makes loans on people's souls?"

"Equity positions. Not loans, but yes, as soon as we get our privacy statutes straightened out," he answered. "It's going to be huge."

"But—I don't think that's ethical."

"Why?" He seemed surprised. "You have a soul, right?"

'Well, yes," she started.

"And it belongs to you, right? Nobody else."

She was still hesitating. "Yes."

"Well, you can do with it whatever you want. Who's to say you can't?"

"Well, it's not a *thing*, I mean, you can't touch it, or—"

"What's a patent? What's intellectual property? You can own those."

"Well . . ." She was thinking carefully. "Those things end *up* being something."

"How do you know a soul doesn't?" He laughed at the look on her face. "Ah! Here we are." He gestured toward a doorway covered in hammered bronze. *Entrez.*

Otero pushed the door open, and they walked into a plain, white room with a white table and chairs. Everything was white—the walls and ceilings, the floor, the table linens and chairs. Only the cutlery was shiny pewter and the glasses, sparkling cut crystal. Sitting down, Tina looked around and said, "Wow. Sensory overload."

"Just wait," said Rix as they all took their places at the table. "Right. Where would you like to eat?"

"I get it," Tina said, slowly looking around them. "This room—"

"Yes," said Rix. "Disney bought a lot of this technology. Actually, we share a member of their board of directors. But it never fails to thrill even me—and I've been everywhere."

"What kind of room is this?" asked Neda.

"Wait!" said Tina. "I know. Rix, pick your favorite place and take us there."

Otero finally spoke. "I never been to Disney, so I'm not sure—"

"You'll be fine," Rix said. "Wait. I like to eat in the clouds. Missy?"

"Yes, sir," said the woman.

"We would like to dine in the sky."

"Thank you."

Suddenly, they were sitting in the middle of the air, far above the Earth's surface. Surrounded by nothing but clouds, their plates, glasses, and cutlery floated in front of them, filled with sushi, hot dogs, and salad. Tina could feel her feet on the ground, but when she looked down, there was nothing below them but sky. Reaching out, she felt around the plate.

"I can feel the table," she said. "But I can't see it. This is *way* cool."

Otero was gingerly feeling around his chair with his feet. "I don't like heights," he said. And then his voice got a little bit louder. "I mean it. I *really* don't like heights."

"Sorry," said Rix. "It does sometimes have this effect on people." Tina rolled her eyes. "We can eat somewhere else," he said. "How about the deck of an aircraft carrier? That one's *fun*."

"How about a nice, quiet garden?" said Neda.

Tina was looking at Otero. "Pussy," she said.

"A nice, quiet garden it is," said Rix. "Missy? Nice, quiet garden."

The room changed into a carefully manicured English country garden, complete with manor house. Their plates were now sitting solidly on a heavy wooden table, and butterflies flew around them in the air. Two ducks walked past them toward a pond in the background.

"You know, you guys are *good*," said Tina.

"Thank you," said Rix, looking at his watch. "Look, we're all on a schedule; time to get down to business. You have something of mine," he said, putting his elbows on the table and leaning forward. "I want it back." He looked straight at Neda. "I realize that you may not be so inclined as to provide me with what is rightfully mine, and so therefore I am prepared to offer you a fair sum of money for, shall we say—doing the right thing?"

"I—what do I have that belongs to you?" she asked, looking confused.

"Your husband, Wilson, and his business partner, Roy Alexander, conducted a business transaction with my office. I paid them to bring some documents into the country for me." Tina thought he was starting to look unpleasant.

"Smuggle, you mean?" said Otero. Neda glared at him. "Might as well say it like it is, Neda, and get to the point."

"Getting to the point is what I plan to do," said Rix. "No, Mr. Otero, I did not pay to have the documents smuggled. The reason I chose to have them come into the country under such secrecy is because their very existence needed to remain secret. There are other—people—who want the papers even more than I do. Serious—well, collectors—if you will. But I paid for them. I can assure you, they're mine."

"So what's so great about 'em?" asked Tina. "What's on these papers?"

"Trade secrets," said Rix. "Personal agreements with public figures—contracts. There is a very small but very discerning market worldwide for this select type of collecting."

"I *knew* it!" Tina stood up. "Porn."

Rix started laughing. "No," he said, "nothing so obvious. But something that could prove as lucrative. If not more so."

"Like what?" said Otero. Rix liked the look on his face; it reeked with interest. *Greed*, he thought. *One of my favorite emotions.*

"The secret to eternal life."

"Ha! Right," said Tina as she sat back down with a huff. "Sounds like a face-cream commercial to me."

"Well, we each have an ultimate potential," said Rix. "Our corporation, Soul Equity, can help you realize yours." He shrugged. "People are complex. They dream about having and achieving many different things. For some individuals, money is everything. For others, it's youth. You name it—fame, freedom, success, talent. People have a million different hearts' desires." He pushed his chair away from the table and stood up, facing the group. "Think about what you could achieve if you could have any dream realized that you could possibly want."

Everyone was silent, until Neda said, "How—exactly—is this possible?"

"Equity on your soul," said Rix, looking surprised. "I really thought you knew when you came here. It's not such a big thing."

"It's like borrowing, right?" said Tina.

"Absolutely," answered Rix. "Like taking out a loan. In fact, I have an offer here for each of you. Just on the off chance that you might be interested." He reached into his inside jacket pocket and produced three legal-sized envelopes. They were glowing—sort of. Each perfectly white envelope was rimmed in sparkling silver with an elaborately lettered name on the front.

"So how does your company make a profit if you exchange money or whatever for a piece of paper?" asked Neda. "What's the deal with the IPO?"

Rix smiled. "Well, if I gave you a fortune and you went out and made a hundred fortunes out of that one, that would make you pretty wealthy, right?"

"Right . . ."

"We have a percentage clause."

"A percentage—"

"And if I gave you power or intellect or beauty beyond belief? We use the little favors, the contacts, the business connections. Believe me, it's lucrative. For every man I've made into a millionaire, I have a hundred who are now billionaires. I have heads of state, I have beauty queens, and I have industry giants, sports stars, movie producers, and bank presidents." He leaned down toward them and put both hands palms-down on the table. "Who wouldn't want to buy stock in that?"

"I'll take one of those envelopes," said Otero. "I'm game."

"*What?*" said Neda, shocked. "That's absolutely ridiculous. You don't know what you're talking about."

"I'll worry about me," he said. "Let's try this out. Give me one of those things." He held out his hand.

A slow smile spread across Rix's face as he handed Otero an envelope. "Anyone else?" he asked cheerfully, looking at the group. "The offer is free."

"No limits, right?" said Otero. "Anything I want?"

"Your heart's desire."

Otero took the envelope and turned it over in his hand; it was surprisingly heavy. "What do I do to enter?"

"It's not a *contest*," said Neda, shocked. "You're giving up some of the rights to your *soul*, for God's sake. Well, not for—you know what I mean. You should think this through."

"Ah." He dismissed her with a flutter of the back of his hand and then stopped, looking directly into her eyes. He was very serious. "I haven't had a soul for years."

"Just fill it out and sign the bottom. I don't need to see it," said Rix.

Otero opened the envelope and took out two sheets of paper. Looking at them, he asked, "What's this say on the bottom? This funny writing?"

"Hmm?" Rix looked at the copy. "You've already been approved—that's a signature. Our principal is not an American."

"I'm doing this soul arrangement thing with a Chinese guy?"

"It's not Chinese." Rix slid a pen across the table. "It's Hebrew."

"I'm doing this soul arrangement thing with a Hebrew guy?"

Rix let out a patient sigh. "No, actually, you're not."

Otero began to write carefully.

"Can I have some more soy sauce?" asked Tina.

There was a knock at the door to the garden, and a square opened up in the air beside their table. Entering the room, the driver of the coach they'd been riding in walked quickly over to Rix and, cupping his hand against his mouth, leaned over and whispered something in his ear.

Rix frowned. "That's unfortunate," he said. The driver turned and walked out through the door in the garden closing the sky behind him.

"Sorry." Rix seemed anxious. "I'm out of time." He reached out quickly to Otero, who was still carefully writing, and touched the pad of one of his fingers.

"Ow!" said Otero sharply as his finger sent a drop of blood down onto the page. "What the hell was what *that* for?" He looked at Rix with his eyes wide.

"Confirmation of identification," said Rix. "Our principal is really quite picky about real identities. We're talking about heart's desires, you see, and the inclination toward cheating does occasionally occur." He slid the paper back from Otero, folded it, and slid it into his right-hand shirt pocket. "Thank you," he said. "I really *do* hope you're happy."

"Happy?" said Otero. "Oh, I'll be happy." He looked taller somehow. "Now—to digress—Neda has something that's 'rightfully' yours. So just to be clear, in regards to this, I think a consulting fee will be in order; speaking as the personal representative of Mrs. Wilson Mason, that is."

Neda turned to him with her mouth open.

"Actually, I also happen to represent Ms. Mason," said Tina. "She wouldn't have a calendar without me."

"I wouldn't have a—" Neda started.

"Done," said Rix, still smiling. "At Soul Equity, we appreciate business relationships."

"Well, all righty then," said Tina. "Rightful is after all, rightful—that's my advice anyway—sometimes people ask for it. About that soy sauce?"

# CHAPTER 37

## MARY'S GRIN, FLORIDA

Micelli was just turning north off the highway at the junction to Monroe Station when his cell phone rang. There was no shoulder on the road once he was off US 41, so he slowed way down to concentrate on his conversation. A New Jersey area code was showing on the caller ID, although it wasn't his mother's number.

"Hello?" he said quickly. It was his aunt Helen.

"Jack," she said with an annoyed tone in her voice, "I've been trying to reach you. Isn't today a working day for you? Why aren't you at your office? Some young woman keeps telling me I have to leave a message when I call there. I don't want to leave a message. I want to speak to you, and I don't like talking on these moving phones."

"Hi, Aunt Helen," he said. "How are you?"

"I'm fine, dear. How's your leg feeling? Is it better?"

*No,* he thought to himself, *it's not. I shouldn't have tried to run along with that bus.* "My leg? It's much better. It's fine. Thanks."

"That's nice, dear. Listen, I'm calling you because your mother has had a little accident. "Don't be alarmed, but she needs to come stay with you for a little while."

"Accident?"

"Yes, but only a little one. You know your mother; sometimes she exaggerates."

"Well, did she have one or not?"

"Oh, yes! Goodness, I was there."

"Well, what happened? Did you say she needs to stay with me?" He could hear coughing in the background.

"Yes, she does. Anyway, she was making toast points for our evening bridge club. We like to have a light dinner. You know, everyone brings something. June Gilliam and Karen Ream were making spreads for the toast points, and I was bringing salad. We were also having a *wonderful* corn salsa that Nancy Soles makes; it's really, really good. She uses frozen corn—" Micelli held his cell phone away from his head and took a deep breath.

"So, Aunt Helen," he interrupted, "Mom had an accident making toast points?"

"Yes, well, there's a reason we ask her to only make the points, you know. Sometimes she wanders. Toast points are a perfect task for her."

"She—had—an—accident—because . . . ?"

"Well, some idiot told her to put something *on* the points. So she tried to use the stove." She was making tsk-tsk noises. "The fire department says it will take a while to get the smoke damage cleaned out of her apartment. It was awful, Jack. They found her on the kitchen floor, completely overwhelmed by the smoke." There was more coughing in the background. For a minute, he felt numb and could hear the words of the old Haitian woman in his head. *She is in the smoke, Jacky-Jack. Surrounded by smoke.* He looked down and saw that his hands were shaking.

"Are you there?" his aunt was saying. "She can't stay with us; Tony and I are going on an Alaskan cruise next week. She can't be totally on her own right now. So I'm sending her to you."

He pulled the car over to the side of the road and stopped it.

"Aunt Helen," he said slowly, "I have a one-bedroom apartment."

"I'm sorry, Jack," she said. "There's just nothing else we can do. I've booked her ticket, and I've given that girl, Frances, the information. By the way, she doesn't exactly answer your telephone in the timely fashion that an employee should. I think you might want to look for someone else."

He looked at his watch; it was 2:30 p.m., and he needed to get to Mary's Grin and find out what was happening with Soul Equity. Maybe he could sleep on the fold-out couch for a while, although the bar that ran down the middle of it came right up through the mattress, and the last time he slept on it, he swore he would never do *that* again. Then he felt bad because he'd been trying to get her to come and visit him for a while now.

"When is she coming?" he asked.

"Saturday."

"That's the day after tomorrow!" he exclaimed.

"It's the best I could do," she said. "It was a special ticket. She gets into Miami at 11:30."

"Well, at least we'll have the day to get settled," he said.

"At night."

"You're killin' me," he said with his forehead on the steering wheel.

"Yes, dear," she said cheerfully. "Well, call me if you have any questions or anything. Bye."

Micelli started the car and pulled back onto the highway. After driving about two miles, he saw a State of Florida sign that read, "Ochopee, one mile." Beneath it was a National Register of Historic Places sign for Monroe Station, a gas and service station built on the edge of the Big Cypress National Preserve in the mid-twenties. Underneath that, someone had stuck up a handmade wooden sign that said—in long-faded paint—"Rednecks and snakes strait ahead." What a *godforsaken place*, he thought, looking down the length of the pothole-filled dirt road. *This has got to be the absolute middle of absolute nowhere.* He had the windows rolled up, but he could still taste the grit as his tires spun dust and small rocks up into the air around the car. Something that looked like a large shadow lay in the road in front of him over by the shoulder, and slowing the car, he could see what had to be at least an eight-foot gator, sleeping near the edge; its large head turned toward the sun. *Just like that,* he thought. *An alligator sleeping in the road.* Geez, sometimes he actually missed Jersey.

Slowing, he passed Monroe Station. Once famous as the only outpost on the road between Miami and Naples, the large, two-story building didn't have enough paint left on it to even know what color it had been. Most of the windows were broken out, and a hole big enough to drive a car through gaped from the side facing oncoming traffic. *You could just drive right in there,* thought Jack. *Maybe that's what somebody did.* A small white cross had been erected and placed next to the road. Squinting, he could read the words "Red Rooster" written on it in neat block letters. The scenery in general made him feel sad in a strange sort of way. In Hollywood, swamps have a sort of murky mystery about them, but here—only about an hour outside the bustling stewpot that is Miami—he felt as if the whole place had just been abandoned and thrown there in some sort of cosmic pile called "Lost Places and Other Junk." He picked up his cell phone again and dialed Neda and then Otero, with no answer. Then, just for fun and no other reason, he called the station in the Keys. Frances answered. She was breaking up.

"Your mother," she said. ". . . smoke . . . weekend . . . SEC . . . pick up papers . . . can't hear you at all . . . Bye . . . Hello? . . . Bye."

He was reading his text directions and trying to decide what to do when he saw the woman standing by the side of the road. The wind was whipping her long skirt around her legs, and he couldn't see her face; she had turned away from him and was looking in the other direction. Holding a large wicker over-the-shoulder purse close to her body, her arms were heavily tattooed. She was extending one arm, and he could see she was holding out her thumb—hitchhiking, trying to travel in the direction he was coming from. Then, as she turned and looked at him, he saw her change the direction of her thumb. *Going anywhere,* he thought and got a bad feeling.

Slowing the car, he rolled the driver's window down halfway and watched as she took the few steps around a large pothole toward the side of the car. Her salt-and-pepper hair was still blowing across her face as she placed a heavily ringed hand on the edge of the window. *Why is it blowing so hard outside?* he wondered. *It was perfectly still only a few minutes ago. Jackyyyyy,* he heard the wind hissing as he looked up into her face.

"You have to be very careful," the woman said, squinting down at him. "If you make a mistake now, we'll have to start all over again." Her skin was weathered and brown, wrinkled at the corners of her eyes and along her neck. There was a streak of dirt that ran alongside her face, from the corner of her mouth to her temple. He noticed her hands were calloused, the nails on her fingers bitten and dirty.

"Mistake?" he said, looking around them at the empty road. A movement on the ground made him lean toward the window and look down. There were three snakes slowly curling around her sandals. Shocked, he looked back at her face, and for just the briefest of seconds, he saw the face of the old woman in Little Haiti. He blinked quickly, and she changed. Now she was smiling at him.

"Who *are* you?" he asked.

"Time," she said slowly. Her smile was gone.

"I don't understand."

"You don't remember me." She pushed her hair out of her face. "Yet." And he felt for a moment that she had once been very beautiful. Closing his eyes, he felt her mouth against his. "Listen," she was saying. "We're so close now; please don't go to Mary's Grin. Just let it happen."

"What do you mean, *happen?*" he asked. *Jackyyyyy,* the wind was singing loudly. He struggled to hear her.

"We've been through this so many times before," she said, shaking her head tiredly. "This time, I decided to try the truth." Her eyes were deep and black. "Jack, listen to me. I'm tired. Don't go to Mary's Grin."

"Get away from my car," he said, looking at her hand on the edge of the window. It was bloated and fat, the veins swelling outward from the skin.

"I'm tired of standing on this road."

"I said get away from my car."

"Look at me, Jack," she said, and her face turned again into the old Haitian woman and back. He closed his eyes and rubbed them with his hands. "We *can't* change the past," she was saying. "We can only change things going forward."

"I don't know what you're talking about." She was making him mad.

"I'm sorry," she said, "but I have to do this." Then she leaned down and scooped up the snakes in her hands and in one great flinging motion, threw them through the open driver's window.

Micelli screamed like a little girl.

# CHAPTER 38

―――⟫●⟪―――

## NORTH MIAMI, FLORIDA

Pascale had never talked to anyone from the SEC before, so when he was given the message that they wanted to speak to him, he was more than mildly interested.

"Really? The Securities and Exchange Commission wants me to call them?" he said to the department secretary when she handed him the note. "Are you sure this message is for me?"

"They probably appreciate the fact that you have a degree in accounting," she said, a little bit more sarcastically than Pascale would have liked. She was drumming the end of her pencil against a folded section of newspaper. "What's a six-letter word for 'purposeless'?"

"Pamela?" he said, walking down the hallway toward his office.

Shutting the door, he walked slowly to his desk. All the message had on it was a name and telephone number. Pamela had checked the "please call" box and written "Security Exchange Commission" on the bottom of the note.

He was about to dial the number when his own telephone rang. Hitting the speakerphone button, he heard his boss's voice. "Pascale?" it said.

"Yes, sir."

"You get a note to call the SEC?"

"Yes, sir."

"Don't worry about it. I'll take care of it."

Pascale paused, uncertain exactly as to what *it* was. "If you don't mind, sir," he said, "why are they calling?"

"Something about an IPO for a company called Soul Equity. For some reason, they seem the think that the FBI is in possession of certain paperwork necessary for their database. EDGAR."

"Who?"

"Not who—what. EDGAR. Electronic Data Gathering, Analysis and Retrieval. It's a publicly available, searchable database that the SEC maintains. They're ready to approve the filing, but they need two more things. They say we have them." He cleared his throat. "Do we have them, Pascale?"

"Well, no sir, I don't believe we do," he answered, holding the blueprint BlueJean had given him in one hand and thinking about the papers in the Scooby-Doo lunchbox in Micelli's safe.

"What's this about a news conference with that BlueJean artist woman who said she was giving you some blueprints or something?"

"She—I went to talk to her, but she's been moved to the psychiatric ward at the hospital."

"Really? That's a shame. She paints with parts of her body, right? I went to an exhibition of hers over at the Fontainebleau called 'Test-y Breast-y.' Marsha wasn't impressed—but then, you know Marsha."

*Actually,* thought Pascale, *I've never met your wife.*

"Yeah," Pascale answered. "Ha ha. Well, that's Marsha for you."

"Right," said his boss. "Well, I'll call Darrell over at the SEC and discuss it. You're telling me everything?"

"Darrell, sure," said Pascale. "Absolutely."

"Because I don't want to be on the bad side of the SEC on this one, Pascale. The FBI needs to be a team player—at least that's the message we're getting from Washington. This IPO is going to be huge—worldwide—and there are a lot of eyes watching it. Wall Street, the Fed, international markets. Christ—no pun intended—we got a call from the Vatican yesterday. Understand?"

"Yes, I think I do," said Pascale.

His boss's tone changed. "Your ass can be gone pretty quickly, Pascale. The FBI doesn't want *any* involvement in this if it means a delay in that stock offering. None. Understand?"

"I—" Pascale started as the phone disconnected with a slam.

Taking a deep breath, he rolled out the blueprint onto his desktop, stood up, and looked down on the schematic. It was a blueprint of Turkey Point Nuclear Power Plant all right, but it was more than that. It was a map. He reached inside his desk drawer and pulled out a pair of reading glasses. Why would the SEC be interested in having this? Stamped in the upper-right-hand corner were the neat letters: Soul Equity, Inc. along with a Mary's Grin address and telephone number. Beneath that, someone had written neatly in blue ink:

*Verified. Authority granted in the form of an exclusive agreement to trade in sovereign souls. Rix, I've made arrangements so that your documents will not be disturbed. You will note the box has been placed inside the container wall of the reactor building. Clever choice for place of safekeeping? Thank you—you owe me one. Should you ever need to retrieve it, access is limited to once every 6 months when the reactor is shut down for maintenance. Your new venture sounds profitable, my friend. Watch your back.*

*So it's not the blueprint itself that's valuable*, thought Pascale. *It's the location of the "documents."* Presumably, possession of them made a difference. But that didn't answer his question about the SEC. What possible knowledge of this arrangement could they have? His head was starting to hurt. He took off his glasses and was rubbing his eyes when he remembered the man in the parking lot. Shuddering, he felt sick, and he remembered the little cat one more time.

"Pascale?" It was his speakerphone. He jumped.

"Yes, Pamela?" he said.

"I forgot to give you a message. A woman named Frances called from Captain Micelli's office at the police station. She hasn't been able to reach him, and she says that she got a call from the SEC, saying that they want to come over and pick up a box or something he has in the safe. She wants to know what to do."

He took a deep breath. "Call her back, and tell her I'm coming over to pick them up," he said.

"Okay," she said. "When?"

"Now."

"Now?"

"Yes," he said patiently. "Now, as in this very minute. Now."

"But it's 5:00 p.m." She was whining.

"You know, Pamela, you can always go and work in your father's dental clinic."

"But—"

"Whatever it takes," he said. "Just get a hold of her and tell her to have those papers ready."

He clicked the speakerphone off and rolled his eyes. She would have been far more efficient as a hygienist; certainly, plaque control could have been her specialty. Tucking the blueprint into his briefcase, he flicked the numerical tumble-lock on the outside of the case to secure it and checked his cell phone for messages. Nothing from Micelli, and this was starting to be a concern. He sighed. Last week, he had met a woman in the bar at Mambo Club on the Beach, and she ultimately told him to "get a life" before putting her cigarette out in his Red Bull martini. He really wished he could. A life would be nice to have right now—any part of one.

\* \* \*

It was dinnertime when Mambo Taffy pulled into her driveway, and her interest was immediately drawn to the black Mustang sitting at the side of the house. First, she noticed that it was a beautiful, expensive-looking car. And second, she noticed that it was parked in the middle of her flower bed.

"Andy?" she shouted as she slammed the front door behind her. "Andy! There is a car in my bougainvillea."

Putting her bag down on the sofa, she crossed the room and looked to see if he was out on the back porch. "Come on in," she said over her shoulder to Friar Bill. "Neda will be home soon. Now, where is that boy?" She opened the kitchen door and looked out onto the porch.

He was standing behind the loveseat, looking into the altar. Holding a small picture in his hands, he turned toward her as she stood in the doorway.

"Maman," he said, "how do you have a picture of my friend?"

She walked over to him and looked at what he was holding in his hands. Inside a small silver frame was a folk-art drawing of a black man dressed in a tuxedo, wearing a top hat and sunglasses. The man's face was painted partially white, like a skull, and he was smiling broadly. She looked at Andy quizzically and then thought for a second about how to answer his question. Andy had always been so special. Early on, she learned not to respond to him with an obvious answer, because Andy's questions were sometimes layered in other truths. The man in the picture was Baron Samedi, Vodou guardian of the gates to death.

She heard the door to the kitchen open, and Friar Bill poked his head out. "This is where you are," he said. "Hi, Andy."

"Hi there, Mr.—church." He looked at Mambo Taffy. "I can't . . ."

"This is Friar Bill," she said gently. "Andy, whose car is outside the house?"

"My friend gave me that car," he said, and his face lit up like a child's.

"This friend?" she asked, pointing at the picture he was holding.

"Yes." His eyes were so blue—so bright and clear. She felt a pain in the middle of her chest.

"Andy," she said, "you sit down now—right here." She patted the loveseat. "We have to have a talk."

"Sure," he said, "but first I have to go put the top up on the car. There's a really bad storm coming. I'll be right back." He got up and went out through the back porch door.

"Well, sure," she answered, looking at Friar Bill. He shrugged. "I haven't heard anything about a storm, Friar, have you?"

"No," he said. "You want me to stay? Or leave?"

"You have to stay," she said. "Neda will be home soon, and we need to sort out these papers she has, and we have to come up with a plan to stop this IPO."

"I agree," he said. "Do you want to have some time alone—with—you know . . ."

Closing her eyes, she suddenly felt faint for just a second. Then, steadying herself, she took a deep breath in through her nose. She could smell water on the wind, and something was telling her to pay attention to those things that only she knew how to hear and see. Yes, her senses told her a storm was coming; it must be her Iwa, she thought. *Why don't you pay attention?* she chastised herself. *Don't become distracted.*

"Andy?" she said as he came back into the porch. "Can you ask your friend to come and talk with us?"

"Mr. Sam-ee-di?" Andy asked. He wasn't sure this was a good idea; his friend would probably show up again wearing that Halloween costume.

When Andy said the name, Mambo Taffy again felt a sharp pain in her chest. "My son will not go with you," she said out loud.

"What?" said Friar Bill. He was sitting in the rattan queen chair across from the loveseat.

There was a crack of lightning across the sky, and Mambo Taffy knew it was a signal for her to gather herself together. "Let me ask you something, Andy," she said as she pointed at the picture. "Has your friend—this man here in the picture—has he asked you for anything?"

"Well, yeah," Andy answered slowly. "There's these papers that belong to him, and I'm going to help him get them back."

*Good God,* she thought, looking at him. *When do you get to stop protecting your child?* Then, taking another deep breath, she felt suddenly old, and for just a minute, didn't know if she really had the energy.

Suddenly, there was a loud pounding against the outside screen door. They all jumped and turned to see Pascale. "Sorry," he said. "I knocked at the front, but nobody answered." Mambo could see a drizzle of rain behind him. "Can I come in?" he asked. "It's getting a little wet out here."

She stood up. "Where are my manners? Please."

"My name is Pascale." He was shaking the drizzle off his jacket sleeve. "I'm with the FBI. Captain Micelli's been working with me on a case involving your daughter, Neda."

"She has told me about you," said Mambo carefully. "My daughter is not at home right now. I'm not sure what her schedule is today."

"Doesn't matter," he said. "I've finally managed to get Micelli on the phone, and he's been held up, but he's going to pick up Neda and meet us back here. I brought some papers with me that belong to her." He motioned to his briefcase and a small box he was carrying covered with duct tape. "Can you put these in the house? We can catch up on the details while we wait."

Mambo and Friar Bill looked at each other. Time was very short now, she could feel it. Her temples throbbed. Perhaps this man was right—a united front could move with more strength.

"How much do you already know?" she asked.

"Soul Equity's stock offering announcement is scheduled for tomorrow afternoon. They moved it up. The SEC has pretty much cleared the way for trading to begin as early as the following day. This IPO will roll out on the New York Stock Exchange under the trading ticker of SEQ. The next day, trading will open on the London Market, as well as Japan; it will be around the world within the next forty-eight hours."

Mambo felt as if someone had slapped her in the face. She was absolutely shocked. "I—I don't know what to say," she said, looking helplessly at Friar Bill. "What can we do?"

Pascale sat down heavily in the wicker chair beside Andy. "By this time next week, every family with an unside down house, every real-estate agent down on their luck, and every kid who can't come up with college tuition will be able to sell part of their soul to help make ends meet."

"I feel absolutely helpless," Friar Bill said. He leaned forward and put his head in his hands. "This is going to be catastrophic."

"We could ask my friend," said Andy.

The group just sat there.

"*What* did you say?" asked Mambo Taffy. She had a strange look on her face.

"I was thinking—maybe—we could ask Mr. Sam-ee-di."

"Who?" said Pascale.

Andy handed him the picture and watched as Pascale went pale. It was the man in the parking lot—the man who made him so sick.

"You *know* this guy?" he said, horrorstruck.

Andy was nodding his head wildly. "He gave me a car," he said. "I like him a lot."

"Baron Samedi is a Vodou spirit or Iwa," said Mambo. "He is the commander of the Gede and guardian to the gates of death."

"I see," said Pascale in a dry tone. "Why don't we just ask the Easter Bunny to help too? Is Santa busy?"

"Your sarcasm doesn't take away from the fact that we have no idea how to stop this whole process," interrupted Friar Bill. "And you know what? If I knew how to contact the Easter Bunny, I might consider it."

"Where is Micelli right now?" Mambo asked, changing the subject.

"He said something about having a car full of snakes," said Pascale. "So he's walking to Mary's Grin."

"You want to talk about the Easter Bunny?" said Friar Bill. "Think about what you just said."

There was another huge clap of thunder, and a gust of wind blew through the small porch, causing a ceramic lamp to tip and fall, sending shattered pieces of pottery across the wooden deck. Zumbie the cat screamed and leapt from the floor onto Mambo's lap. She stroked him for a quick second and then laughed. "Looks like we have ourselves more than one kind of storm."

She was still smiling when the lights went out.

# CHAPTER 39

## MARY'S GRIN, FLORIDA

Although Neda, Tina, and Otero were still sitting in the English country garden, the conversation had suddenly grown quite serious, and the atmosphere had altogether changed. The pleasant look on Rix's face had been replaced by one showing some strain, and he was leaning toward them now with an almost hungry look on his face.

"I have only a very short time," Rix was saying, in a measured, careful tone. "So, to finalize the deal with the documents—am I to understand, then, that we are all in agreement?"

"About what?" Tina said, her mouth full of sushi.

He sounded exasperated. "You *will* turn over the documents that belong to me," he said, looking at Neda. "The documents that Wilson Mason was supposed to *deliver—to me.*"

"Look, I know what you're asking," said Neda. "But I need to think about—"

Rix slammed his fist down hard on the table in front of them, causing Tina's sushi to leave its plate and roll over toward Otero. "We had a *deal*," he sputtered. "Wilson was supposed to give the documents to *me*—not to the church. He made a switch at the last minute—at Big Daddy's Bar—and he left me *no choice.*"

Somewhere out in the hallway, they heard a loud crash.

Neda couldn't speak. "What do you mean, you had no choice? Are you saying—are you saying that you were involved in his shooting?"

Rix looked back over his shoulder toward the place where the door had once been; Neda saw sweat beginning to bead up on his forehead. *"Are you a thief too?"* he hissed.

She was completely shocked. "Am I a *what?*"

"I had a deal with Alexander to bring my papers into the country, and your husband, Wilson, decided to do a little business of his own. Overcome—*apparently*—by some sort of altruistic wave of conscience or whatever," Rix said, rolling his eyes, "Wilson contacted the church about the papers." There was more noise in the hallway, and Neda could hear the sound of running. Rix continued. "All right—yes! I sent one of our people to the monastery on the pretense of working with the order. Friar Allen was in the car with the Master and went down to the Keys with him, to see if he could somehow *intercept* the papers. At the last minute, Wilson panicked, and that idiot friar shot him." Again, he slammed his fist down hard on the table. "I *will* have my documents!"

"Hey!" Otero interrupted, holding up one hand. "Calm down."

"How was I supposed to know that Wilson gave the papers to Neda?" Rix was sputtering now. "Who knew he was going to get shot? Then, there's a hairpin turn in the road, and my trigger-happy, underperforming employee tries to take the corner at some ungodly—no pun intended—speed. Well. Accidents happen."

"Accidents *happen?*" she shouted. Neda couldn't help herself. In a burst of realization, she knew then, looking at Rix, that after all these months, after all her loneliness and pain, after all the stupidly squandered time that she and Wilson had lost together, well—she could barely stand the thought that she was sitting in front of the person who made a decision that resulted in her husband's death. She would have cried if she hadn't been so mad. The FBI might not know who killed her husband, but now, she did.

"You're *never* going to see those papers," she said, shaking.

"You *stupid,* petty, little people—" Rix was sputtering.

Behind them, the door in the air opened. Rix looked flustered for a second and then tried to compose himself as the figure of a woman entered the room.

Neda was still staring at him, thinking about what she would do, and didn't notice that Otero and Tina were staring at something else. *Shoes.* It was almost as if the shoes walked into the room by themselves. They were red patent-leather shoes, reminding Tina of the ones that Dorothy wore in *The Wizard of Oz,* but these were sparkling and spitting light back up into the room with each crisp step that the woman took. Although they were sitting on the grass, each stride the woman took clicked with a sharp resonance that seemed to tear into the air. It hurt Tina's head. Neda looked at Otero and watched as his eyes started at the shoes and then went slowly upward to the woman's long, slim legs; followed by a short-enough red skirt with a matching, too-tight, long-sleeved jacket. The woman was stunning. Even Tina couldn't think of anything to say.

"Rix," the woman said. It was a statement, not a question. Tina noticed that her lipstick matched her shoes. Tina could never quite get that right. The woman had the blackest hair any of them had ever seen; long, straight, Oriental-almost hair hanging lushly down her back, slightly curling like lazy smoke around her elbows. "Have you completed our business agreement?"

Rix cleared his throat—hesitantly. The group looked from him to her and back again.

"My dear. No," he started, swallowing heavily. "You're—unexpected."

This should have been when the woman said something, but she didn't. She just stood there, waiting. Staring at her, Neda thought that she had the most beautiful clear skin, with eyes as black as her hair. The effect was striking.

Taking a few steps away from Rix, the woman began to move in a slow, small circle, turning her face outward toward the walls, with her chin up and her head tilted back.

"No," she said flatly. "Our guests have decided *not* to do business with us."

"She's blind," Neda whispered to Tina, who was nodding, and they watched as the woman stopped and then slowly faced them. Neda put her finger to her lips and looked at Otero. Tina had her hand over her mouth and was holding her nose closed with her thumb and forefinger.

"I'd like to introduce you to the principal of our company—and," he cleared his throat. "My wife, Satanaele." His face was gray with seriousness; Otero thought he looked awful.

"Your wi—" Neda started.

"Even the blind can see," the woman said quietly, turning her face toward Neda. "It just depends on how you define sight."

Neda was looking into the woman's eyes; there was something different about them—something unsettling. Then she saw what it was: There was no pupil in the middle of the iris—which was black anyway, but the effect was odd and cold at the same time.

The woman continued, speaking slowly and pausing between her sentences. "I see, for example, that there are three people in the room—not counting Rix, who may or may not actually *be* a person—depending on how you categorize humanity." She took a step toward them. "I see that there is one man and two women. I see that one of you is small." Her nostrils flared, and she smelled the air. "I see that one of you is very frightened and that one of you has cancer of the throat."

The group looked at each other. No one replied.

"One of you—the man—likes knives," she smiled, keeping her lips together. Then, after another pause, she added, "*I* like knives."

Otero could hear a slight hissing noise, almost like steam. Then the woman turned away from them and took a few steps toward Rix. As she walked, static sparks of electricity flashed around her ankles.

"I'd like to see her walk through a gas station like that," whispered Tina.

The room seemed to vibrate almost to the point of shaking. The woman walked right up to Rix, almost touching him, and then stopped and said in a shrill tone, "We are *out-of-time*. Do you realize what that means?"

He rolled his eyes back and moved his face away from hers. Looking at Neda, he said, "My apologies. My wife can be an—" He cleared his throat. "Well, she can be an effective communicator."

"Am I to understand that we have *no deal?*" her voice echoed.

Neda stood up and placed her hands on the table. Responding in even tones, she said, "Right now, I'm sick and tired of hearing about business deals and papers." Then she paused and stood as tall as possible, crossing her arms across her chest. "So that I am perfectly clear, we have *no* agreements—of any kind. Be it *up* agreements, *down* agreements, or *sideways* agreements. We still have no deal. In fact—to save everybody time—we do not now, nor will we ever have *agreements.* Questions?"

They waited; the woman looked down at her feet, took a deep breath, and then held both arms up over her head and snapped her fingers.

Suddenly, the room that was a garden disappeared, and they were in deep space. The blackness of it all was startling; around them stars and galaxies were sprinkled like powdered sugar against the backdrop of eternity. It was utterly terrifying, utterly beautiful, and utterly cold. To Neda, the logic of knowing that they were still in a room on solid ground wasn't strong enough to stop her feeling disoriented and a little bit sick.

Tina gasped, and Neda thought Otero looked panicked at best; talk about fear of heights. She was trying to fight off the dizziness when she heard a low, throaty laugh and realized that the woman found Otero's fear funny.

"Stop it," Rix said. "I'm almost there."

"You're not *almost there*," she said. "You're pathetic. Your garden party approach to business is juvenile."

Neda felt the room shake again and tried to steady herself. The woman was right, this *was* juvenile, and Neda decided she wanted it to stop.

"The pathetic thing," Neda said, "is that you would think your little universe room here would frighten me or anybody into going along with whatever it is you want."

There was another undeniable tremor throughout the building.

"I already knew what your answer would be," said Satanaele, standing in the middle of a supernova and facing Neda. "You're not as smart as you think you are. In fact, there's very little that's redeeming about you at all. Married to a drug dealer, a liar—your *real* mother knew all this too, when she left your grubby, dirty, little self on the floor of that toilet."

Neda felt as if someone had punched her in the stomach. Tina was next to her and took her hand; she could feel Neda shaking.

"Right. I think we need to leave now," said Otero.

The woman turned her sightless eyes toward him. "We went to visit you at your home this morning—*Cutter.*" She was almost purring. "You were out, but there was a dead dog in the street in front of your house. Hit by a car, I think, because she was laying in the gutter. A small, black chow—just an ugly, worthless dog. Someone must have left her out. Someone who didn't care about her."

It was Otero's turn to gasp. He'd let his dog Anna out in the morning and was certain she was back in the house before he left. She *must* have been in the house. She *had* to be in the house. He didn't know what to say or do, and he felt a huge lump of panic inside his chest. He just stood there, looking like he was fighting off tears. Dear *God*, no—what if he'd forgotten to put her back in the house?

"If you touched her—" he started, unable to breathe. "If you touched my dog—"

Tina had seen some dangerous looks on people's faces and knew this was one of them. It was all getting to be a bit much. "Look, Mrs. Satan-ettesky," she interrupted, "thanks for lunch. Your place is nice.

Et cetera. Et cetera. Can we cut the stars? I think our business here is finished."

"*Lastly,*" the woman said, turning toward Tina, "the little freak—speaks. Small isn't better in your case, Miss Tina—it's *less*. No one ever watched you dance because you were *attractive*. They watched you dance so they could laugh at how grotesque you really are."

With that, Tina took a resolute step onto the corner of Orion's belt, reached up with a small but very tightly closed fist, and punched Satanaele right in the face.

Staggering, the woman fell back against Rix, who deflected her by holding out both hands as he started to move toward the place in space where the door must be. But Tina was spitting mad, and she kicked her leg out, stomping down as hard as possible on those Dorothy shoes at the same time as she took another swing. She looked like a pint-sized buzzsaw of ferocity, and Otero, still mortified over the comments about Anna, thought to himself, *Now* this *is effective communication.*

Then, unbelievably, Tina fell to all fours and did a full-body roll toward Satanaele's legs, knocking her completely off her feet. Someone screamed, and as Rix bent down to pick Satanaele up, the door to the room opened in the sky. Rushing past them toward the light, Otero brought his elbow down hard against the back of Rix's head, knocking him to the floor along with a shrieking, flailing blur of red suit and black hair. Then, Otero, Neda, and Tina bolted through space and out into the hallway beyond. Neda was sure she could feel the entire building shaking as they ran through the corridor away from the chaos behind them.

"It's all *too late*," Satanaele was shrieking and laughing at the same time.

*       *       *

It was starting to get dark now, and Micelli was walking to Mary's Grin. Without his car, that seemed to be the only remaining option. There was little else that frightened him in this world other than snakes. Just about anybody could have thrown just about anything into his car, and it wouldn't have stopped him from continuing—but snakes were different. He never really understood this reaction; there was no childhood trauma to remember in his life, no horrific encounter in the woods, no painful bites in his past. He just plain hated snakes, and deep in his heart of hearts, he knew that they just plain hated him back. It didn't even have to be a real snake. A picture of one was enough to make him leave the room. He had to turn the television off if there was a snake on it; not just go to another channel—he had to turn it off.

The whole episode with that crazy woman and her snakes had left him extremely annoyed. Now he was going to have to get a new car. Thoughts rolled through his mind as he walked toward the fish camp and Soul Equity headquarters. He figured he had about three or four miles to go, and so he picked up his pace. He didn't want to be out here walking in the dark. No, sir, not with the gators and bugs and—*snakes.* The very thought of it made him break out into a cold sweat.

*Stupid woman.*

She hadn't seemed surprised when he threw open the door and jumped out of the car toward her. Rather, he thought the look on her face more closely resembled one of *satisfaction.* And while he was wriggling around, shaking out his sleeves, and jumping up and down, she had calmly walked to the other side of the road and once again held out her thumb—in the opposite direction from the one he was going.

That was fine.

The toes of his shoes kicked up a puff of dust with each step, and he was glad that he'd remembered to pick up his cell phone before he jumped out of the car. Actually, *glad* wasn't a big enough word. He was able to make a few calls: one to the office, where Frances breathlessly told him that his mother would be here soon: then she brought him up to date about Pascale collecting the Scooby-Doo lunchbox. He wasn't too happy about the whole arrangement, but it was better than letting the Securities and Exchange Commission pick the box up. After Pascale told him that the IPO had been approved and trading was going to start the following day, he knew they needed to come up with something quickly. He told Pascale he would pick everybody up and meet him at Mambo Taffy's later, but now that he no longer had a car, that wasn't going to be easy.

*Idiot, piece-of-work woman.*

The thing was, he probably could have gotten the snakes out of the car somehow, maybe with a big stick, but what if one of them had left little snakes under the car seat or somewhere? Or what if there had been two snakes stuck together, and he just hadn't noticed that? Both of these were possibilities. Once the snakes had been physically placed in the car, how could he *ever* really know that there wasn't the smallest likelihood that an extra one wasn't still in there? Micelli was not a man who took chances.

*That car could rot.*

He'd been putting on a little weight lately, so he decided to try a short jog. His leg was aching, but he needed to pick up the pace. The sun was just touching the horizon, and Mary's Grin was probably just around the corner, so he started to do a fast walk. It felt good, actually, and it took his mind off of the fact that he was out in the middle of gator country, miles away from the nearest human being, running in front of the dark. Stuff of nightmares, one might say; sometimes Micelli hated his job.

*Jackyyyyyy,* the dark seemed to be saying with a snaky hiss.

He turned a corner in the road and was enveloped by a hummock of oak trees draped in long, swinging nets of soft, hanging moss. Massive philodendron clung to the sides of the trees, each stalk entwining back onto itself, creating philodendron bridges in between the old giants. Huge, golden spiders the size of his hand created webs that glistened against their embroidered legs, stretching strands of sunlight into sticky bands of bug-laced jewelry. It was always so spooky to see this kind of scenery in swamp movies. Not that he was a regular watcher of swamp movies, but Micelli thought it was spookier when it was real. *Like most things,* he guessed. He was out of breath now, and he had a stitch in his side as he slowed back into a walk, holding his hand against his lower back. *Oak trees live to be eight hundred years old,* he said to himself. That made him feel suddenly insignificant somehow. He wondered if the trees knew he was there, running down that road.

# CHAPTER 40

## KEY LARGO, FLORIDA

Pascale was frustrated. For the third time, he'd been unable to reach Micelli on his cell phone; voicemail was a ludicrous invention, and he hated it. They were sitting on the back porch at Mambo Taffy's in the dark now, unable to decide what to do. The inevitability of the situation was beginning to set in.

Candles flickered around them, and a mist of rain had begun. "We only have a few hours left," said Friar Bill, looking glum.

Nobody said anything.

Mambo looked at Pascale. "Isn't there anybody you can call? You're the *FBI,* for heaven's sakes. Can't you think of *one* reason—any reason—that you can use to delay the start of trading?"

Pascale looked down at his feet, shaking his head. "The FBI supports the Securities and Exchange Commission on this one," he said. "It's not going to be stopped."

Mambo slapped both hands against her knees. "Then we will have to do it ourselves," she said matter-of-factly.

"How?" Friar Bill said.

"Andy," she said quietly, turning toward her son, "do you think your friend will help us?"

"Well, sure," he said. Then he frowned and looked at Pascale. "Mr. Sam-ee-di wants some papers in that little box there." He pointed at the coffee table. "He'll help us if you—we—give them to him." He stood up to go into the kitchen. "Does anyone want a tuna sandwich? I'm a little bit hungry."

"Gentlemen, I suggest you discuss our options," Mambo said, standing up to follow Andy. "You have six minutes and four tuna sandwiches to make up your mind." As she walked into the house through the swinging kitchen screen door, Andy glanced at them for one quick second and ran after her.

Pascale looked at Friar Bill. Neither man spoke, alone in their own thoughts. There was a small scratching sound on the screen door, so Friar Bill got up to let the cat out. At the door, he stepped back, and looking toward Pascale quizzically, motioned with his hand to come to the door. As the two men stood there looking into the drizzling evening, car lights appeared to approach from the road, and the sound of a revving engine along with screeching tires followed.

It was the black Mustang that had been parked alongside the house earlier. But now, it seemed to be driving erratically up the street toward them, zigzagging across the road. They watched as the rear fishtailed on the wet street, clipping a garbage can near the driveway next door that had been set out for collection.

Pascale winced. He was thinking about the paint job on the car. "What's going on?" he whispered.

"I don't know," said Friar Bill. "That can't be Andy. He's in the house."

The car jumped the curb and drove through the back yard next door, around the side of the house and came out onto the main road with a trampoline stuck on top of its roof.

Pascale's eyes went wide. "Did that car just drive under the trampoline?"

Andy came back out onto the porch with a plate full of sandwiches at the same time the trampoline drove up Mambo's driveway, through the side yard, past the screened porch, and out again onto the road. As it passed them standing in the doorway, they could hear a man laughing wildly. "Uh-oh," Andy said, as the three of them watched the trampoline head down the street.

"Andy, who's driving that car?" asked Friar Bill.

"It's probably my friend," Andy answered. "I don't think he drives very much. Sandwich?"

Mambo Taffy came back out through the kitchen door and peered through the screen to see what they were looking at. "Is he here?" she asked.

"Somebody—someone—is driving Andy's car around the block," said Pascale.

"I think it's Mr. Sam-ee-di," said Andy, as the car once again drove past the screen. At the rear of the yard, the driver slammed on the brakes and slid through the muddy yard to a jerky stop, causing the trampoline to tip forward off the car and land upside down flat on top of Mambo's vegetable garden.

Mambo pursed her lips and gave Andy a long look.

The driver's door swung open, and a tall black man emerged wearing a dark purple tuxedo and a white top hat with sunglasses. Half of his face was painted white like a skull, and he was holding his sides with laughter. Taking two steps toward the porch, he turned back to the car and reached inside, removing a small bottle of what looked like some kind of liquor and a long, black cigarette holder. Then, semi-staggering, he walked toward the house, gingerly stepping around several mud puddles—giggling the entire time. Under his arm he carried a folded white umbrella.

Pascale was shocked. It was the man he had seen in the parking lot at the marina. "*This* is your friend?" he asked Andy.

"Well, yeah—don't be scared," Andy said. "He just likes Halloween—I think. I've been meaning to talk to him about that."

They heard several heavy footsteps on the outside wooden stairs, and then the man stepped into the room. He was taller than Pascale remembered and not quite as menacing. But nevertheless, it was quite a sight. Friar Bill quickly retreated to his chair, looking as if he might flee into the house. Mambo remained pensive, and Pascale was just standing there with his hand on the now-closed door.

The man looked slowly around the room over the top of his sunglasses and then reached inside his jacket pocket for a cigarette. He pulled out a pack of Marlboros, removed one, and stuck it into a cigarette holder. Putting the pack back into his inside pocket, he removed the top hat, shook water from the brim out onto the floor, and then placed it back onto his head. In the candlelight of the porch, he looked just like the drawing in the picture frame that Mambo Taffy had earlier. So this was Baron Samedi, Vodou guardian of the gates of death. The group was silent as the man held the cigarette holder out over one of the candles and took a long, slow puff, blowing the smoke out slowly toward the ceiling.

"You like tuna?" Andy said, holding the plate of sandwiches toward him.

The man burst into an explosion of laughter that startled everyone. "Pas ce soir, mon ami," said Samedi. *Not tonight, my friend.* "Where are my papers?" He leaned toward Andy with palpable eagerness. "I know they are here—shall I have them? Are you giving them to me?"

"This is the important part," said Mambo quietly. "He can't take them. We have to give them freely."

Friar Bill cleared his throat. "Mr. Samedi, is it? Well, ah—what we want to know is, can you stop the Soul Equity IPO? Can you keep the company from going public?"

Samedi took another long puff on the cigarette and looked thoughtfully at the group. "Perhaps," he said very slowly. "I can *see* the *papers?*"

"I don't trust him," said Pascale quickly.

At that, Samedi turned to look at him, causing Pascale to double over instantly in agony. "See?" He was trying to breathe and holding both hands over his stomach. "I told you."

"Let's have a look," said Mambo Taffy. "Andy, go get the box from the kitchen."

"But—" Friar Bill started.

"He can't take them," she interrupted. "Let's see what we have. Andy—go on." She turned to Samedi and made a motion toward Pascale. "Leave him alone," she said. "Some people don't understand."

Samedi made a small nod, and slowly Pascale stood up. "*Understand?*" Pascale said breathlessly. "Understand some Vodou spirit-guy who's supposedly in charge of the gates of death? What's to understand here?"

"Death itself is not a bad thing," Mambo said almost kindly. "Why don't you sit down? Come over here." She pointed to the loveseat next to the friar.

"Death is merely change," said Samedi, shrugging his shoulders. "Part of a continuing path."

"So why do we need gates and stuff?" asked Andy, walking back onto the porch and fiddling with the duct tape around the outside of the box. Mambo watched Samedi carefully.

"The gates are a metaphor, Andy," she answered. "Why don't you get a knife so we can get the tape off the outside of the box?"

"You want a knife *and* a fork?" he asked.

"I said metaphor, not fork. Just get one knife—from the kitchen." She rolled her eyes and looked at Friar Bill. "*You* try and explain metaphor to him."

"First you could try and explain it to me," he said. "What's all this got to with Soul Equity's IPO?"

"I think I know," said Pascale. "You can't sell part of a soul and still have the whole thing—*continue*. Right?" He looked at Samedi a little fearfully.

"Right enough," Samedi answered. He wasn't laughing anymore.

"Your job is to watch over this—path—and now some guy has started this company that will effectively stop thousands, if not tens of thousands, of souls from—*continuing?* Is this something that was part of the whole deal with souls in the beginning? And you can't stop it unless we *want* it stopped? Am I right?"

"Not literally," Samedi said, beginning to smile. "But perhaps—metaphorically."

Andy came back into the room with the knife, and they watched as he worked to cut a clean seam around the top of the box.

"I thought you were involved with Soul Equity," said Pascale to Samedi. "You dropped their business card that night by my car."

"No. You could say we are—longtime competitors. I only came to warn you about them," he answered. "I believed you might give them my papers."

"Ta da!" shouted Andy, standing back in slightly dramatic pose as he flipped open the tin lid.

# CHAPTER 41

---

## MARY'S GRIN, FLORIDA

Micelli finally made it to the fish camp and was tired and thirsty. He was standing there trying to figure out what to do next, looking at the lake in the quiet of the evening at the exact moment that Neda, Otero, and Tina burst from the lobby entrance and ran across the dock toward him. The sight was quite startling, as the three of them appeared to just jump out of the sky above the lake and hit the ground running. At that same moment, an entire building appeared at the end of the dock as well. Micelli had serious doubts about believing what he was actually seeing.

It was clamoring, and the suddenness of the accompanying sound created complete and utter pandemonium. From all directions, people appeared to be running and shouting. As Micelli saw Neda and the group running toward him on the dock, there seemed to be instant people and instant noise everywhere.

"Keep going! Keep going!" shouted Otero as Neda and Tina ran past Micelli, hardly noticing him. Not knowing *what* was going on, Micelli turned and ran after them. There was a huge rumbling sound behind them coming from the building, and it seemed to be almost vibrating. Micelli looked back over his shoulder in time to see one of the large plate-glass windows from an upper story burst outward and fly into the sky. They ran to the edge of a nearby hummock and jumped into the shrubbery.

As they tumbled roughly to the ground, Otero landed on one side of him and Neda on the other. "What the hell?" Micelli started as Neda leaned over and kissed him on the mouth. "*What* the hell—" He smiled.

"It's good to see you, buddy," puffed Otero. "Your timing is perfect. Where's the car?"

"I got a sticker branch up my pants," complained Tina from somewhere behind them.

They peered over the top of the lantana bush they were crouching behind and could see Rix standing near a group of men on the edge of the dock. The men were looking up toward the top of the building, gesturing, and shaking their heads as Rix gave a murderous glance toward the edge of the hummock.

"One of those guys has a gun, look," whispered Neda.

"A couple of 'em have guns," Otero whispered back. "Micelli, where's the car?"

Micelli cleared his throat. "I—well, I walked."

"You *what?*" Neda's eyes were big.

"From *Miami?*" said Tina. "How'd you *do* that?" She was wriggling around and making little "ow" noises. "I got a goddamn sticker bush up my butt."

"Can you stay down?" Otero said in a too-loud voice.

Micelli noticed that Rix had turned toward them, listening.

"Shhhh," he said to the group. "I'll just—I'll have to explain later. Right now, we have to get out of here."

"How the hell are we going to do that?" said Tina. "There's people everywhere. Look—there's that awful woman."

They peered over the bushes again and saw Satanaele walk slowly out of the building, brushing her suit and pushing back her hair. She stood on the dock, and a group of people came running over to her.

"Hey," said Neda, "what about the bus?" She motioned, and they could see the tour bus; it was parked about a hundred yards from them, on the other side of the people on the dock.

"There's absolutely no way we're gonna get to that bus through all these people," said Tina. "No friggin' way."

"Well, what other choice do we have? We can't *walk* back to Miami." She gave Micelli a look. He smiled weakly.

More people came running onto the dock, and they seemed to be organizing into groups. Then, as they watched, another large pane of glass fell from the side of the building into the water, and the hysteria started all over again.

"We gotta go while there's still chaos," said Micelli. "Once things calm down, we don't stand a chance."

"I'll get the bus," interrupted Otero, "and I'll come back and pick you guys up."

Micelli rolled his eyes. "How the heck are you planning to get *to* the bus?"

"I can be invisible," Otero said. And something about the look on his face said he wasn't kidding.

"Oh, fer—" Micelli was shaking his head.

There was another huge rumble, and the building seemed to tip a little. Several women in the area of the dock screamed and started to run back toward the fishing cottages. Rix was shouting something to the men around him, and even Satanaele seemed to be preoccupied in the frenzy.

With that, Otero stood up in the bushes and calmly walked out and into the rushing people.

Neda couldn't watch.

"Mother," Tina said.

The group looked on as Otero hunched his shoulders and moved toward the bus at the same pace as whoever was passing him at the time. As people ran past, he ran with them. As people were standing, he stood for just a second and looked at whatever they were looking at. He kept his head up, made no eye contact, and carefully made his way across the dock area. After several minutes, they lost sight of him in the crowd.

"I can't see him," said Tina in a worried tone. "Where is he?"

"I'll be dammed," said Micelli.

Neda opened her eyes.

"Who knew?" said Tina. "Little did I ever think that—uh-oh."

Neda didn't like the look on her face.

"What?" she said with some urgency. "*What?*"

Tina pointed. Satanaele was gesturing toward the bus. Luckily, there was so much panic around her that no one seemed to be paying any attention. Then, as they peered through the lantana bush in horror, Rix turned and noticed what she was doing. His eyes scanned the dock area, and they all noticed at the same time that the bus had begun to move.

"Show time," said Tina.

Rix grabbed the shoulder of a man next to him and was pointing at the bus, but the man didn't seem to understand what Rix was saying. More glass was falling from the building, and it had begun to tip even more now. Neda thought it looked as if it might topple over and wondered how that could be possible.

The door to the bus shut, and it started to glide toward them.

Just when it seemed that Rix might get someone to figure out what he was saying, Satanaele took off across the dock and walked up to him, slapping him on the back of the head. He turned toward her, visibly angry, and she slapped him again, this time in the face. The two of them began to argue furiously.

In the background, the bus was steadily moving now, inching its way through the chaos.

"Come on, baby," Tina was saying. "Come on."

"Look at the water!" Neda shouted, and the three of them actually stood up. At the far edge of the lake, the shore had begun to crumble and fall into the water, sending a wave toward the now-tilting building. As they watched, the crumbling began to widen on both sides, sending more and more water toward dock and the building.

"What's happening?" shrieked Tina, and they could barely hear her over the roaring of water and the chaos of screaming people running in all directions.

The bus was very near them now, and they ran toward it flat out. Micelli couldn't see Rix or Satanaele or anyone through the rush of air and the roar of glass amid the screaming of people. He was holding Neda's hand and pulling Tina along by her sweater as the bus pulled to a jerky stop in front of them and the door opened. There was dust and brick and drywall flying through the air, and for a minute, Micelli didn't know if they were going to be able to get the bus away from the dock before everything and everyone got sucked down into the growing cavernous hole that the lake was becoming.

"Drive!" Micelli was shouting as they fell into the bus and scrambled to crawl over each other and get away from the door. "Freakin' drive!" Otero floored it. The bus lurched hard to the left; there was an awful grinding sound. For a minute, it looked like the bus was actually going *backward*, and then they were driving uphill somehow. Seated on the floor, Neda and Tina hunkered down in between the sofa and the coffee table as Micelli held on to the sides of a big leather armchair.

The bus was alternately tipping sideways and fishtailing along the dirt road, spitting up clods and rocks, adding to the mayhem around them. They lurched horribly as the left rear wheel dropped into a steep pothole, jarring the bus and sending anything inside I that was not tied down flying. For a few minutes, Micelli wasn't sure the bus would keep going; all of nature seemed bent on stopping them as Otero gunned the engines around falling oak branches and uprooting pine trees.

"Hang on," he shouted through the open door between the two cabins. "I gotta drive over some stuff."

"Can you hear that sound?" Neda said to Micelli. She looked afraid. "What *is* that?"

"I'm trying not to think about it," said Tina.

What started as a low hum had become a loud shriek. The sound was all around the bus, coming through the air, searching for them, wanting them, trying to touch them. It was as if the sound had become a thing itself—something physical; and then it became a cry, and the bus was pushed sideways off the road, down into a large section of field. Tina was thrown upward, her bare thigh scraping along the sharp corner of the glass coffee table. Squeezing her eyes shut, she felt sick with pain. It felt as if a giant hand had just pushed them off the road. Otero was frantically trying to fight with the steering wheel and hit a tree stump, sending the wheel spinning sharply on its own.

Tina started to cry softly. Behind them, out the back window, she could see that the entire building had sunk into the lake, which had now disappeared into one huge, cavernous hole.

"Holy Mother!" She was wide-eyed. "Jesus, Mary, and everybody else!"

Neda looked stricken. "My dear God. What is this?" she said. "What's going on?"

Otero, who'd been driving as hard and as fast as he could, slowed the bus to a stop and came back into the cab with them. They stood there watching as an unbelievable sight unfolded behind them.

"That's my heart's desire," he said breathlessly.

"Your *what?*" said Neda.

"That guy in the room, Rix. He said I could have anything. Remember?"

Neda touched him on the arm. "What did you ask for, Cutter?" she said quietly.

"A sinkhole," he answered. "On the day before the IPO."

"You traded your—" she started.

"It ain't about me," he interrupted, his voice sounding husky.

"What's a sinkhole?" asked Micelli.

Neda looked at him, questioning. "I forget—you're not from Florida. I guess they don't have sinkholes in New Jersey." She felt like crying.

"It's where they take too much water out from the ground and so, like everything just collapses," said Otero, walking back toward the driver's seat and then starting the bus.

"I lost a Volkswagen once," interrupted Tina, wiping the blood off her leg with a cloth napkin. "No shit, really. It was there when I went to bed, and it was gone in the morning. People lose houses. Once, I heard of a whole supermarket disappearing."

"My God," said Neda slowly, "I never would have thought of asking for a sinkhole. But Pete, you could have asked for anything. That Satan woman—she said something about throat cancer?"

"Like I said," he answered, looking down at the floor, "it's really not about me. We all got dues we gotta pay, you know? I owe a few. Anyway, the sinkhole was the only thing I could think of that would wipe it all out. Without their building, their records and their security, well, I thought maybe I could make a difference." They were silent for a minute. "Neda," Otero continued, "do you realize that Wilson stopped those papers from being given to Rix? That was a brave thing to do—a really brave thing."

"Fill me in," said Micelli.

"Turns out Wilson was a decent human being after all," said Tina, opening the refrigerator and looking inside. "You didn't know what was going on," she said, looking back at Micelli. "Wilson was making a deal to turn the papers over to the church when he got shot." She reached in and came up with a vanilla cupcake covered in sprinkles. "Ooh!" she said, popping it into her mouth. "Kind of fitting that his memory gets fixed by the guy he double-crossed," she said, wiping frosting off the corner of her mouth and looking at Neda. "I guess that means you can love him again."

"I always have," said Neda quietly.

Micelli placed his hand on top of hers. "I'm sorry," he said simply, not moving his hand.

"I know," she answered, not moving hers either.

They sat that way for a long time and then Tina shouted, "Hey! Doritos, anyone?" And the bus turned down the street to Mambo Taffy's house.

# CHAPTER 42

## KEY LARGO, FLORIDA

The reaction was instantaneous as the top to the Scooby-Doo lunchbox came off. First, there was one great sigh of anticipation from the group and then one great release of air as they looked down into the little box and saw just one small, square piece of paper sitting there. Just one.

"Is this all Neda asked you to put in the box, Andy?" said Mambo reaching down and picking it up. Her brow was furrowed as she turned it over and looked at both sides. "For some reason, I thought there would be many papers in here."

Andy looked dumbfounded. "No, Maman," he said, "there were a lot more." He was staring down into the little box like he believed that one single act alone would recreate the missing papers. "I don't know what happened to them."

"They are no longer important," said Samedi. He was smiling. "So they have gone." He opened the white umbrella and stood on the porch with it open over his head. "If you give me that one piece of paper and the blueprint that is in the other room, this stock or IPO game can stop."

Pascale looked past Samedi and into the garden behind him and saw that the Mustang had started its engine, and the front headlights had come on.

"Game?" said Pascale, looking back at Samedi. "That's what this is? A *game?*" He was standing now, and he looked angry.

"Life is a game, in the sense that it has rules," Samedi said, smiling broadly. He walked over to the screen and looked out at the car and up into the sky. "Yes. Everything has rules. Even the Earth itself." He looked back at them and thought they looked small. "What do you think gravity is? It is a rule. What do you think happens when the sun comes up in the morning and you wake from your bed and you eat your breakfast and you yawn and you scratch your bottom? Those are the rules that you play by while you are living. You sleep. You eat. You *itch*. You are *alive*." He gave a great bellow of laughter and took a long swig from the bottle he carried. "You will have different rules later."

"All you need is this one piece of paper and the blueprint?" said Pascale.

"Can we see what's on it?" said the friar.

Samedi laughed again, harder this time, and Andy wondered if everyone else could hear him laughing like he could. "Why not?" Samedi said finally.

They looked at each other, and then everyone was quiet. Finally, Mambo broke the silence with a statement of fact. "The one thing we all want is for the IPO to be stopped. Regardless of what is on that paper."

Pascale could hear a car engine revving out in the back yard.

"You all know I'm right," Mambo finished. "Andy, go get the blueprint."

"The blueprint's a map," said Friar Bill, turning toward Pascale. "It shows the location of an agreement worth many souls—perhaps hundreds, even thousands—to something called Mbweto. It's the basis of what keeps Soul Equity going."

Andy got up and left the porch. At the door, he turned toward Samedi and asked, "Do I still get to keep the car?"

"Mon ami," Samedi smiled. "Go."

It was raining harder now. No longer misting, the drops came down with tropical Florida strength. *Robust rain,* Mambo called it when the children were little, trying to make a word game out of a bad storm. Andy grew up thinking she was calling it "robots rain" and for years could not explain to her why he had nightmares about machines being in the back yard whenever it was raining. Now, looking at the sky beyond the little screened porch, Mambo Taffy knew a storm was coming that would scrape the sky clean. Thunder, although a way off, was coming too.

Andy came back onto the porch carrying the blueprint and placed it on the table in front of Mambo Taffy. She waited a moment while she seemed to be considering what she was about to do; then she took a deep breath and stood up to face Samedi. Without saying a word, Pascale and Friar Bill stood up at the same time, and Mambo reached into the tin box, removed one small piece of paper, and handed it to Samedi.

"We give this to you freely," she said quietly.

Together, the group watched as the guardian of the gates of death closed his fist around the paper. Pascale heard a sound like a loud clap. Then, unexpectedly, Samedi started to giggle, because no matter serious they might have all been, Andy was making gestures behind their backs with a tuna sandwich. Considering the unwavering rules of life's game, Samedi had to give points to Andy, because using his own sweet wisdom, Andy knew the greatest truth of all: life was not to be taken too seriously, no matter what the situation. Of all the human beings Samedi had met over all the eternities that he had walked between his gates and the face of the Earth, Andy was one of the most innocent and funny. Above all else, Samedi truly loved funny. What else did they all share?

Suddenly, there was an unbelievably huge crash in the back yard. Running to the screen door, they could see a bus sliding sideways through the mud-slicked grass into the side of the parked Mustang. Injured, the Mustang jumped up, raced its own engine, and pulled forward, driverless. As Mambo, Pascale, and Friar Bill stood in the doorway, the door of the bus opened, and four people fell out into the yard, laughing and screaming. In the rain, it was hard to see who they were, and the sight they made was unforgettable. Squinting, it looked to Pascale like one of them was Micelli, and he seemed to be locked in an embrace with a very muddy Neda Mason. Andy's eyes almost leapt from his face as he saw Tina struggling to get to her feet. Throwing open the door, he ran through the pouring rain to her side and jumped on top of her just as she was just standing up. *They look like puppies,* thought Mambo. *Not a bad thing to look like.* She remembered feeling like a puppy once.

Turning back to the porch, she saw that Samedi was gone.

They hit the house like Army Rangers.

"Turn on the TV, turn it on!" Micelli was shouting as he slid from the back porch door across the room toward the kitchen. Neda was laughing and covered in mud; she hugged Mambo, who tried to squirm away from her soaking daughter, to no avail.

"We don't have any pow—" Mambo started as Otero ran past them toward the television in the corner of the living room and turned it on, flipping through the channels to the local news station. "—er," she finished.

The news lady was speaking. "For more on this breaking story, we go to Bryan Daniels at Mary's Grin. Bryan?"

The camera showed a young man standing in the middle of a somewhat chaotic situation, but it was dark and hard to tell exactly what was going on. "Police have put up a barricade here at Soul Equity headquarters in historic Mary's Grin. Behind me, you can see an incredible sight. A huge sinkhole opened up about an hour ago, swallowing the entire lake as well as the headquarters building itself. A sinkhole on this scale has *never* been reported in this part of the state. We have reports of several fatalities, including that of the founder and CEO of Soul Equity, Rix Roman. A company spokesperson has issued a statement canceling an IPO of the company's stock, set to begin trading tomorrow morning."

Otero looked at Micelli with wide eyes. "Holy shit!" Micelli said.

There was a knock at the front door; keeping one eye on the television, Neda went to open it. Standing there, dripping with rain, was Jean Alexander.

"I found the key to a safe deposit box," she said to no one in particular. "So, this is where everybody is." No one said anything. "Look," she continued, looking at Neda, "I know how you feel about my husband. But there are some things I thought you should know. Can I come in? It's wet out here."

Neda stepped back from the door without speaking, and Jean took two strides into the room, shaking rainwater off her sleeves. "Wow!" she said with slight sarcasm, looking at all the people in the room. "Thanks for the invite."

"I don't like that lady," Tina whispered to Andy. "Isn't she the one who hurt your hand?"

"Roy had some woman stashed in the Cayman Islands," Jean said, throwing her dripping purse down on the sofa. She ran her fingers across her cheeks and fluttered the water out of her eyelashes. "All those trips to buy jewelry for the store? That wasn't all he was paying for."

"I'm sorry," Neda said.

"Don't be." Jean was breezy. "I got the account numbers. Roy was partners with that Friar Allen guy; they were smuggling stuff for a company called Soul Equity." She looked at Pascale. "And where did you go?" Her question was petulant. "I'm carted down the hall at the hospital and thrown into a locked ward and you just—what? Go to the grocery store?"

"I didn't—" he started.

"Did you check on me?" she demanded. "Did you even *try* and help me out?" She was jabbing at Pascale with her finger, making the bracelets on her arm clink together.

Otero interrupted. "Those guys were partners years ago. Roy and Allen. I knew 'em both."

"Was there anything else in the safe deposit box?" Tina interrupted.

"What is it that you think I need to know?" added Neda.

*She isn't being very pleasant,* thought Micelli.

"Roy kept tapes from the answering machine in his office. He recorded calls with your husband." Jean was looking at Neda with her head cocked and one hand on her hip. "Can I have some juice or something?"

"I'll get it," said Tina, jumping up and leaving the room. "Be right back."

In the kitchen, she opened the refrigerator and removed a large can of tropical punch. Reaching under the counter, she pulled out a gallon bottle of vodka that she and Andy had been tapping regularly over the past few days. Filling the glass halfway with vodka, she topped it off with a small amount of punch. Plopping in three ice cubes, she walked back into the dining room and handed the drink to Jean.

Neda was sitting at the table with Mambo and Pascale. Everyone else was standing, and Jean was walking back and forth excitedly between them.

"Thanks," she said, taking the glass from Tina.

"—other tapes," Micelli was saying. "Are you saying that Wilson was double-crossing Roy? Wasn't Wilson in on the Soul Equity deal?"

"Listening to the tapes, it sounded like he was in at the beginning, but then, for some reason, he was having second thoughts," Jean answered. "He kept trying to get Roy to give some of the papers to the church. To Friar Rene or Master or somebody." She waved her hand dismissively in the air and took a big gulp of the juice. "Woo," she said, looking down into the glass.

"Something had been bothering him," Neda said, sounding tired. "He wasn't sleeping, and he seemed tense. Then he had this meeting at

Big Daddy's, and he said that if Roy called looking for him, I was to say that I didn't know where he was."

"Roy knew about the meeting anyway," said Jean, taking another long gulp from the glass. "He sent Friar Allen along. They thought Wilson was going to make a deal with the church and cut them out."

"It was a trap," said Pascale. He looked at Micelli. "Call your office and have Crocodile Lake searched. My guess is we'll find the gun that killed Wilson in the water. The windows were partially open when the car went off the road."

Micelli was watching Neda closely and saw tears in her eyes.

Jean continued. "Wilson said on the tape that it was about more than money. He said that it was about people's souls. Mothers and fathers. People with futures ahead of them; people just down on their luck or whatever. Desperate people with no other hope. He said the whole Soul Equity thing stunk, and he wouldn't have any part of it." She gulped the last of the glass and looked at Neda. "He said he hoped to have a son one day, and he didn't want him to grow up in that kind of world."

Neda put her elbows on the table and her head in her hands.

"Wilson was right to be afraid," said Micelli. "That's why he hid the gun in the bushes. Just in case." He looked at Pascale. "You need to run a check on gun permits in Jersey. Tie the gun back to Friar Allen—or whoever he was."

"Is it hot in here?" said Jean, looking around.

Friar Bill spoke for the first time. "I guess that makes our Wilson a sort of honorable smuggler."

"Isn't that an oxymoron?" asked Mambo sadly.

"No, that stuff is really addictive," interrupted Tina.

"That's Oxy-contin," said Micelli, rolling his eyes, "not oxy-moron."

"Hey!" Andy said sharply. "Don't be calling Tina any names."

Jean started giggling. "You guys ought to hear yourselves. This is like the six stooges or something." She had one eye closed and was pointing her finger at each of the people in the room, counting them. "Five—no, seven stooges." Then she jumped and pointed to herself. "Eight. Eight stooges." She burst out laughing. "Isn't there a song about that? Ninety-eight stooges on the wall or something? Take one down, turn it around . . . ?"

"That's bottles of beer," said Tina.

"I never said *anything* about being queer," Jean giggled, falling down with a hiccup. She looked startled for a moment as she sat on the floor of the dining room. "What happened to the chair that was here?"

Mambo reached over and touched Neda's hand. "How are you, my dear?" she asked quietly.

"I always knew these things about Wilson, Maman," Neda said. "I loved who he was in his heart." She wiped the tears away from her eyes. "He died believing in a better world."

Friar Bill was still staring at the television. "This is incredible," he said, looking at the images coming in from Mary's Grin. "This is simply unbelievable."

"*Believe* then," said a booming voice behind them. Turning, they saw Samedi standing in the kitchen doorway. "One of my favorite words. It has so much *possibility* attached to it."

"Who the hell?" started Micelli.

"The paper you gave me is for Rix," said Samedi gleefully, almost rubbing his hands. "An old competitor is now *mine*."

"The paper in the box?" said Mambo.

"*That's* what was in the box?" said Otero. "An equity contract on Rix's soul?"

"So he's—"

"He is dead." Samedi was smiling. "Don't put too much importance into what things are called. He is allowed to *continue*. This is my job, you see. And I'm good at it."

"And the blueprint?"

Samedi took a long drink from his small bottle. "If you give it to me, no one else will be able to find the license." He wiped his mouth with the back of his hand. "Soon, people will forget."

"License?" said Micelli.

"Something about rules," said Mambo Taffy with a knowing smile.

"Hey, what about that Satanaele woman?" asked Tina. "And what happened to those shoes?"

Samedi laughed. "Oh, she'll always be around," he said. "But she realizes that these short-term gains don't add up to much. Without mortal money and a respectable front, she won't be causing trouble for a while."

"So, can I have them?" Tina asked. "The shoes I mean."

He was laughing harder now. "Why do you want to have the shoes?" he said, bending over and looking closely at her feet.

"I've got this idea for a new act," she said. "I'm gonna be Dorothy, see? Like in *The Wizard of Oz*, and I'm gonna have these wires from the ceiling attached to my dress so I can make it fly off me in the wind. And I'll just be standing there in these great shoes, clicking my heels and making those sparks fly." She was still talking and waving her arms as Samedi reached back toward the kitchen door.

"One last thing," he said, pushing the door open.

A small black dog ran into the room. Otero gasped and sank to the floor with his hands out. The dog scooted past Samedi toward Otero, taking a nip at his ankle as she ran past.

"Anna!" scolded Otero as he stroked her head and wiped her eyes with the corner of his shirt. "I'm sorry—"

"Dogs don't like me," said Samedi. As if on cue, Anna growled softly in the back of her throat. Samedi shrugged. "Rules again. I don't always get to make them."

"Well," said Neda as she walked past Samedi into the kitchen and on toward the back porch, "let's get this done."

Andy started to follow her, but Mambo made a motion with her hand. "No, leave them," she said. And they watched as Samedi followed her outside.

The two of them were alone on the porch.

"Is this what I'm supposed to do?" she asked, picking up the blueprint from the table. Then, taking a deep breath, she placed the roll of papers into his outstretched hand. As she looked down, she saw that the fingers closing around the blueprint were small and young. Looking up, she saw Alais standing there holding them. He smiled at her with a big, open, happy smile.

"Thank you," he said simply.

She felt her throat closing, as tears started to run down her face. "From Wilson," she managed to say.

"For many others," he answered as he began to turn away. She wanted to reach out and touch him, but he was beginning to fade, beginning to become transparent, and then all she could see was the smile on his face. She knew that was just in her mind.

"My headache is gone," Mambo said in the other room.

Neda was still standing in the middle of the porch when Micelli walked up to her and touched her elbow lightly with his hand.

"I have to pick up my mother at the airport tomorrow night," he said softly. "Do you want to come with me?"

"You can't go by yourself?" she asked.

He leaned over and put his lips very near to hers. "I don't want to go by myself," he said, pulling her toward him and kissing her.

\* \* \*

"Come here," said Andy, running past them, dragging Tina by the hand. "There's something outside next to the house I want to show you." They clattered over the wooden deck, down the steps and out into the garden behind the house. Turning the corner, Andy stopped suddenly, with a look of confusion and disappointment on his face.

"Oh, An-bee!" Tina said in a breathy voice behind him, "I can't believe it!"

There, in front of them on the lawn, sat Tina's lime-green Mustang GT—in perfect condition.

"You had it fixed!" She was jumping up and down. "Oh, baby, this is great!"

Startled, Andy looked around the yard for the black Mustang. Not seeing it, he held his hands out away from his sides with the palms up and shouted, "Surprise!"

Tina jumped toward him, and the two of them fell against the trunk. Andy had a breast in each hand and was kissing her when he opened his eyes and saw Samedi looking at him over her shoulder.

"*Mon ami!*" Samedi winked. A haze of cigarette smoke circled his head. "I almost forgot." He held out a heavy envelope to Andy. It was long and edged in silver, with the word "OTERO" written in script across the front. "Can you return this to your friend for me?" he asked. "Tell him not to sign such things again."

Andy smiled as Tina, sitting on the trunk lid, nestled her head against his chest. "Sure," he said. "What is it?"

"Not much in the bigger scheme of things," said Samedi, tipping his head back and looking up into the night sky. "But everything to one man. Then he was whispering. "I found a few money orders," he said sideways to Andy. "I put them in the trunk for you." Placing his hand against the car, the trunk popped open slightly underneath Tina, and pieces of paper began to tumble out onto the grass.

He touched Andy lightly on the shoulder and was gone.

*　　*　　*

"I feel dizzy," said Jean, sitting on the couch in front of the television with Pascale. News lady had a red crawl going across her chest, and she was standing at the edge of a large, black sinkhole. The crawl read: Sinkhole destroys entire lake, building. Jean slumped against Pascale's shoulder. "Do you know if there's any more of this good punch?" she said, looking down into her empty glass.

"How about if we go get some coffee somewhere?" Pascale answered.

"Who?" she said brightly, sitting up. "You and me?"

"Why not?"

Squinting, she looked at him for a long time. "I've got an espresso machine at my house," she answered, running her finger up the buttons of her blouse. "Want to look at some art?"

*　　*　　*

"So what about this Mbwento?" said Friar Bill, leaning against the dining room wall. The small room was bright with light from the open kitchen door, and every lamp in the living room seemed to shine against his face.

"I think he's gone," Mambo said, tilting her head and squinting. "For now, anyway. I don't have a headache anymore."

A rush of air moved through the room past them and Otero appeared, breathless. "Did you see me just now?" he asked.

"See you?"

"Yeah." He was bouncing up and down on the balls of his feet. "I just walked through the room twice. *Right past you.*" He pointed at the floor. "There. Right there."

"Well, no," said the friar. "But we—"

"Ha! I was *invisible*," Otero said, sticking his chest out and smiling. "You didn't know that about me."

Friar Bill started. "I don't—"

"No," Mambo said, interrupting and reaching out to touch Otero's arm lightly.

Searching his face, she could see the knife reflected through his eyes. "We *didn't* know that about you." She was almost purring. "How *very* interesting."